MYRA DUFFY

THE HOUSE AT ETTRICK BAY

To David and Ivan,

With best wishes,

Myra Duffy

Published in 2010 by New Generation Publishing

Copyright © Myra Duffy

First Edition

The author asserts the moral right under the Copyright, Designs and Patents Act 1988 to be identified as the author of this work.

All Rights reserved. No part of this publication may be reproduced, stored in a retrieval system, or transmitted, in any form or by any means without the prior written consent of the author, nor be otherwise circulated in any form of binding or cover other than that in which it is published and without a similar condition being imposed on the subsequent purchaser.

British Library C.I.P.
A CIP catalogue record for this title is available from the British Library.

MYRA DUFFY

THE HOUSE AT ETTRICK BAY

AN ALISON CAMERON MYSTERY

www.myraduffy.co.uk

Also by Myra Duffy:

'When Old Ghosts Meet'

THE ISLE OF BUTE

The isle of Bute lies off the west coast of Scotland, less than two hours from the city of Glasgow. It has been occupied for over five and a half thousand years but rose to prominence in Victorian days when its proximity to Glasgow made it a favoured spot for the wealthy to build summer houses and the not so wealthy to enjoy the delights of the seaside in the many rooms available for rent during the holiday season.

The northern part of the island is Highland in appearance but the southern part is lowland and fertile. Ettrick Bay is on the western side of the island and here the mile curve of sandy beach looks over the tiny island of Inchmarnock to the great Sleeping Warrior of Arran.

Characters in this novel bear no relation to any persons living or dead. Any such resemblance is co-incidental.

PROLOGUE

At Ettrick Bay, the sun is going down, the rippling light casting long shadows across the water. Along the sand, the oyster catchers gather, shrieking in the gloaming. No boats disturb the tranquillity of the steel grey waters lapping at the shore.

The cattle in the fields beside the long path look up, startled by the sound of plough horses returning home. In the darkening sky, the stars appear one by one as the pale crescent moon casts a ghostly light across the fields ripe with corn.

High above the bay, Ettrick House stands brooding, steadfast against the autumn winds. Couch grass and bindweed choke the once well tended flower beds and the long sweeping drive is pitted and potholed. The windows are shuttered, dark.

Alone in the silence of the empty house he sits nursing a glass of whisky, gazing at the pictures he sees in the flickering flames of the fire set against the chill of the evening.

Now, in his old age, the ghosts come back to haunt him. They give him no rest. And he wonders if tonight will be the night when at last she is found.

ONE

She lay on her side, as though asleep, one arm crooked under her head as a substitute for a pillow. Sunlight filtered into the deep trench at the bottom of the lower gardens, illuminating her outline.

She looked quiet, at peace, in this most tranquil of places high in the hills above the calm waters of Ettrick Bay so far below. If you looked closely you could see a few bits of what looked like pottery in the grave beside her, tiny remnants of a life lost. Her legs were curled up under her like a child's, though even my untrained eye could see she was a fully grown adult.

'How do you know it's a female?' I asked.

Morgan Connolly, the archaeologist in charge of the dig, looked up. It was hard to make out his expression behind the long red beard he sported, an apparent extension of his mass of curly hair. But he seemed happy to answer my questions.

'You can tell by the shape of the pelvis,' he said, bending down to my height as he pointed it out to me. 'And the shape of the skull also helps, though that's less useful.'

How long she had lain there, I wondered, as I watched the team go about their work. It must have been a long time. All that remained now were the bare bones of what had once been a living, breathing person.

Little bits of lichen clung to her feet and a tiny creature or two scuttled away into the remaining darkness, fretting at being so disturbed.

The archaeologists clustered round the trench did not share my concerns as they chattered excitedly about this discovery.

'Stand back.' The order from Morgan was firm. 'It's essential the site isn't contaminated.'

My daughter Deborah moved away reluctantly and came over to join me.

I turned to the slim young woman standing beside me. A terrible thought had suddenly occurred to me. 'Is it a murder victim?' I whispered.

Penny Curtis smiled and shook her head. She pushed back the lock of her long brown hair which had fallen over her face, leaving a little streak of mud on her forehead. Her large grey eyes were shining.

'Unlikely, though Morgan will be able to tell soon. It's much more likely to be an old skeleton.' She waved her trowel around, spattering earth over her yellow safety jacket. 'It's possibly a very old skeleton indeed.' She frowned and consulted a map she pulled out of her back pocket. 'But there's no record of a cemetery anywhere round here, so it is unusual and a great discovery.'

She smiled at me again, 'There's nothing we archaeologists like better than finding something like this. Don't worry.'

She looked over at Morgan who was talking animatedly to the other member of the excavation team. Brian March was still in the trench, standing beside the skeleton. In complete contrast to Morgan he was stout, which made him look smaller than he was and his head was shaven. A single gold earring glittered in the light as he scrambled up out of the trench, hoisting up his faded blue jeans as he did so. He looked more like a professional wrestler than an archaeologist.

Penny said, almost as though speaking to herself, 'Morgan will be incredibly pleased.'

'Why?' I could understand a find like this would be important to an archaeologist, but she spoke as if this skeleton was very special indeed.

She folded up the map and sighed. 'Morgan's been searching for the big discovery for some time now. He's had this theory for years that there was a Roman settlement on Bute somewhere. This high ridge is one of the more likely spots. No one else credits his idea so if he's proved right, it will be a major coup.'

I looked around me. Yes, I could well understand this stretch of land, high in the hills, would be an ideal site for a community to settle and to feel safe.

As though reading my thoughts she pointed over the fields to where the land began to curve steeply upwards. 'You can see the raised beach from here. A great place to build a settlement in ancient times.'

I knew enough about the academic world from my husband Simon to realise that if Morgan was proved right and this was the major find he had so long searched for, his reputation would be made. Papers by the score, conferences in overseas universities: he would be an expert whose opinions would be sought on every occasion. The academic world would be at his feet.

I became aware Simon was speaking. 'What happens next, Morgan?'

Morgan frowned and scratched his head. 'First we have to excavate the skeleton and discard any extraneous material. You often find bits of animal bone in an old site like this. Then we have to date the skeleton and assure the local police it's ancient enough for this not to be a murder enquiry.'

I looked away from the activity of the trench and down the sweep of hills towards the half circle of the bay. It was shaping up to be a perfect West coast afternoon. The sun blazed down from a cloudless sky and the heat was becoming so strong you could almost smell it on the strengthening brine from the bay. But I shivered in spite of the warmth and draped my jacket back over my shoulders.

This might be all in a day's work to these professionals, but it was the first time I had ever seen anything like it. How had the skeleton come to be here, in the grounds of this house at Ettrick Bay?

I heard my husband's voice again, as though from a distance, so engrossed was I in my own thoughts.

'Alison, are you all right?'

I turned to face him, shaking my head.

He grasped my elbow. 'Perhaps we should move away from here and let them do their work?'

I stood still, unable to move. Simon was concerned about this discovery. And so was I.

How could I have known when we agreed to help my friend Susie with this house at Ettrick Bay it would turn out like this?

TWO

It all began with a call from a friend asking for our help. It wasn't the first time she had asked for help, but Susie Littlejohn and I have known each other for a long time. We've enjoyed the highs and lows of life together since we first met many years ago at teacher training college.

And it's not every day someone you know well unexpectedly inherits a house.

'Please, please Alison,' Susie implored me across the miles, 'if you and Simon could go down and check it out for me. I'm sure it will all be straightforward. There can't be many problems with a holiday home on Bute. I can't possibly leave America at short notice.'

How could I refuse? A trip to the island, even in February, would make an enjoyable day out. I was sure Susie would be happy for us to make use of her holiday home over the summer.

Her exchange to a school in America from Strathelder High, where we both teach, was proving a great success and for whatever reason (though I had my suspicions) she was reluctant to make the journey back at the moment.

Surely it wouldn't take much time to check out the house Susie now owned? She had helped me out on so many occasions in the past, it was the least I could do.

'I don't remember much about it,' she had said, 'but we did spend a lot of time there during the summer months when I was very young. I must have been about five or six the last time we visited. It's a sort of lodge house I think.'

She paused. 'Some distant relative or other of my father owned it. I do remember there was plenty of space to play outside the house. I can't believe I've inherited it.'

'Can't you remember anything else about the place?'

'Not really.' She paused. 'I can't recollect why we stopped going down there. I haven't been back to Bute since.'

We chatted a little more about the house, then wandered on to other topics.

I crossed my fingers Simon would be happy to come with me when I explained the circumstances. I was now eager to make the trip: Susie's vagueness had made me more than a little curious about her inheritance.

So, one misty February morning of damp and rain (not the weather I would have chosen) we found ourselves in the offices of Laidlaw and Cummings in Montague Street in Rothesay, the main town on the island of Bute. It seemed as if the meeting would go much more smoothly than I had originally anticipated. Susie, to give her credit, had managed to deal with much of the essential documentation by fax and by e-mail. We anticipated few problems.

It had been a rush to leave Glasgow. Although it was half term at Strathelder High, where I teach English, there was still a lot of catching up to do before I could thankfully close the door of my classroom and take advantage of the few days' break.

At least I'd managed to fit in a trip to the hairdresser before we left. At my age it gets harder to keep up the illusion of naturally blonde hair and though I keep it short, the grey seems to be showing through with increasing frequency.

I was even luckier Simon had, after a fair bit of persuasion, decided to come with me. As he is stockily built, a legacy no doubt of his early youth when he played a lot of rugby, I find his presence re-assuring in all sorts of ways. His dark hair and colouring can make him look menacing, though he's really very good natured. He would be very helpful in dealing with the lawyer should there be any difficulties.

Simon works in a college which seems to exist in a state of permanent crisis. If it's not funding issues, it's a problem of too few students or too many students or students wanting to do courses that are not available. Sympathetic though I am, I've learned over the years to tune out much of what he says.

His mind was made up after yet another difficult staff meeting. He said, 'I feel I deserve a rest before the next assault,' and so we made the journey together from Glasgow to the ferry terminal at Weymss Bay for the short crossing to the island of Bute.

The offices of Laidlaw and Cummings, set halfway along Montague Street, were more spacious than they appeared from the plain wooden entry door, the highly polished brass nameplate its only adornment.

We were greeted on our arrival by a young woman, slim and delicate featured, her long blonde hair tied back severely in a knot on top of her head. She was clad in a very short blue skirt and a white tee shirt that only just covered her midriff, very much at odds with the severity of her hairstyle and her lack of makeup. The outfit was most unsuitable for the weather, never mind the staid offices of a lawyer.

Cassie Milne, as she introduced herself, was cheerful enough. 'I'm Mr Laidlaw's secretary,' she said smiling at us. 'He's expecting you so I'll take you straight through.'

We were ushered up a narrow stairway into a room decorated in cool tones of blue and cream. The décor and the pale blonde furniture made it look bright, even on an overcast day such as this. But though the furniture looked good, it was not exactly comfortable, as I discovered when I sat down on one of the high backed chairs. Mr Laidlaw himself was happily ensconced in a large black swivel chair of battered leather which looked very comfortable indeed.

I soon realised why Cassie was so lightly clad. The temperature in the room was hot, very hot. I shrugged off my rain jacket as I went in.

'Mr and Mrs Cameron,' Cassie said loudly and then slowly retreated from the room. She didn't close the door completely, though Mr Laidlaw didn't seem to notice.

The lawyer was a desiccated man of rapidly advancing years, judging by his white streaked hair. He looked at us over his glasses as he stood to greet us.

'I think you'll find everything there,' said Simon, passing a folder thick with paper over the desk to him.

We sat in silence as Mr Laidlaw carefully withdrew each document and examined it scrupulously before adding it to the collection of papers already sitting on his desk. Over many years of teaching, I've learned the trick of reading upside down and I could see Susie's signature on several of the documents already on his desk.

I gazed round the room as we waited for him to finish. A few certificates hung on the walls and there were several framed photos of Bute, but apart from these the room was extraordinarily bare.

'Everything seems in order,' Mr Laidlaw said as he continued leafing slowly though the large pile of papers.

Out of the corner of my eye I had seen him glancing up as Simon and I quietly discussed the best way to get to Ettrick House, but he said nothing. He continued to countersign and fuss over the never ending number of documents seemingly essential to the transaction.

He paused and tapped his pen on the desk. 'Does your friend know exactly what it is she is inheriting?' He gazed at us expectantly.

I shook my head. 'We're only here because Susie is unable to return from America at the moment.'

Mr Laidlaw smiled again. This time a low chuckle came from somewhere deep in his throat. 'Best to prepare her, I would think.'

'Prepare her for what?' I said.

I could see Simon was becoming restless with the slow pace of this meeting but I was intrigued by the lawyer's remarks.

Mr Laidlaw hesitated for a moment. 'Well, it's likely some work will be done up there soon …she might want to know…'

Simon shifted restlessly in his seat. He was anxious to be off and wasn't interested in what might be no more than local gossip. 'Yes, yes, well, I'm sure Susie will investigate everything when she comes back,' he said.

Mr Laidlaw grimaced and continued to shuffle the papers. 'As you wish.'

We had obviously upset him by our lack of interest.

Simon was determined that once we had had a quick look at the house, as Susie had instructed, we would catch the evening ferry back to the mainland. But we were rapidly discovering time on the island was more or less elastic. Or perhaps Mr Laidlaw was being over particular, even for a lawyer.

'You don't know anything about the house?' The lawyer was trying hard to engage our attention again.

'Only what Susie remembers,' I said, anxious to break this deadlock. 'I think she spent a lot of time there as a child. Her mother was widowed young and some of her father's relatives helped out by having Susie over during the long summer holidays.'

I frowned as I tried to recall anything else of interest Susie might have told me but that was about as much of the essentials of the story as I could remember at the moment.

He chuckled again, his good humour restored. 'It's a well known house on the island. A wonderful place in its heyday, though latterly it was allowed to go to ruin. The last Mr Ainslee was a bit of an eccentric, you know. The family never really recovered from that business with his aunt.'

'Yes, yes,' Simon butted in, looking pointedly at his watch. He obviously feared that Mr Laidlaw might embark on a long history of the house. While this might be of interest to Susie, it wasn't to us, his look said.

The lawyer looked a little crestfallen again at this interruption but all he said was, 'Well, it would seem that your friend Ms Littlejohn was the only heir who could be tracked down. I warn you, the place has been empty for quite some time.'

Behind me I was sure the door creaked slightly. This time, Mr Laidlaw heard. 'Yes, yes, Cassie, what is it?'

For a moment I thought that she was going to pretend she hadn't been listening, but she suddenly realised we knew she was there because she came right into the room, her face noticeably flushed. 'I wondered if you wanted some tea.'

Mr Laidlaw looked at us over his glasses. 'Well, would you like some tea?' It was clear he felt he had now been cornered into making this offer and it would be rude to ignore Cassie's question.

To Mr Laidlaw's evident relief Simon shook his head and looked again at his watch.

This instruction of Susie's 'to drop into the lawyers and pick up the keys' was rapidly turning into a full day's work.

Mr Laidlaw waved her away and this time I heard the door shut firmly. 'No thanks, Cassie, we're fine at the moment.'

Mr Laidlaw looked apologetically at us. 'I'm not from here myself, so I still find it strange how much the island likes to know all the details of everyone's life.'

I wasn't the least bit upset by Cassie's behaviour. In a small community, any small community, it's good to know who your next neighbours are going to be.

He returned briskly to the business in hand. 'Anyway, let's get you started.' He pulled out a map from the top drawer of his desk which, like his chair, was a very battered affair, much out of place in these sleek modern offices.

'I've marked the way up to Ettrick House on this map and I've written down some directions. I'm sure you'll find it easily. Any problems just give me a ring.'

He traced the route on the map with his finger as Simon said impatiently, 'It all looks very straightforward.'

This time Mr Laidlaw stood up and shook each of us by the hand.

As we left his office in a flurry of goodbyes, I was surprised to see Cassie scuttling back to her chair.

It was no concern of mine what she was up to and I dismissed it from my mind. Probably she was keen to have the most up-to-date gossip to pass on to her friends.

By 12 o'clock we were back out in Montague Street, with the map supplied by Mr Laidlaw and the keys to this surprise windfall of Susie's.

'Well, that wasn't too bad,' said Simon heartily. 'Let's go and check this place out for Susie and then we can come back and have some lunch in Rothesay.'

'I think I'll pop into the shop and buy some milk and some coffee to take up with us,' I said, still cross at being cheated out of my cup of tea. 'I'll see you back at the car.'

'Oh, all right, but be quick.' He hurried off in that urban way so at odds with the slow pace of life on the island.

I didn't take long to make the basic purchases and I did include a packet of biscuits. As I came out of the shop immediately opposite the offices of Laidlaw and Cummings, I was surprised to see Cassie standing by the door to the office, talking earnestly into her mobile phone.

'Hello again, Cassie,' I said raising my hand in greeting as I passed her.

She gazed at me with a look of horror and snapped her phone shut, then turned and went straight back into the office without a word.

Well, that was certainly odd. I hadn't said anything to upset her as far as I knew. Why should she want to end her phone conversation so abruptly on seeing me?

I shrugged. Probably it was no more than a co-incidence. Much later I would remember this small incident and realise it was part of the puzzle that was Ettrick House.

THREE

I walked along Montague Street, deep in thought. I was on my way to meet Simon at the Albert Pier, delayed by only one or two brief stops for window shopping. I pondered why Cassie had reacted so strangely and then I remembered my suspicions about her listening in to our conversation with Mr Laidlaw.

As I expected, Simon was standing by the car checking his watch.

'Right, Alison,' he said, opening the passenger door. 'Let's get up to this Ettrick House and back on the ferry.'

The rain had cleared, as it does so quickly on the Atlantic coast. A weak sun lightened up the Shore Road as we drove out of Rothesay, along through Ardbeg towards Port Bannatyne. In the sheltered curve of the bay only a few small boats bobbed about on the water, the rest being tucked up snugly for the winter in the boatyard at the end of the village.

Nothing stirred. It was as though the whole village was asleep. There were no other cars in sight as we drove past the playing fields and rounded the corner alongside Kames Castle.

When we reached the old ruined church at Knockencroyf we came to a stop at a fork in the road. There was a choice of routes, both inconveniently signposted for Ettrick Bay.

'Any ideas on which one we take?' Simon asked, peering out through the windscreen.

'Not really.' I knew from long experience not to make any suggestions.

'Get the map out, Alison and let's have a look at those directions we got at the lawyer's.'

I dutifully opened the map and wrestled at the same time with the directions we'd received from Laidlaw and Cummings, without much hope of the instructions making a difference.

There was silence for a while as Simon worked out which road would be better to take. I gazed out of the window. Fields stretched in all directions as far as the eye could see. There was no evidence of water from here, no help in deciding which road would lead us to Ettrick Bay.

Apart from the bleating of a few early lambs and their suspicious mothers in the nearest field, there was no sound. Suddenly I spied a row of little cottages beyond the next clump of trees.

'I could go and ask at one of the cottages,' I suggested brightly. 'There's smoke coming from the chimney of that middle one, so there must be someone at home.'

'No need - we'll manage, I'm sure.' Simon went back to studying the map.

'Got it. We go right, take the road past Colmac Bridge, continue alongside the farm, and then it's first right at the Ettrick smithy.'

In a few minutes we had passed the smithy, long since disused, and turned up the hill. As we climbed the steep, winding road I looked back and could see the bay stretched out behind us, the water shimmering steel grey along the line of the sands in the pale spring light.

The only building to be seen was long and low, set a little back from the shore. From the evidence of the cars parked there and the little swing park beside it, it was a tearoom, a place that might prove very useful. I noted it for future reference.

Simon stopped the car again, pulling over tightly to the verge, though I doubted that there would be much traffic on this road apart from the odd farm tractor.

'We must be close by now,' he said, consulting the map again.

I looked up ahead, but could see no evidence of a house.

'Did Susie say anything else about the place, give you any description?'

I shrugged. 'Not really. I'm not sure she remembers much about it herself, to be honest. She was very young when she used to visit here. She did say she thought it was a kind of lodge house, though.'

'That's not much help. I suppose we should have asked for more information from Mr Laidlaw.'

I made no comment. It was too late to go back now. There was nothing for it but to continue on the road up the hill and hope we had made the right decision. Since leaving Port Bannnatyne, we hadn't seen a single living soul, no one to stop and ask for directions.

We bumped over a decidedly shaky bridge signposted Kilbride, where the waters rushed down in a noisy torrent after the heavy winter rains.

'Don't think it's far now.' Simon sounded more confident than I felt. 'We go up Glen More and take the first turning on the right again.'

The tarmacadam road had run out. The way was now rutted and potholed, haphazardly filled in with large stones. Hadn't the lawyer mentioned something about building here? If this was where a new road was planned it was long overdue for upgrading.

Yet why would the council spend money on this when there were so many other well used roads in Argyll and Bute needing attention? I wished we had let Mr Laidlaw tell us more instead of rushing off as we had.

We turned right and suddenly found ourselves on a short track, thickly overgrown with hedging and brambles, deep holed from seasons of rain and ongoing neglect.

Simon eased the car onto the grassy verge, carefully checking for any ditches. Large wooden gates, firmly shut and bolted, faced us.

'It must be a house built on an old estate. Probably this Ainslee was one of the workers: the factor or something.' I could think of no other sensible answer.

Simon moved round behind the car and I followed him. With some effort he inserted one of the largest keys in the gate lock.

A light rain had started again. I put up the hood of my jacket.

'Come and give me a hand, Alison,' he said.

Together we pushed hard until at last the heavy gates creaked open. Immediately to our right stood a trim little lodge house. Even its shabby exterior and peeling paint couldn't disguise its charm. It sat at the bottom of a road which swept round to the left and out of sight. Old fashioned rose bushes ran rampant round its door giving it the promise of a wonderful summer retreat.

'Oh, it's really pretty,' I said, picking my way carefully through the overgrown grass towards the front door. 'Look, I think there's a date on it.'

'Yes, here it is.' I peered up at the lintel. 'It was built in 1850. I'm sure Susie will be pleased with this. It'll make a great holiday home and it looks to be in pretty good shape. A bit of cosmetic work and it will be fine.'

I moved round to the side and rubbed at the grime on the front window with my hand to get a better view of the inside. I could see very little but the room appeared completely empty. It was the kind of place Sunday supplements describe as 'having serious potential.'

Already I was looking forward to a holiday here. I was sure even Simon wouldn't object to this for a short break.

'Isn't Susie lucky,' I sighed, 'to have a place on Bute.'

There was no response. Simon had walked a little further up the road and disappeared from view. I heard him say in a very loud voice, 'Bloody hell, Alison, come and look at this!'

Startled by his tone of voice, I abandoned my inspection of the lodge house and hurried up the road to find him.

'Where are you?' I called. 'What's happened?'

'Over here, past the trees.'

I followed the sound of his voice and hurried round to the spot where he was screened by a copse of ancient trees and overgrown hedging.

He was pointing shakily ahead. I followed the direction of his hand. The little lodge house had been no more than that: a lodge house. And what we had thought was the road was in fact a sweeping drive.

I found myself looking at the Victorian mansion that was Ettrick House.

FOUR

'There must be some mistake, Alison, surely?'

Simon scratched his head. A huge Victorian mansion loomed before us, dark and brooding, set amid trees which sheltered it from the elements and any prying eyes. It seemed to fill the whole landscape.

I tried to recall exactly what Susie had said. Had I misunderstood? The house we could see in front of us through the smirr of rain was not by any stretch of the imagination a 'holiday home'.

I turned to Simon and opened my mouth to speak, but closed it again as I saw the expression on his face. We stood together in silence, trying to make sense of what was in front of us.

The house was solidly built of grey stone. A mock turret on the north side gave it the appearance of a lopsided fairy castle, as though the builder had decided on one style and then run out of enthusiasm or of money.

The number of windows I counted gave some indication of the scale of the house. There were four bay windows, two on the lower floor and two on the upper and we could see the tops of other windows on what appeared to be the basement of the house, mostly obscured by the top terrace of the garden.

'Let's move round to the back.' Simon broke into my thoughts.

As we walked slowly up the drive we could see how large these windows were. Close up, the elaborate wrought iron balconies of the bay windows looked perilously close to crumbling away. The position of the house, high above the bay, had exposed them to years of salt water. Neglect had damaged them beyond repair and long smears of rust blotched the walls below.

Ivy rampaged unchecked along the side walls, creeping into every crack, eating into the eaves where it was shady. The windows stared back at us, blank eyed.

It had been a long time since the terraced gardens had had any attention and the flower beds were choked with couchgrass.The lawyer had been right: this building was in a sorry state.

So this was Ettrick House? It looked sad, forlorn, as though it had entirely given up any hope of rescue.

As we explored, we discovered our first impressions had been right. The top terraced gardens half concealed the basement of the house, probably the old servants' quarters. Light was not a priority for servants when Ettrick House was built.

The remainder of the gardens encircled the house in a sweep of lawns as far as the eye could see. They were sadly overgrown and all traces of the original layout was long gone. Thistles and weeds rampaged through what might have been at one time well tended flower beds.

'There's more round here,' called Simon. He had gone ahead of me to the back of the house.

As I picked my way through the long grass to join him, I saw the old kitchen garden was a mess of straggling plants whose origins had long been forgotten. We peered in through the grimy windows of the old outhouse attached to the main house at the back. Whatever purpose it had once served it was now some kind of storage facility and all that remained were some old tools, an ancient boiler and a few rusty canisters.

We walked together in silence: no words seemed adequate for what we were seeing. Against the brick wall at the far end of the kitchen garden several old apple trees were struggling in to bud. They must have provided the house with a goodly crop at one time, but the few green shoots they had managed to produce this early in the year only served to show how neglected they were. There was evidence of ancient onion beds, of trailing plants of strawberries now gone to riot and winter vegetables rotted in the soil.

The wind had suddenly risen and was sweeping in from the bay with a smell of seaweed and brine. It had a sharp bite to it and I pulled up my coat collar.

'Let's go inside,' said Simon. 'Goodness knows what we'll find in there.'

I was as baffled as he was. 'When Susie said she had inherited a house, I didn't think it would be any thing like this.' Neither, I suspected, did Susie.

We had a quick look at the rest of the outside and then returned to the front of the house.

'Let's get out of this rain.' Simon repeated as he retrieved my bag from the car and started fumbling with the set of keys.

As he attempted to decide which of the many keys on the ring might open the front door, I once more tried to remember as much as I could about Susie's last phone call from America confirming arrangements. The phone call that had resulted in Simon and I standing, cold and damp, outside this vast mansion.

'Do you remember me talking about the Ainslee family?' she had said. I've now found out my mother was actually a relative: a very distant one of course.'

'I do seem to recollect you told me something about the place.' I struggled to recall this story among the many Susie had told me over the years.

'You know how it is,' she said vaguely. 'We hadn't seen Robert Ainslee for years and years. I think my mother must have fallen out with them. Or perhaps she was too much of a poor relation. She was connected in some way to his wife's sister-in-law. Or was it her father-in-law's cousin?' As usual, Susie was short on the details.

'And so...' I paused, waiting for her to tell me more.

'Well, I was surprised as anyone to get the call from some firm called Inheritors Ltd. Apparently they track down missing heirs. I thought it was a joke at first or one of those telephone scams, but no, it was true. Apparently Robert and his wife had no children. Both she and her baby died in childbirth and he never re-married.'

'And there were no other relatives?'

'Apparently not - all I had to do was meet with their representative, sign up with them and that was it.'

'But don't you want to see this house?' I was truly amazed. If someone had left us a property on Bute, the proverbial wild horses wouldn't have kept me away.

'It's not that simple, Alison.' Across the miles I could picture her standing at the phone, fiddling with one of the long dangly earrings she favours. Susie reminds me of nothing so much as a little bird with her quickness of movement and her sharp featured face. She was making it very clear that in spite of this unexpected inheritance she wasn't going to give up her exchange year to America so easily.

I sighed, resigned to what was to come. 'And you want me to go down to Bute to sort it out?'

Now Simon and I were standing outside this gloomy house high up in the hills above Ettrick Bay, about to open the door to who knew what.

I gazed around as Simon continued to struggle with the large bunch of keys. Wifely words of encouragement would not be well received.

From the bottom of the steps leading up to the door the house looked even more neglected. At a quick glance I could see broken tiles on the porch, rotting window frames and spidery cracks in the walls above the entrance.

I shivered. Perhaps this wasn't such a great windfall after all. If this was what Susie had inherited she was welcome to it. There was something brooding about the place that spoke of the long dead. I don't think of myself as particularly affected by places but there was something strange about this house. I was beginning to regret we had agreed to help, but it was too late now.

I should have listened to my instinct, should have helped Simon have a quick look around the house and then locked it up, never to return. But I didn't.

'Got it.' Simon waved one of the keys triumphantly.

'Let's hope so,' I muttered. I was chilled through and couldn't bear to spend more time out in the cold.

We walked up several steps to what appeared to be the main door, though it was located at the side of the house.

I frowned. 'Why is the entrance not grander, at the front of the house?'

'Think about it, Alison,' said Simon. 'Look at the road.'

'Of course. This circular driveway was built for a horse and carriage. The horse couldn't turn the way a car can now.'

Two stone lions guarded the door, their teeth bared to frighten any intruders. But the passage of time and the effects of the salt water had weathered their faces and one of them had lost its nose. They looked sad rather than fierce.

'If Susie wants to live here she'll have to find money to do some repairs fast,' muttered Simon as he turned the oversized key to open the massive wooden front door.

With a mighty groan it gave way and we almost fell into a vast entrance hall dominated by an ornately carved oak staircase.

It was the smell of the place that struck us immediately: the damp, musty odour of a place sadly abandoned, where the windows hadn't been opened in a very long time. The once beautiful wallpaper was pitted with mould and in the far corner above one of the doors a long strip had started to peel away, exposing bare wall beneath. I shivered again. The house felt cold, desolate. There was no welcome for us here.

The floor was of marble, ornately designed, but it was water stained and many of the tiles were cracked or had pieces missing. I went over to the bottom of the staircase and ran my hands over the carved newel. What little carpet remained on the stairs was frayed and worn and the thin line of lighter colour on each tread showed the stair rods had been removed at some time.

This was worse than we could have imagined. What on earth would Susie do with a place like this?

'The inside's every bit as imposing as the outside then,' said Simon.

Doors led off in all directions. 'Let's have a look now we're here,' I suggested. 'Susie will want a full report.'

Simon grumbled, but he didn't refuse. He was as intrigued as I was. 'We can go round the ground floor,' he said, 'but I'm not starting to go through this whole house. It's enormous and we don't have time if we're going back to Glasgow tonight.'

We looked round, wondering where to go first. By mutual consent we made for the nearest door.

In spite of the overall condition of the house the elaborate cornicing in the main rooms was almost intact and the marble fireplaces hadn't been gouged out, as so often happens. The remains of badly stained and musty carpets covered some of the floors, in others there were only bare boards which echoed to our footfalls. We moved round cautiously. I sniffed hard and then coughed as the overpowering smell of decay hit my nostrils.

I stood on the carpet in what seemed once to have been the dining room and I swear I felt it squelch under my feet, though Simon dismissed that as my imagination. A few pieces of furniture remained: two broken chairs and the top of what appeared to be a mahogany table propped against the wall. Here too was that smell of mildew, of rooms unheated for many years.

In one of the rooms at the back, which might have been the old morning room, a wire hung from the ceiling without a bulb, let alone the luxury of any kind of shade. In the corner an old couch and a couple of broken armchairs, their stuffing spilling out, did nothing to make the place feel any more comfortable.

In spite of all the decay I could imagine what this house must once have been like: finely furnished, the ceilings ablaze with glittering chandeliers illuminating the details of the ornate cornicing.

'Has it been empty for long, do you think?' I whispered.

Simon stopped. 'Why are you whispering, Alison?' he said crossly.

I had no idea. 'Perhaps I don't want to disturb the ghosts,' I said.

'Come on, let's see what else there is.' Simon moved off at a brisk pace and I followed close behind. I didn't want to lose sight of him.

Everywhere it was more of the same: faded, frayed carpets, a few pieces of old, rather than antique, furniture. In the fireplace in the largest room, the old drawing room, the desiccated carcass of a dead bird lay. It seemed to be appropriate for this house: death and decay.

As we made our way through room after room the air of neglect became overpowering, oppressive. Everywhere there was that strong smell of damp: the kind of damp that seeps into your very bones.

I opened the door to the room next to the drawing room. This was better furnished than the rest of the rooms with a couple of sofas, a few chairs, a small table and a bureau. There was no doubt it was a library: floor to ceiling dark wooden bookcases filled every wall. Through the mullioned windows I could see they still held some books but I could only guess they would be like everything else in this house, rotting on the shelves.

'The owners must have fallen on hard times,' I said, gazing round.

'Mmm, it does appear they had to sell off anything of value.'

'I don't see this as a place for Susie to enjoy a holiday break. How would you begin to heat it for a start?'

A two bar electric fire sat incongruously in the marble fireplace. 'This looks as if it's one of the rooms Robert Ainslee retreated to as his fortunes declined,' I mused.

The drawing room and the library overlooked the sweep of gardens to the front of the house. Although it was surrounded by thick bushes and trees, the house was so high up you could see over the terraced gardens and the pastureland below down to the long arc of Ettrick Bay. It was little wonder the house had been built on this site.

At the back the house was even gloomier, and here were more rooms. We peeped into the first two: one a huge empty space and the other the makeshift kitchen, furnished only with an ancient cooker, a sink and an old fold up formica table.

'The kitchen's a bit small for a house this size?'

Simon laughed. 'The original kitchen will be in the basement. Whoever last lived here evidently decided to create a kitchen up here for comfort.'

'I've no intention of finding out about the other kitchen,' I said, remembering the door to the basement we had spied under the stairs.

In spite of the resolution to 'have a quick look', we were now far too intrigued by this massive house to abandon our exploration. Without a word we started to climb the stairs.

But upstairs there was even less to see. Our footsteps echoed again on the bare floorboards and there was no furniture except for a few stray pieces in one of the many bedrooms.

'Come and see this, Alison.' Simon was standing at the door to the last of the bedrooms.

I peered over his shoulder. Someone had been using this room because it contained a bed, a table, a huge mahogany wardrobe and a few shelves. There was still a smell of damp but it wasn't as strong as in the rest of the house. And the décor looked more modern, though by more modern, I mean some time in the 1960s. I thought about my own comfortably warm house with its squashy sofas and fitted carpets and felt a pang of pity for whoever had had to live in this place, end their days amid all this faded grandeur.

'Looks as if the last person here used this bedroom and a couple of the rooms downstairs.' Simon was very matter of fact about it all.

I shivered again. 'This place is really creepy,' I said. 'Let's go.'

'Nonsense,' was Simon's curt reply. 'Come on; let's see what the rest of the place is like.' He strode ahead of me. He had evidently forgotten his earlier lack of interest and was now exploring enthusiastically.

'Look at this.' Simon called me over to the large bay window in one of the empty bedrooms. The smirr of rain had lifted and from this huge window you could see further down over Ettrick

Bay, past the island of Inchmarnock and over to the Sleeping Warrior of Arran beyond. Far below we could see a couple of hardy souls walking along at the edge of the water, throwing sticks for their dog, but from this distance it would be impossible to say who they were.

Simon was prowling about the room, peering into cupboards. I began to suspect he would be perfectly happy to spend time here if it could be made more comfortable. But no amount of cosmetic work would make the place appealing to me.

By now the light was fading and darkness was beginning to settle round the house. Soon it would be impossible to see.

I followed slowly, careful not to lose sight of him. We hadn't thought to bring a torch with us and now, in the deepening gloom of the February afternoon, long shadows lurked in every corner like malevolent ghosts. We should have looked for the electricity supply as a priority instead of wasting time wandering round all these decaying rooms.

It was the same everywhere: room after room resplendent with marble and carved wood, but empty, chilly. We went into the bathroom.

'Careful where you step, Alison,' said Simon, pointing to the floor round the bath. A large damp patch in the centre of the room looked as if it might give way at any moment.

Rather than risk hurtling through to the floor below I stood in the doorway and craned my neck to see. There had been some attempt to modernise this at one time, but it would have been better to let well alone. The suite was dark blue, the bath badly stained: not somewhere you would want to use unless desperate.

Simon turned on the tap in the basin and a thin stream of brackish water gurgled out.

'What was that?' A sudden noise, a scratching, made me stop. We both listened, scarcely breathing.

'Don't be silly, it's probably only mice. Or rats.' Simon grinned as he spoke. I didn't think it was funny.

How was I going to tell Susie this had all the makings of a terrible mistake?

'Let's go,' I said. 'I've seen enough of this place to let Susie know she wants to get rid of it as soon as possible.'

From his silence I could tell Simon didn't agree with me.

'What now?' I asked Simon but he merely shrugged. He had no answer either.

No matter what ideas Simon might have, I didn't see myself spending any holidays here. Even the little lodge house had lost its appeal.

We made our way back downstairs, sidestepping the most frayed parts of the carpet.

'I'll have a last look round here to check we haven't missed anything,' he said, 'and I guess we should try to locate that electricity supply for next time we come.'

I failed to understand what we could have missed but there was no way I was letting Simon wander off without me into the deepening shadows. And I ignored the promise of 'next time.'

'I'll come with you,' I said, more eagerly than I felt.

Simon ferreted round in the cupboards in the hall till he found the source of the electricity supply.

'Do you think you should touch it?' The jumble of black cables looked very dangerous.

But Simon wasn't to be deterred. 'Nonsense, it's perfectly safe,' was his muffled reply from somewhere deep inside the cupboard.

He emerged at last and went over and flicked on one of the switches on the wall. Light appeared, a very dim light: it made the place look gloomier than ever, so poor was it.

'Well, they installed electricity,' said Simon as he dusted himself down, 'but they didn't let it interfere with their other discomforts.'

I went through and gazed up at the ornate ceiling in what had once been a splendid dining room. The frieze round the walls was adorned with all kinds of fruits: lemons, oranges, pineapples, cherries in a random sequence. A few had crumbled away and the plaster lay on the floor where it had fallen. I contemplated trying to rescue these bits and pieces but quickly decided against it. That was a task for another day, should we ever return.

'Are you coming, Alison?' Simon called from the hallway. 'This is some house. Are you sure it's really Susie's?'

'So it appears.' I hurried to join him.

I was surprised. Susie had never in all the time I had known her (and it was a very long time) indicated in any way that she might be an heiress. To be fair, she seemed as surprised by what had happened as anyone.

We weren't sure what else we could do. When I phoned her later I would try to find something positive to say.

'It's not my idea of a holiday home,' I said to Simon. The very idea of spending even a night in this place made me shiver. There was something about the atmosphere of the place. In Ettrick House my active imagination was working overtime.

'Why don't we abandon this exploration meantime and head down to that tearoom we spied on the way up? I could do with something warm and comforting,' I suggested. 'We've time before the ferry.'

Before Simon could reply there was a loud pounding noise.

We looked at each other.

'What on earth was that?' I said.

'How should I know?' Simon answered, not unreasonably.

Again it came, even louder this time.

'It's the front door, Alison. We've got visitors,' he said.

The knocking grew louder and louder as we approached till I thought the door, solid as it was, would come crashing in.

Simon wrenched the door open and was confronted by a man of indeterminate age.

Indeterminate because most of his face was covered by a long beard which seemed to reach up into his long glossy mane of curly red hair.

'Yes?' said Simon, with more courtesy than he felt, I'm sure. Was this a local beggar who thought he'd chance his luck?

The man smiled, showing a row of white teeth. 'Hello. Are you the new owners of Ettrick House?'

I was about to say, 'No, we are opening it up for a friend,' when something in his manner made me hesitate. Instead I said, 'We're just here for a short while.' No need to let him know the house would soon be empty.

'So will you be here for long?' he persisted.

I could see the frown on Simon's face. Perhaps I should say nothing more.

'Why are you interested?' Although Simon sounded meticulously polite, I could hear the steel in his voice.

The young man smiled, not at all put out by Simon's unfriendly manner.

He extended a hand in greeting.

'Sorry, I should have introduced myself properly. My name is Morgan Connolly and I wanted to let you know we would be starting on Monday about 8 o'clock.'

Simon stared. 'Sorry? I don't understand. Starting what?'

I couldn't make sense of this. Had Susie ordered workmen in? But how would she know what needed to be done?

'Oh, it's all in order,' said the man hastily and he waved a large sheet of paper. 'We've brought all the necessary permissions.'

He grinned engagingly. 'We'll try not to disturb you. We even bring our own tea.'

We gazed at him, speechless. What on earth was he talking about?

'I don't understand. What do you mean? What permission?' said Simon.

The man pointed to the large white van behind him. 'We're the archaeologists and we're coming to start work on the site at Ettrick House.'

FIVE

'How are we going to break the news to Susie? I said.

We were comfortably ensconced in the warmth of the Ettrick Bay tearoom, feasting on bacon rolls and hot sweet tea. After the chill of Ettrick House, the food tasted like nectar.

Simon shook his head, his mouth too full to speak.

I stared out of the window. The rain had cleared once more and from the comfort of the tearoom we could see a red and purple streaked sunset, hope that good weather was on its way. The pale moon had already risen and the sea lapped slowly at the long stretch of glistening sand curving into the far distance.

'It's strange Mr Laidlaw didn't mention an archaeological dig was planned for the bottom of Susie's garden. I mean, it's not the kind of thing that happens every day, is it?'

'Possibly he didn't know.' Simon started on his second bacon roll. 'He did suggest something was happening. But he didn't give us any details.'

I was about to say, 'Because you cut him off before he could tell us anything' then decided it would be better to keep my opinions to myself.

I was sure Mr Laidlaw had been more than anxious to alert us to the proposal to build a wind farm on the site at Ettrick Bay. We hadn't given him the opportunity.

'Anyway, you heard what Morgan Connolly said.' Simon gestured to his cup for a refill. 'By law they have to have archaeologists examine any site of interest they find. It's a condition of the exploration for the building of the access road to this wind farm.'

I didn't dare to think how Susie would receive the news that she might be about to have a wind farm situated beside her new inheritance. And I couldn't imagine how a wind farm could be built in a spot as beautiful as this without a lot of protest from the local community. Perhaps that was still to come.

The smiling young waitress appeared at our table with another generous cup of steaming coffee. 'Anything else you would like.'

'No, thanks.' I shook my head. In the refrigerated cabinet beside the counter I could spy an array of tempting cakes. I resisted, promising myself that next time I would indulge.

I didn't find Simon's words convincing. The road up to the house wasn't busy. A few farms were dotted about, but I didn't understand how there could be much of historical interest there.

Simon sat back in his chair. 'Alison, forget it. All we have to do is let Susie know what's going on. That's our obligation finished with.'

'At least Morgan seems a nice young man,' I said as I put down my empty cup.

'Mmm,' Simon was non-committal. 'We'll see.'

I thought back to the encounter at the house. Morgan had been happy to chat and told us in some detail about his plans for the excavation at the site.

'That's an unusual name, Morgan,' I had said.

He grinned. 'My dad was well into classic cars. Lucky I wasn't called Ferrari - that was his favourite.'

I smiled. We all choose names for our children without thinking about the consequences.

'Anyway,' he went on, 'I'm usually known by my nickname 'Red'. For obvious reasons,' he added, pointing to his mop of red curls. 'You can choose what you call me.'

Morgan would be fine for me: I didn't see myself calling him 'Red' somehow.

I thought about our youngest daughter Deborah. Morgan seemed exactly the kind of young man to appeal to her.

'Alison, are you listening?' Simon broke into my thoughts.

'So we're going back up to Glasgow tonight?' I changed the subject.

'Of course. There's no way we can stay unless we organise to bring down some home comforts.'

This was sounding increasingly as if Simon thought we would return to Ettrick House - and soon. I had to come up with a good reason to avoid returning to the house for a holiday, well aware my 'feelings' about the place wouldn't be a good enough reason for Simon.

I considered our bank balance. Could we stretch to a holiday abroad on the basis that the weather in Scotland could be unpredictable and the heating in Ettrick House was less than adequate?

As Simon finished his coffee I thought again about our visit from the archaeologists. Morgan Connolly explained he was in charge of the project.

'We're only here for a preliminary visit,' he had said. 'We won't be down again until Spring when we'll be starting properly.' He turned as if to leave and then suddenly came back. 'Are you staying on here?'

'Absolutely not,' I said as Simon replied, 'Oh, we might come down for a short break in a few weeks' time.'

Morgan smiled again. It lit up his whole face and made him look handsome in spite of his quantity of facial hair. 'And you definitely won't be back before then?'

'It's hard to tell,' I replied, puzzled by his determination to pin us down to an exact date. 'We're doing a favour for a friend. She might come over to the island before us.'

In spite of his charming manner, I wasn't prepared to say too much to him.

'Don't worry, we'll still be here. I expect this survey will take several months.'

Morgan beckoned to the others. 'Let's head on out, you guys. We'll keep these good folks posted.'

They all jumped into the old white van where the lettering had faded, so that what had once said

"Strathmore Archaeological Services" now bore the bizarre legend "Stat more logical vices".

'We'll look forward to meeting Susie Littlejohn later,' were Morgan's parting words.

I tried hard to stifle a laugh. I wouldn't want to upset them if they were going to be Susie's neighbours for a while.

The van spluttered into life at the third attempt and stuttered off in a pall of smoke as Morgan leaned out the window, waving to us.

'If their van is anything to go by, they won't be very professional,' Simon had muttered.

I returned to the present and to Simon, who was now sitting back with the contented expression of a man who has been well fed.

I had a sudden thought. I opened my handbag and raked through it.

'What's wrong, Alison?' said Simon.

'I've left my house keys behind. I took them out of my bag when we were in the library.'

Simon looked cross. 'Why on earth did you do that? If we don't catch the next ferry we're going to be pretty late back in Glasgow.'

I was adamant. My school keys were on the key ring and in spite of Simon's enthusiasm it could be some time before we came back to Ettrick House. 'It will only take a few minutes. And I do need them.'

'Oh, if it keeps you happy,' Simon sighed as he saw the expression on my face. We went over to join the queue to pay the modest bill before heading out to the car park.

The man in front of us turned sharply, bumping into Simon and causing him to spill the change he was carefully counting out.

'Oh, so sorry, I do apologise.'

I looked in astonishment. 'Harry?'

'Good Lord, is it you, Alison? What are you doing here?'

Of all places to bump into Harry Sneddon, recently retired from Strathelder High School, the tearoom at Ettrick Bay seemed one of the strangest.

Harry grinned. He looked a lot better than when I had last seen him, shambling out the door of the school after the 'retirement event' traditional for all those departing the trials of teaching.

His white hair which once flopped carelessly over his eyes was now cut short and he seemed to have gained an inch or two in height, though that must surely have been my imagination. He sported casual clothes of quality, unlike the worn suit and down at heel shoes which had once been his trademark attire for school.

A bigger surprise was to come.

'I'm living on the island now. Have you met my wife, Greta?' He said this with a wicked gleam in his eye. Was Harry, the confirmed bachelor, indeed married?

'No, I haven't had the pleasure,' I managed to say as a tall handsome woman came walking towards us. My first impression was one of elegance. She was as formally dressed as Harry was casual, in a blue wool two piece suit. Her mass of grey hair was swept up into a bun at the back of her head, not a hair out of place. Her piercing blue eyes regarded me coolly. At least Harry hadn't married some young thing. If anything, Greta appeared to be several years older than he was.

If Greta was the cause of Harry's transformation she had done a good job. She extended a hand in greeting as I turned to include Simon in this surprising group.

Harry said, 'What brings you here, Alison, in the middle of February. I would have thought sunnier climes would have suited you at half term?'

I explained briefly about Susie unexpectedly inheriting a house on the island.

'Good for her,' said Harry. 'Where is it?'

'Up in the hills behind here,' I replied. 'It's Ettrick House.'

I sensed Greta stiffen beside me. 'I thought that was still all in dispute,' she said coldly.

I shrugged. 'Apparently not. It seems to have been decided Susie is the only living relative, distant though she is.'

'Indeed. She's not from the island then?' This seemed to trouble her.

Before I had a chance to explain, Simon tugged at my sleeve. 'Sorry - we really have to go. Alison wants to go back up to Ettrick House. She's left her keys.'

'You must come and see us sometime,' said Harry. 'We're living out at Ardbeg.'

'Yes, and if you'll excuse me, I have to drop in some books at the charity shop. I'll see you outside, Harry.' With a quick nod in our direction she was gone.

Harry raised his eyebrows, evidently embarrassed by Greta's sudden departure. 'Sorry about that. Greta's mother died a couple of weeks ago and Greta has had to go through all her papers and belongings. It's upset her more than I would have imagined. Her mother was over ninety and had been in a nursing home in Largs for some time, but I suppose no matter when it happens it's a shock. And she's an only child, so it falls to her to sort things out.'

Harry appeared so worried about what we might think I hastened to re-assure him. We parted with promises to be in touch.

'We'll catch up with you next time we're down,' I called over my shoulder as we left.

We headed back to the car. Once out of the warmth of the tearoom, the wind chill took your breath away. It was still too cold for a walk along the beach, beguiling though it looked in the pale moonlight.

'Fancy Harry marrying after all these years,' I mused as we climbed into the car, 'though I must say Greta is a bit of a cold fish. Ah well, it takes all sorts.'

We left the car park with another car close on our tail. It was time for everyone to go home then, I thought.

We bumped our way in the car back up the potholed road to Ettrick House. Here the darkness was inky black. The moon had disappeared behind the clouds and as we approached the house its dark outline, framed by the windswept trees, made it look even more forbidding than before.

Simon stopped the car beside the front door.

'Aren't you coming in with me?'

He laughed. 'Yes, if you like. But I really don't know why you are so frightened of this place. It's only a big house.'

We opened the door more easily this time, trying to remember where the first light switch was. I kept close behind Simon as he fumbled about in the dark in the downstairs cupboard, switching on the electricity supply. This dim light in the hall was of little help.

'Next time we'll bring some torches,' said Simon, brushing a cobweb from his hair as he emerged.

'I don't see Susie living here,' I shivered, pulling my coat tightly around me. 'Not unless she can raise the money for a complete makeover.'

'The archaeologists will keep her company,' grinned Simon. 'They seem just her type.'

'Wait a minute.' I stopped. 'Simon, how on earth did Morgan know Susie's name?'

Simon shrugged. 'You must have told him. Come on; let's find your keys and leave.'

Although I replayed our conversation in my head several times I was sure I had done no such thing. All I had said was that we were here on behalf of a friend. I was sure I had given nothing else away. At no time had I mentioned Susie's name.

I was about to argue when Simon said, 'Let's hurry, Alison, if we want to catch that ferry.'

Unfortunately finding the keys took longer than anticipated. I was sure I had left them in the library but a search of the room failed to find them.

'I need to retrace my steps,' I muttered, aware that time was passing rapidly and Simon was becoming more and more tetchy. Eventually I found them lying on a little table in the makeshift kitchen.

'Got them,' I said coming out and waving them triumphantly.

'Right, let's go.' Simon took my arm and propelled me to the front door.

We went down the steps into the forecourt. I felt almost light hearted to be leaving, which was ridiculous and I was so deep in thought it took me a minute or two to register what Simon was saying.

'What the hell has happened,' Simon exploded.

As I was still behind him, I was at first unaware of why he had shouted.

Then I saw for myself. Our car, which had been parked as close as he could get to the main door, was no longer there.

We both stood stock-still for a moment, as though expecting it miraculously to re-appear. But there was no doubt about it. The car had vanished.

SIX

'Are you sure you parked it here?' I knew it was a stupid question. But where on earth was the car?

Simon didn't answer me. He was too busy gazing at the empty space as though the car might suddenly re-appear.

'Perhaps the handbrake wasn't on securely?'

Simon glared at me. 'Alison, you saw me park it, you got out of it at the same time as I did, we went into the house together. So these suggestions of yours aren't at all helpful.' I knew he was berating himself for leaving the keys in the ignition. But who would have thought there would be any danger in doing so in a spot as remote as this?

We stood there, at a complete loss. How could a large object like a family saloon vanish into thin air?

'Did you hear anything while we were in the house?' Simon was as baffled as I was.

'Not a thing.' I tried hard to think of any noise I might have heard. But from inside the thick walls of the house it wasn't likely we would have heard a car start up. Besides, the very idea that someone might come all the way up here on the off chance of stealing our car was ridiculous. No, there must be a simple explanation.

We looked around but the darkness was almost impenetrable. The only light was from the moon which peeped in and out of the thickening cloud.

The wind had strengthened and the trees behind the house were bending and sighing in a most alarming fashion. I pulled my coat more tightly around me. Thank goodness I hadn't left it in the car.

'Let's have a look round the outside of the house,' said Simon, determined not to believe what was happening. 'It might only be someone's idea of a joke.'

I gripped his hand tightly as we went round to the back of the house. In the dark we had to pick our way carefully. At this time of year the grass was treacherous underfoot and the spiky bramble bushes had made inroads everywhere. We kept as close as we could to the driveway.

The exploration didn't take long: there was no car here.

'Are you thinking what I'm thinking?' I ventured.

'Probably,' said Simon gloomily. 'How on earth are we going to get out of here with no car and not even a torch to light our way?'

'Perhaps there might be some candles in the house?'

'In this wind?' Simon was dismissive.

We walked slowly to the end of the drive, trying to spot a friendly light from a nearby house, any house, but the only lights looked to be very far away. With no idea of where we were, even I had to admit it would be foolhardy to try to walk to one of them.

'We could phone for a taxi?' I suggested helpfully.

'Indeed we could, Alison,' Simon shook his head. 'Unfortunately my phone is in the car.'

As was mine, together with my handbag, my scarf and gloves and everything else of use.

We stood in silence, trying frantically to think of a solution. We couldn't stay out in the dark and increasing cold.

Simon said. 'There's nothing else for it, Alison. We'll have to stay here for the night.'

He was right. There was no alternative. We didn't know how to get back down except by the very bumpy road we had come up in the car and the danger of straying off that path was something I didn't want to contemplate. Up in the hills of Ettrick Bay the darkness was complete.

Awful as it might be to stay over in this forbidding house, it was going to be even more dangerous to try to make our way down to Ettrick Bay.

Reluctantly I followed Simon as he again unlocked the massive door. In the dark it took him a few minutes of fiddling about with the key ring and I was relieved when I heard the click of the key in the lock.

I was feeling more than a little guilty. If I hadn't insisted we return, we would by now be comfortably settled on the ferry on our way back to Glasgow. I had no idea how we would manage to pass the night in Ettrick House, but I did know I wouldn't have much sleep.

Once inside, in that gloomy hall, we had to make a decision about where we should go. This time Simon's first action was to seek out the electricity cupboard though it was difficult to know if the lights were a help, sparse as they were.

'Let's go through to that library at the front,' he said. 'I suspect it was the room old Ainslee used most.'

Unfortunately this was one of the rooms lacking a supply of electricity. There was a bulb in the holder in the ceiling but it had long since died.

'We can either have light or we can have somewhere to sit down, unless you want to start pulling furniture around. Let's use the library: we can leave on the light in the hall and keep the door open.'

'Whatever you think.' I was too cold and too tired to argue. Look how much my last bright idea had helped us.

From memory this room boasted a couple of ancient sofas, a table and some chairs: luxury compared to the rest of the house.

'Ouch,' I bumped into something solid as we tried to find our way round the room. It was the small bureau.

'Do you think there might be some candles in this?' I asked more in hope than expectation.

Simon wasn't listening. He was too busy trying to move the few pieces of furniture around to give us some degree of comfort.

I pulled at the drop down front of the bureau, but it was securely locked, as were the three drawers. Short of searching for a chisel, I wasn't going to get much out of this piece of furniture.

'Come and give me a hand, Alison.'

Simon had managed to push the two old sofas together and with a last effort we pushed them into a corner as a makeshift bed.

We sat about in silence for a while until Simon said, 'We may as well try to get some sleep.'

It seemed the only sensible thing to do so we settled down as best we could. Without any bedding, we had to make do by putting my coat on the joined up dusty sofas. It was hardly a solution and we lay down cautiously.

Every creak, every noise the old building made startled me into wakefulness each time I tried to doze off. And I was so cold. I kept as close as I could to Simon, sure the beating of my heart could be heard with every tremor of fear I experienced. Better perhaps to stay awake, then there would be no surprises.

Tired out by the events of the day, exhaustion at last overcame me. In spite of my fears I drifted off to sleep sometime during the night.

As I did so, in that half world between sleeping and waking, I wondered about the bureau.

Why was it locked? I would try again in the morning to open it. Susie wouldn't mind.

SEVEN

The morning light filtered slowly through the grimy windows in the room where we had spent the night. We had considered pulling down the heavy dark red chenille curtains hanging at the windows then, almost as quickly, dismissed the thought. The dust of the old sofas was enough to contend with. Every time I had wakened during that long night it had been with a bout of sneezing.

I raised myself up cautiously on one elbow. For a moment as I came to I felt groggy and wondered where on earth I was. Beside me, Simon lay sound asleep.

I slid off the sofas and stretched to rid myself of the aches and pains from the uncomfortable position I'd been lying in during the night.

I went to the window, rubbed at one of the panes of glass and looked out. The sun was up and a glorious day of blue skies and bright sunlight greeted me. Beyond the neglected gardens the rolling slopes down to Ettrick Bay looked green with the promise of Spring.

The water in the distance sparkled in the sunlight, little motes of light dancing on the waves. It was still cold, but somehow the sunshine lifted my spirits. We would soon be out of here and on our way home.

'Morning, Alison,' Simon stretched and yawned. 'What time is it?'

'After 9 o'clock,' I replied. 'Can we start soon?'

Simon sat up and ran his hands over his head, a gesture that made his short straight hair stand alarmingly on end. 'I guess we've no option. There's nothing to eat or drink here. At least we'll be able to see our way down to the bay.'

Preparations for leaving didn't take long, though Simon made a great show of checking everything was shut down before we left.

'We wouldn't want to have to come back up here again in case we'd forgotten something, would we, Alison?' he said, his voice heavy with irony.

As Simon locked the door, I started to walk slowly down the drive towards the lodge house.

In this sunshine and from a distance Ettrick House didn't look so forbidding. Instead it appeared dejected, as though aware how badly it had been treated.

Still chilled from our uncomfortable night, we started to walk briskly past the lodge house and onto the road outside, pausing only to wrestle open the heavy wooden gates. As we walked along we debated what could possibly have happened.

'I don't see someone coming all the way up here on the off chance there might be a car to steal,' I said.

'Nor do I.' Simon was as perplexed as I was. 'We'll report it to the police as soon as we get down to the town. We can phone for a taxi from the Ettrick Bay tearoom.'

'With a bit of luck they might let us have some breakfast with a promise to pay later.' The very thought made my mouth water and I quickened my pace.

We each took a deep breath and steeled ourselves for the walk. My shoes weren't ideal for what lay ahead but there was no way I would let Simon go without me. I tried to keep up as best I could, leaning heavily on him when we came to any bumpy part of the road. Thank goodness we were going downhill.

The morning had kept fair and the wind of the previous night had died down, leaving only the gentlest of breezes. We stopped a couple of times on the way, leaning on the fence to survey the newborn lambs gambolling in the fields. The mother sheep looked up, moving protectively towards their offspring and staring at us fixedly. They didn't see many walkers up here at this time of year.

Half way down we turned onto the rutted path that led alongside a huddle of trees.

'Look,' said Simon pointing downwards. 'Thank goodness we decided to stay up at the house last night.'

Along the length of the road there ran a deep ditch, mostly covered over by the remains of last year's grasses. 'It would have been all too easy to stumble into one of those by mistake.'

I shuddered. The thought of being left out in the open with one of us injured was even worse than the night we had spent in Ettrick House.

Simon looked at his watch. 'Let's move, Alison. We can see without any problem now.' He grasped my elbow to hurry me on.

'We should sing as we go to keep our spirits up...' I suggested, but a withering look from Simon made me stop in mid sentence.

We were well away from the house now. I turned back to have a last look, but from where we were standing it was hidden by the trees. A secret place, well disguised from curious eyes.

I was lagging behind again, pleased to be in the sunshine and glad to be out of the house. I stopped again for a moment to catch my breath and watch as far below on the bay a little sail boat made slow progress.

I heard Simon give a sudden shout. Where was he? A moment of panic before I realised he had moved round the corner of the road, screened as it was by high hedges.

I ran as best I could in the circumstances, stumbling a couple of times in my less than adequate shoes, to catch up with him.

He was standing at a passing place on the road scratching his head. There, in the indent and neatly parked, was our car.

I couldn't believe what I was seeing. Who would steal a car to leave it a mile or so down the road?

'It isn't even damaged,' Simon muttered, more to himself than to me, as he walked round it examining the bodywork and running his hands over the tyres for any signs of vandalism.

'Ah, but are the keys there?' I was sure it couldn't be as simple as this.

Simon opened the unlocked door and peered inside. 'Yes, the keys are still there in the ignition. Come on, Alison, let's try it out.'

I didn't need to be asked twice and opened the passenger door quickly as Simon slid into the driver's seat.

The car started at once. There were no visible signs of wear and tear, no signs of its having been taken for a joy ride. It was all most odd.

We were too relieved to worry about explanations. We had our car back and the rest of our journey would be easy.

Now we had to go into Rothesay, report what had happened to the police and try to return to the mainland as soon as we could.

Several times on the way there I opened my mouth to say something to Simon, but he was looking ahead with grim determination.

So I said nothing, but when I thought about it, why would anyone want to take our car unless they wanted to cause us problems? Did they hope we would set out to look for it and come to harm? If not, what other reason could there be?

My feelings of unease increased. It all looked so tranquil here, yet there was something sinister going on.

There was more to this house at Ettrick Bay than we knew.

EIGHT

We wanted to return to Glasgow as quickly as possible. I had to contact Susie urgently about Ettrick House, to find out what her plans were. I didn't want any more to do with this strange place she had inherited.

We had to inform the police about the disappearance of our car, so Rothesay was our first stop. We slid into a parking space outside the police station in the High Street.

Simon rang the bell on the desk while I idly read the wealth of posters adorning the walls. For such a crime free island there were a lot of admonitions.

The door to the office swung open almost immediately with a 'Can I help you?'

P.C. Killop was young, but most professional. As we recounted what had happened, his expression gave no sign he thought we were two slightly eccentric visitors from the mainland who were possibly reaching the age of being forgetful.

'And where exactly was your car parked?'

'Right outside the house, Ettrick House,' Simon replied.

'We're looking after it for our friend,' I added helpfully.

His head came up sharply. 'Ettrick House, out at Ettrick Bay?' There was an edge to his voice which made me start.

'Yes.' Simon frowned. 'Is there a problem?'

'No, no,' but the tone of his voice made think there was indeed some difficulty he wasn't telling us about. Perhaps anyone who ventured up there had their car stolen? As we waited for him to explain, he seemed to collect himself and smiled again at us.

When every detail had been noted down he assured us we would be contacted as soon as there were any developments. Although he promised to keep us informed, I wasn't too sure this 'crime', if it was a crime, was a high priority.

'At least we have the car back without a scratch,' I said as we headed for the ferry.

Simon made no reply, but I could see he was far from pleased.

We managed to catch the lunchtime ferry back over to Wemyss Bay. It was a smooth crossing, much appreciated by both of us. The journey to Weymss Bay only takes about half an hour, but once you're out of the shelter of the bay there are times of the year when the journey can be a bit rocky.

We were greeted like long lost travellers by Motley, our cat, when we opened the door of our house. Compared to Ettrick House, it felt tiny, but at least it wasn't spooky. Besides, although cats aren't the most demonstrative of creatures, even cupboard love is sometimes appreciated.

'Shall I try Susie now?' I asked Simon, looking at the clock.

'You'd better leave it for a while yet. Were you thinking of trying to contact her at school? Not a good idea, Alison.' He frowned.

'No, she might think there's something seriously wrong if I do that.'

We decided to have something to eat and I'd try phoning her much later to allow for the time difference.

I was in luck. Susie was at home when I called later that night.

'Hi, Alison - I didn't expect to hear from you so soon. How did it all go?'

'Well, Susie, there are no immediate problems.'

I thought it prudent to begin cautiously. How to tell her what had happened without alarming her? 'It's just that, well, the place is a bit bigger than I expected. But perhaps it's because I didn't fully understand what you were telling me.'

'What do you mean, Alison? I know the lodge house appeared big to me as a child.'

'Yes, there is a lodge house, that's true,' I said slowly, 'but it's more what's attached to the lodge house.'

'Oh, for goodness sake, Alison, stop beating about the bush and tell me straight what's happening. No matter how bad it is, there's nothing I can do about it at the moment.'

I told her.

For once my friend was lost for words. When she recovered, her amazement was genuine. 'What! You're joking. Surely there must be some mistake.'

She shrieked down the phone so loudly I had to hold the earpiece at a distance.

'No, Susie, there's no mistake. It's all yours. I suspect when you visited as a child you lived in the lodge house: the main house is well screened by trees, so you may not have been aware that there was any other building there.'

As there was no reply I went on, 'I thought that in the circumstances you might want to come over and see for yourself?'

'You know I can't, Alison,' she wailed. 'I'm at a very critical stage in sorting out the continuation of this job…'

Her voice tailed off. She was obviously torn between whatever was happening in America and the lure of this vast estate she'd inherited.

'And,' I replied sternly, 'what else is happening that you're not telling me about?'

There was an embarrassed laugh and then a pause. 'Well, there is this man that I've been seeing. Nothing serious you understand,' she hurried on, 'but I don't really want to come away at the moment. Our relationship has reached a certain stage, if you know what I mean.'

I was impatient with her. 'Susie, I don't think you understand. This is a mansion you have acquired. There are decisions to be made. I can help, but there's a limit to what I can do…'

She cut in to my tirade.

'Please, please, Alison, I do need your help. This is a great opportunity for me and I don't want to mess it up. The house will still be there when I come back.'

'Oh, so you are planning to return?'

I meant my comment to sound sarcastic, but across the miles the sarcasm must have been lost. I now wasn't sure if she was talking about an opportunity for employment or for romance. I rather suspected the latter.

She sounded as if she thought I was creating a problem where there was none. 'Don't be silly, Alison, you know I'll have to come back at some stage. Please, please help me. I'm sure you can manage things until June,' she pleaded, 'and I'll have to come back then anyway.'

It was hard to refuse when I knew how much the exchange to America meant to her, whatever form it might be taking at the moment.

'Fine, Susie, I'll speak to Simon about it but no more than that,' was my final word on the subject, though I suspected, as her effusive thanks came down the line, she had somehow managed as usual to persuade me to agree. Susie has that effect on people. And I find it hard to say no.

We chatted briefly for a few more minutes and she promised to phone me at the weekend. At this distance, the house at Ettrick Bay had assumed an air of unreality for her.

'Remember to check your e-mail,' I scolded her as we signed off.

I was determined that love of her life or not (and knowing Susie I rather suspected not) she would have to understand the implications of her sudden inheritance.

It was only after I'd put the phone down I realised I had completely forgotten to mention the archaeologists.

As luck would have it, I didn't have the opportunity to call Susie back that night to tell her about the excavations taking place on her property. No sooner had I replaced the receiver than the phone rang again, startling me. It was Deborah.

'Mum, I'm coming home for a few days if that's all right,' she said.

I was concerned by this brief call, though I tried not to show it. We would find out soon enough what was going on. 'Fine by me. Is something wrong?'

There was a moment's silence and then she replied hesitantly, 'Not really: I feel I need a break, that's all.'

I knew better than to question her further. She can be a bit prickly: the artistic temperament I suppose, though Simon in his usual way dismisses that as a lot of nonsense.

I hoped that there wasn't something wrong with this new job in London she had started. It had taken her so long to find something she liked after several years of dropping in and out of various art courses.

I put the phone down, took a deep breath and went through and said to Simon as casually as possible, 'Deborah's coming home for a few days for a break.'

He looked up from news section of the Sunday paper he was wrestling with. 'What's the matter now?'

I shrugged. 'Don't know, really. I expect she'll tell us when she arrives.'

'She'll have to fend for herself, that's all. I've a busy week ahead of me.'

'I'm sure she won't trouble you at all. The spare room is all ready.'

It was one thing for Deborah to say that she would tell us what was going on when she came home, but the result was I hardly slept all night.

I went in to school the next day feeling the effects. Monday is one of the heaviest days on my timetable and, as was only to be expected, we were short of staff yet again, so my only free period was swallowed up by a 'please take' for third year boys.

I was so annoyed I made little pretence of trying to interest them. They can be a handful, but I was in such a bad mood there was not a murmur of dissent when I set them an interpretation. I must be more fiercesome than I think, in spite of being smaller in stature than most of them.

There was a staff meeting at the end of the afternoon about changes to the content of the courses for the upper school next term 'in order to make it all more relevant for our less able pupils' as our head of department put it.

'Make it so easy that any of the little blighters could do it more like,' my colleague Malcolm muttered in my ear, but then he is always cynical about any new initiatives.

To complete a less than perfect day I was caught in the rush hour traffic, with the usual delays on the Kingston Bridge made worse by several minor accidents. By the time I reached home I was in need of a few days' rest myself.

Deborah hadn't yet arrived, but that was nothing unusual. I made a half hearted attempt on the spare room. I suspected Motley had been in again, sleeping on the bed, even though we do try to keep him out.

Simon arrived first.

'Smells good,' he said sniffing the air appreciatively. I didn't confess it was a ready made meal from a well known supermarket, hastily enhanced with some herbs.

'Do you want to wait till Deborah arrives or do you want to fix a sandwich to keep you going?'

'I think I'd rather have a drink,' he replied. 'Do you want one?'

I shook my head. 'I may have one later.' It all depended on what Deborah might have to tell us.

He took off his jacket and loosened his tie. 'As you wish. I'll go and change first.'

Time wore on. Simon by now was on his second drink, not a good sign at the beginning of the week.

I began to wonder if I had mistaken the date. Maybe she'd said she'd be here next Monday? I kept popping between the kitchen and the sitting room where Simon was watching the television news.

The weather forecaster was predicting another day of torrential rain in a cheery manner at odds with the grim forecast when the door bell rang and there was Deborah at last.

I greeted her with a hug and a kiss. She looked much better that when I'd last seen her. She was dressed almost respectably, in a pair of jeans lacking her usual trademark holes and safety pins. Last time she'd visited, she'd been wearing a strange combination of layers and layers of black clothes. I hadn't realised there were so many different shades of black.

She came through and hugged Simon.

'Hello, dad, really good to see you.' Then she hugged me again. This was unusual, because Deborah is the least tactile of all three children. It took both of us by surprise.

'Great to see you, Deborah and dinner's ready. Shall we eat now? '

'I'd rather you sat down for a moment, mum. There's something I want to tell you both.'

My heart started pounding. What on earth was she going to say? My instinct had been correct. I knew that there had to be a reason for this visit. And here it was.

She looked from one of us to the other, swallowed hard and then it all came out in a rush, 'I have to tell you I've given up my job.'

My worst suspicions were confirmed.

A frown crossed Simon's face. 'What do you mean, Deborah?'

I looked at him, trying to give him a warning sign. I didn't want a full scale crisis on my hands just yet. But he was too busy gazing at Deborah to notice me.

She shrugged, 'What I say. I've given up my job. I made a big mistake. It wasn't for me. This isn't what I want to do.'

I was sure she was trying to be brave about it, but she sounded so laid back as though she was announcing she'd prefer tea to coffee. I knew Simon would be furious.

'You can't leave.' Simon had regained his composure and I could hear warning bells. He and Deborah have a habit of rubbing each other up the wrong way. They are too alike in temperament.

Deborah looked defiant. 'Well, I have. It's too late now. I've told them I'm not coming back.'

She turned to me. 'If it's all right I'd like to move back in for a while.'

After the initial shock Simon calmed down, especially as Deborah began to look distinctly tearful.

'And what do you plan to do?''

Deborah visibly brightened. 'Oh, there's no problem about that. I've been accepted for teacher training college in the autumn. There's going to be another teacher in the family.'

Simon opened his mouth to make a comment, but at another warning look from me he closed it again. Now was not the time for picking over what had happened. That could come later.

Around midnight as we went up to bed, Simon said, 'I hope we're not going to have to put up yet another wrong choice. Teaching isn't the easy option some people seem to think it is.'

'Give her time, Simon,' I said soothingly, 'she's only arrived and it's all been a big decision for her.

She's probably been thinking about this for some time, but didn't want to tell us. And it's a long time till the autumn. She may yet settle on something else.'

There was no reply. I continued, 'It must have taken some courage to admit that she was wrong. I suspect that's why she left her job instead of talking to us about it beforehand.'

'I suppose so,' was the gloomy response, but I could tell he wasn't convinced. 'I hope this isn't the start of them all trailing home again'

'Don't be ridiculous,' I said brusquely. 'Maura is perfectly happily settled in Kent with Alan, and Alastair wouldn't dream of giving up his post at the university in Canada. You know how much research suits his temperament. He's more likely to end up as the eternal student.'

And that concluded the conversation for the moment.

The next day we went off to work even more subdued than we usually are in the mornings. There had been no sign of Deborah at breakfast, but then I hardly expected her to appear so early. Now she had told us what her plans were, she would keep herself to herself for a few days.

Fortunately Simon was too pre-occupied with the day ahead to discuss matters, for which I was grateful. As head of department in a large further education college, he does carry a lot of responsibility, but it seems to me they're always lurching from one crisis to another, which makes me glad I'm in a school and I can still close the classroom door against the ever increasing bureaucracy.

We saw very little of Deborah for the rest of that week. She stayed in the spare room mostly, emerging only at mealtimes. We only knew she was there because of the incessant loud music that thumped through the house. Whenever we tried to use the telephone, the upstairs extension always seemed to be engaged.

'I'm going to have to speak to her,' said Simon on more than one occasion when he had tried unsuccessfully to phone a colleague. 'Why can't she use her mobile for these interminable calls?' I managed to dissuade him. I was sure it wouldn't last and she would emerge sooner or later.

I was becoming more and more concerned about our promise to Susie about Bute. I did want to help her, but every time I thought about what had happened to us, a shiver ran down my spine. A car couldn't disappear on its own. Someone had been, at the very least, trying to frighten us.

This 'tiny bit of help' Susie had requested was turning into a full time job, a feeling confirmed by her next contact.

'Alison,' she wrote in that curiously abrupt fashion people use in e-mails, 'I've been thinking about Bute. If the place is as enormous as you say and there's likely to be all this archaeological work going on, maybe it shouldn't be empty.'

I breathed a sigh of relief. Everything was going to be fine. Now we could stay at home over Easter and book a summer holiday somewhere hot and exotic. And we'd be around if Deborah needed help.

Alas, it was all short-lived, because as I scrolled down the text I realised to my dismay Susie had a different plan from the one I had envisaged.

Her e-mail continued, 'I hate to ask you and Simon this because I appreciate how much you've done already.'

My heart sank as I read on, 'Could you possibly go down and find out what's been happening? I've an appraisal in just over two weeks and if all goes well I'll be able to apply for funding to stay on here for another year. AND I REALLY WANT TO DO THAT - THIS MAY BE MY LAST CHANCE OF A REAL LIFE!'

She said little else, she didn't have to. The capital letters in her last sentence made her feelings clear. I closed down the computer with a feeling of despair.

Torn in all directions and with a dread of going back to that house in Ettrick Bay, I needed some time to myself to think through exactly what I should do.

How was I going to tell Simon we were off again so soon to the house at Ettrick Bay?

NINE

Easter was early, too soon after mid term for my liking. Deborah was still with us, certain she'd made the right decision about her future. I was less convinced.

She had gone back briefly to London to sort out various projects to do with her job, but had returned more determined than ever that she wouldn't go back in spite of their pleading that she stay on. I wasn't sure if it was the job she disliked or living in London, away from all her friends.

Her presence round the house had a decidedly dampening effect, like a vague unease you can't quite explain. I'd even tried enlisting Maura to talk to her. If she wouldn't listen to us perhaps she'd pay attention to her big sister. This plan didn't work either because Maura refused to get involved.

'Listen, mum, you'll have to let her sort it out for herself,' Maura had said firmly in spite of my pleading. 'She's made a decision and she'll come round all in her own good time.'

'We'll have to do something,' growled Simon one night as we sat and tried to watch television, which wasn't easy with loud music thumping overhead.

'Give her some breathing space, as Maura suggested,' I said more calmly than I felt. 'She needs some thinking time. In the autumn she'll be off to teacher training college.'

I could tell Simon wasn't sure this would happen.

'She could try to find a part-time job, get back into the world that way.'

'I think you're exaggerating a bit, Simon,' I protested. 'She's been in touch with lots of her friends.'

'I can tell that by the size of the last phone bill,' he replied.

The Saturday before we were due to leave for Ettrick House we sat in the kitchen reading the papers and having coffee. I broached the subject of our holiday on Bute.

'Would you like to come with us to Bute? The house is certainly big enough for all of us.' I didn't say it was big, but it was also semi-derelict.

'Bute?' She frowned. If I had suggested the frozen wastes of the Arctic that might have sounded more appealing, judging by the way she reacted. 'You're going down there for the whole of the Easter holidays?'

'Think about it.' I knew better than try to persuade her. She made no reply but went back to perusing the fashion pages of her magazine.

As Easter approached with the prospect of final exams soon after, the school became a frenzy of activity. Students you had to berate constantly to hand in the scrappiest of homework now laid siege to you in corridors, asking obscure questions about whatever text they'd chosen to study. Most of it is panic and it's those who don't have to worry who panic most.

There's always a staff meeting the last day of term. Not that anyone is in any mood for serious discussion.

'It's no more than a way of ensuring that we all turn up and don't try to skive off early,' hissed Malcolm who was sitting beside me. I glared at him. Chloe Newcomb, our newish head of department, needs all the support she can get.

It wasn't a long meeting and we took our leave of each other with wishes for a good holiday. As I gathered my papers together, Chloe came up to me.

'Any word from Susie recently?'

I couldn't lie but I did wonder where this question was leading. I said guardedly, 'We are in touch by e-mail. Why do you ask?'

'The Head seems to think that she'll be staying on out there for another year and I want to think in time about a replacement.'

'But Susie is a guidance tutor. Very little of her time is spent teaching in the English department surely?'

'That's as may be, but the part-timer who's here at the moment is pregnant and I don't want to keep on making temporary arrangements. I mean, what if Susie does get an extension for another year?'

'Oh, I don't think that's likely,' I replied, with more conviction than I felt.

I'd have to contact Susie about this turn of events. There was no way she'd want to risk her position in the school, California or no California.

This had to be our final trip to Ettrick House. It was up to Susie to come back and sort things out. There's a limit even to the best of friendships.

I hurried home as quickly as I could. Unfortunately it was the end of term for everyone and the build up of traffic was horrendous. I seemed to catch every red traffic light. At least it gave me time to reflect, not least on the stress of living in this urban environment. The traffic seems to get worse as more and more houses are built on every tiny strip of land. Easter in Bute was looking much more appealing, in spite of my reservations about Ettrick House.

When I finally reached home, Deborah was lazing on the sofa in the living room with a pile of books and magazines strewn all around. Several coffee cups and an empty plate occupied every inch of space on the table nearby.

She was engrossed in some daytime soap on television which seemed to involve a lot of weeping and hand wringing. She looked up when she saw me and smiled. 'Hi, mum, had a good day?'

To my astonishment she uncoiled herself from the sofa and added, 'Fancy a cup of tea? I'll make it. I have to tidy up this mess anyway.'

I nodded, being lost for words. What had come over her?

I watched as she briskly shuffled the magazines into a tidy pile and gathered up the cups and the plate. Balancing them carefully, she headed for the kitchen. I sat down on the nearest chair. This wasn't at all like Deborah. I hoped she wasn't preparing me for more bad news.

I lifted the remote control to kill the sound of the television. Peace and quiet was what I needed now. I put my head back and I must have nodded off because the next thing I remember was Deborah coming into the living room with the tea on a tray and a plate neatly set out with digestive biscuits.

She said with a kind of studied casualness, 'There was a phone call for you to-day - Strathmore Archaeological Services - someone called Morgan Connolly? He wanted to speak to you, but I told him we'd be down to-morrow, so he said he'll speak to you then. He and his team are going back to the island.'

My ears pricked up at the word 'we'. 'So you've decided to come down with us then, Deborah?'

She opened her eyes wide in astonishment. 'Of course I'll be coming. I think the change of scenery will do me good,' as though there had never been any doubt about the matter.

My suspicions were raised. 'So what else did Morgan say when he called?'

'Not much,' she replied vaguely with a wave of her hand. 'We chatted about this and that. He sounds interesting. I think I'd like to see what's going on. He has said I'd be very welcome. They're always looking for volunteers on these digs.'

There had been no need for me to worry. As far as Deborah was concerned it looked as if Bute would have attractions of its own.

We set off for Bute the next day without Simon. He had come home with yet another crisis in his department to be resolved. He had to stay on in Glasgow for a day or two.

'I'll try to join you later in the week,' he said gloomily.

I decided not to wait for him. There was absolutely nothing I could do to help and I was fretful on Susie's behalf about what might be happening at Ettrick House

I packed the car with all we needed for our stay, hoping fervently that I hadn't forgotten anything, since there were precious few creature comforts at Ettrick House. If only I wasn't so disorganised, I thought to myself, as I loaded up the final boxes.

I did try. The drawers in the house were full of lists, but most were half worked through and then carelessly abandoned, to be found months later when it was too late.

Simon had agreed to follow on as soon as he could, taking the connecting train from Central Station and the ferry across to the island. His disappointment at having to remain in Glasgow was evident.

As we set out the roads were almost empty. I'd only had to waken Deborah three times and we left a mere ten minutes later than intended. Even the seemingly endless road works on the M8 had mysteriously disappeared.

At the ferry terminal at Weymss Bay we were first in the line of cars. The early morning air was clean and crisp and the sight of the seagulls whooping and swooping over the water lifted my spirits considerably. Now that we were on our way, I was determined this break on Bute would do us all good. I told myself sternly that my worries about Ettrick House were no more than the product of my over active imagination. Apart from the episode with the car, what could there be to alarm me?

'Fancy a coffee in the Seaview cafe?' I asked Deborah. She might have managed to crawl out of bed but I suspected she was not properly awake.

'Good idea, mum,' she responded. 'I could do with a shot of caffeine.'

We settled down at a table by the window, watching as the queue of cars grew longer and congratulating ourselves on our early arrival.

Suddenly a battered white van I recognised swung off the main road and edged its way into the queue. Several people jumped out and slammed the doors behind them, their shouts carrying in the crisp morning air. Joking and laughing, three of them darted across the road and pushed open the door of the cafe.

The tallest of the three smiled as he saw me and came over to our table.

'Hello there, Mrs Cameron, I thought it was you.'

'Good morning,' I said, as Morgan Connolly pushed back his hair off his face in that engaging way he had.

Deborah looked from one to another, questioningly.

'This is Morgan Connolly, one of the archaeologists I told you about,' I explained to her. 'This is my daughter Deborah.'

I wasn't surprised by Morgan's sudden interest in Deborah. I suspected that it was curiosity about Deborah that made him approach me in the first instance.

Deborah put on her most winning smile, 'Hiya, Morgan. We spoke on the phone last night if you remember? I'm sure what you are doing must be very interesting,' she said, very demurely.

'Are you going over to the island now?' he enquired, fixing her with his sharp hazel eyes.

'Yes, we'll be there for the whole two weeks of the Easter holiday.'

'Then I hope we'll see you,' responded Morgan with a mock bow. Before he turned away he added, 'You could come and see the site, if you're really interested. Remember what I said about needing volunteers?'

Deborah's eyes opened wide. 'I'd like nothing better,' she said and sounded as if she meant it.

Oh, I thought, is this the way the wind's blowing?

'I look forward to that then, Deborah.' His gaze held hers for a few moments.

One of his colleagues called over, 'What are you for, Morgan? A bacon buttie or two?' and then there were guffaws of laughter.

Morgan looked at Deborah apologetically. 'They're trying to wind me up,' he said, 'they know fine I'm a vegetarian.'

'So am I,' replied Deborah delightedly.

'That's something else we have in common,' he said, winking at her as he spoke. I swear Deborah blushed.

He nodded over to where Penny Curtis and Brian March were starting to carry food from the self service counter.

'You'll have to excuse me. I'd better go and keep the others in order or goodness knows what I'll end up with for breakfast.'

I looked at Deborah who was staring fixedly after him in a way I wasn't happy about. This time I was going over to Bute for a break. There was no way I wanted any more complications in my life. The problems of Ettrick House were more than enough.

I drained the last of my coffee and stood up. 'Come on, Deborah, we'd better go.'

'I haven't finished yet,' she protested.

I was resolved we would be out of the cafe before Morgan could re-appear and join us.

'We're first in line,' I said firmly, 'so we should be there in case they start loading early.'

As CalMac run their ferries like clockwork to a tight time schedule, there was no chance that they would start early, but I held my ground.

'Oh, all right then,' said Deborah, 'but you can be such a fusspot, mum.'

As we left, Morgan waved over and called out, 'Bye, Deborah, see you on the other side, so to speak.'

She laughed in a way that seemed to me out of all proportion to the joke he had made, but I supposed I should be grateful he had cheered her up.

Once on board, we locked up the car and went on to the upper deck. It was a wonderful morning, one of those magical West coast mornings that lifts the spirits. Scarcely a ripple disturbed the water and the ferry glided effortlessly away from the pier into the Firth of Clyde.

'Let's go out on deck,' I said. It was too good a morning to waste a minute indoors. As we reached open water only the gentlest of breezes ruffled the feathers of the lone seagull perched on the railings.

'He must be hitching a ride,' said Deborah. The seagull fixed us with a steely glare, annoyed we had no titbits to offer.

As we passed the lighthouse at Toward, I could feel all my cares slipping away. Too bad about anyone else, Alison, I told myself. Think of this as a well deserved holiday and enjoy it.

We docked in Rothesay in good time. There had been no sign of the archaeologists on the journey.

'Where do you think they are?' muttered Deborah several times, peering this way and that for a sight of their van.

'They were probably so busy showing off in the Seaview they missed the ferry,' I said.

Deborah looked at me strangely, but she said nothing.

I was eager to see Deborah's reaction to the house. I'd told her very little about it, but then as we hadn't said much to each other over the past few weeks, I hadn't had an opportunity.

I drove confidently out through Port Bannatyne. There were few boats in Kames Bay: it was as yet early in the season. The little Post Office, newly refurbished as a Post Office and General Store, was busy with customers and the children in North Bute Primary, not yet on holiday, were out playing in the school yard. Otherwise the village was quiet.

As we headed up the hill with Ettrick Bay behind us, I could see Deborah craning back to look at the view. If she's impressed by this, I thought, what will she think when she sees the house.

Deborah and I got out of the car to push back the gates. 'We'll go straight up to the main house,' I said as I settled back into the driving seat. I smiled as I weighed up what her first words were likely to be.

As Ettrick House came into view, Deborah let out a little scream of astonishment. But then so did I.

Down at the bottom of the gardens, there was a huge trench, surrounded by an assortment of heavy equipment. What on earth was going on? Surely the archaeologists hadn't been allowed to do this? As we came closer, I saw that that was indeed what was happening.

Wait till Morgan and his team arrive, I thought grimly.

TEN

Someone had been in the house. As soon as I opened the door, I could sense it, could feel there was something different about the place. Simon and I had checked everything before we left and I was absolutely certain we had carefully closed all the doors. Now the doors to the library and to the little kitchen were partly ajar. There was something else. I gazed round, trying to decide what was wrong. Then I spotted it - a small pile of mud lying beside the door leading to the basement.

I stood still for a moment in the centre of that vast hallway, furiously trying to collect my thoughts, listening intently in case the intruder was still somewhere in the house.

'What's wrong, mum?' asked Deborah, coming up behind me

What should I say? If I told her of my fears we would have to think about going back into the town to find accommodation for the night. I took a deep breath before I spoke. Now was not the time for hesitation.

'I'm trying to remember where everything is,' I lied, hoping she believed me.

She didn't seem to notice my disquiet. She was too absorbed in looking around her in some awe.

'It's quite a size, isn't it? Imagine Susie owing all this.' She was very impressed and it does take something special to impress Deborah.

There had been no sign of the archaeologists or I might have asked them if they had seen anyone about the place. Or if any of them had been in the house. Even as the thought occurred to me I realised how ridiculous it was.

How could anyone get in through that stout wooden front door without a key? Why would Morgan or any of his team want to come into the house anyway? There was nothing of value left here. Their only concern was what might be found at outside the house, down at the bottom of the extensive gardens.

I thought back to the last time I had spoken to him at the trench. He had been very specific about his plans.

'There's something important here, I'm sure of it,' he had said. 'This could be the opportunity I've been looking for.' His belief in what he was doing was written in the determined look on his face, the glint of excitement in his eyes. No, Morgan's interests were firmly located in what he might discover in the grounds of Ettrick House.

'You didn't tell me it was like this.' Deborah was wide eyed with amazement as she turned round to face me. 'Where do we start?'

I came back to the present. 'Yes, it is overwhelming.'

She didn't seem to find the vastness of the house disturbing, but started wandering slowly from room to room, marvelling at the space.

'Surely Susie won't want to live here all on her own?' she said several times. 'And what a lot of work it needs. Though I suppose if they do build an access road she would get some money in compensation?'

'Not nearly enough to do the work required on this place,' I said.

As Deborah seemed so enchanted with the house, I began to fret at my own timidity. Surely there was nothing to be frightened of here. And yet, and yet...

My fears were confirmed when we came into the library where Simon and I had spent the first night. At first glance all seemed as we had left it: the sofas returned to their place by the window, the little table positioned between them. It took me a few minutes to determine what was wrong. I looked closely at the little bureau in the far corner. There was something different about it. I moved over to inspect it more closely.

I was right: there was something different. It had been expertly forced. The top drawer was ever so slightly open, only noticeable if you looked closely. Whoever had been here had left in a hurry, possibly disturbed by the sound of our car coming up the driveway. No, I wasn't thinking straight. If the intruder had been here when we arrived how would he have escaped without us seeing him?

I pulled open all the drawers but they were empty. Nothing in the top drop down section either. I was cross with myself. Why had I not prised it open when I'd had the opportunity? The answer was simple: I had been too eager to escape after our disturbed night. Now I would never know if there had been anything of importance in the bureau.

'What do we do now?' Deborah re-appeared in the room. Fortunately she didn't notice my concerns.

She whirled around, dancing on tiptoe, seeming to find the space liberating.

Then she stopped suddenly and went over to rub the grimy window and peer out. 'I wonder where the archaeologists are.'

'Oh, they'll be here soon enough,' I said, 'and I'll want to see exactly what it is they are being allowed to do.'

If Deborah heard me she gave no indication.

'Let's go outside,' she said, hopping from one foot to the other.

'Fine, but let's sort the place out first.' Some fresh air would do us both good and give me an excuse to question Morgan when he arrived.

There was nothing to be frightened of here, I sternly told myself, determined to make the most of these few days on the island.

We set to, trying to make the place as comfortable as we could. 'We have to decide which rooms we want to use,' I said, aware our choice was in reality limited.

Deborah went to and fro, examining everything, until we decided it would be best to keep to the drawing room, the library and the smallest of the bedrooms upstairs. By mutual consent we agreed to avoid the bedroom used by Robert Ainslee in his last days.

We had no choice but to use the makeshift kitchen on the ground floor. I had no intention of going down to explore the basement - that was one task I would leave to Susie.

We unpacked the extra duvets I'd bought and made up the airbeds, re-arranged what furniture there was and added our fold-up chairs and table.

The electricity in the house had been shut off when we left last time. We had to make sure we could get it on before dark: I didn't want to be left in the vast expanse of Ettrick House without proper lighting ever again, though this time we had at least had the sense to equip ourselves with several torches and a stack of batteries in case of an emergency.

After a few failed attempts Deborah and I managed to find all the switches in the right order and could once again have the dubious comforts of the two bar electric fire. The vast drawing room had a real coal fire but lighting it wasn't a skill I remembered, even if I'd known where to find coal. Somewhere in the basement, no doubt.

The cooker was gas, an ancient affair which might prove lethal, but it was either that or a trip back into Rothesay and neither Deborah nor I could face the journey again at the moment. After we had cleaned it of the worst of the grease and grime, lunch was a pretty scrappy affair of baked beans on toast. At least there was plenty of milk for tea. As the house lacked a fridge, we'd be making several trips into town.

By the time we had generally organised our chosen rooms, it was late into the afternoon.

'Come on, Deborah, time for a walk. After all, that's part of the reason we came here.'

Deborah agreed much too quickly for my liking. I was a little suspicious about her motives, but at least I didn't have to contend with a surly refusal.

We kitted ourselves out in the stout walking shoes and warm fleeces we had brought with us. The sun might be shining but it can still be cold in Scotland at this time of year and I was taking no chances.

'Are the archaeologists likely to be working here today?' she asked with an air of innocence.

'Couldn't say,' was my reply. I had no way of keeping track of their movements, no matter how interested Deborah might be.

It took both of us all our efforts to close the heavy wooden door. When we walked down the steps I realised we had been right to opt for warm clothes. In spite of the brightness of the day a cold wind was blowing in from the northeast and sweeping up across the pastureland.

Outside, Ettrick House appeared brighter in the spring sunshine. In the terraced gardens a few snowdrops and purple and yellow crocuses had managed to poke their heads bravely through the tangle of weeds.

'So where do you suggest we start, mum?'

Deborah's voice came muffled through the collar of her jacket she had turned up against the wind.

'I think we should have a look around the grounds first. Last time Dad and I didn't have much of a chance to explore.' No more than a little lie I told myself, neglecting to say why we hadn't explored much last time. I hadn't mentioned the episode of the missing car to her.

'Fine by me,' Deborah replied and we went towards the first of the terraces. I smiled as I saw her pat one of the stone lions as we left.

Inevitably we were drawn down through the other terraces towards the ditch the archaeologists had been digging, though I felt a bit guilty about snooping around when they weren't on site.

When I said this to Deborah her reply was clear.

'Oh, for goodness sake, mum,' she said, 'don't fuss so. After all we're in charge here, not them.'

'I suppose so.' I wasn't too sure.

As it turned out there wasn't much of interest to see. On closer inspection we could see there were several large machines set ready for work. A collection of tools was lying neatly stacked under a makeshift canvas shelter, a sign they intended to continue very soon. Even the length of the trench wasn't as impressive as I'd thought from a distance, though the spoil heap had increased in size since I had been here. While we were peering down into the trench, trying to look as if we knew what we were looking for, a voice behind us startled us both.

'Interesting, eh?'

We turned round to see Morgan standing there, grinning widely and showing his fine set of pearl white teeth. He might have the appearance of a scruffy archaeologist but underneath he was a very good-looking young man.

'What a fright you gave us,' I replied. 'We didn't hear you arrive. I'm afraid we're not at all sure what we're looking at. Perhaps you can explain to us what's going on?'

'Yes, I would very much like to know.' Deborah was showing an enthusiasm I wouldn't have expected, but whether it was interest in the archaeology or in the archaeologist was hard to determine.

Morgan was obviously pleased to have an audience, especially one so anxious to know what was happening.

'It's no more than a trial trench,' he explained. 'We've permission to dig a few of those, to try to determine if there really is anything of interest.'

'It seems pretty big for a trial trench,' I muttered, but he caught what I said.

'It's a big site,' he replied without the slightest trace of irony. 'We're very hopeful of finding what we're looking for.'

'And what have you found?'

Deborah peered into the hole in the ground as if she expected some momentous discovery.

'Early days yet,' Morgan grinned, 'but we have had some interesting finds, enough to convince us it's worthwhile going on.'

'And if you do find something exciting, what happens then?'

In my role as Susie's representative, I didn't want her to come back and find that all the terraced gardens had been dug up by archaeologists in the vague hope that there might be something of 'interest'.

'That depends on a lot of things.' Morgan stroked his beard thoughtfully as he spoke. 'This is to be the access road to the wind farm if the permissions come through. Although,' he went on hastily, 'your friend would be compensated for the loss of any of her land.'

I think he was considering how much more he should tell us. Possibly he detected the note of anxiety in my voice.

'If there are any significant finds then we'd have to get a further order to proceed with a more substantial excavation.'

'Is it likely that you'd be refused?'

Morgan paused for a moment and looked from me to Deborah. 'No-o-o,' he said. 'If there are any finds of significance we'd be given permission without much trouble.'

Without much trouble for you I thought, but I said nothing.

'I think I'll go for a walk around the rest of the grounds,' I said. 'Are you coming Deborah?'

Morgan leapt in before she had a chance to reply. 'Or you could stay and I'll explain more about what we are trying to do.'

I sighed. I recognised the signs only too well. I'd be going for that walk on my own.

Penny and Brian came strolling down the gardens to join Morgan and I left them chatting animatedly as I wandered off. I had neither clear purpose nor direction to my walk, but you could see the house from whatever path you took, so there wasn't much chance of getting lost.

I stopped before I entered the little coppice of trees that circled the house at the back and looked over. Deborah was engrossed in conversation with Morgan and he was nodding in reply, standing close to her. I knew that these archaeologists had a job to do and far was it for me to interfere: it wasn't even my property, for goodness sake. But Morgan seemed to be ingratiating himself with Deborah in a way that wasn't entirely to my liking.

I didn't stay out as long as I had intended. The wind had swung round and was blowing directly off the bay, creating a distinctly chilly feel. I was tired and hungry.

There was no sign of Deborah nor of Morgan as I passed the trench. I hoped they wouldn't be long, because I didn't relish spending time on my own in Ettrick House as darkness fell.

I went through the trees, expecting to find another exit from the estate but I encountered a solid stone wall, much of it tumbled down. This was obviously the limit of the property that belonged to Ettrick House and beyond I could see only more trees and hedging on a very steep incline. Further exploration could wait for another day and I turned to retrace my steps.

As I came up to the front door I was relieved to see Deborah sitting on one of the stone balustrades by the side of the main entrance.

'I didn't want to come after you, mum, as I wasn't sure which direction you'd taken.'

'Very sensible,' I replied, 'now we can both have something to eat.'

Morgan had made a great impression on her, because once we were inside, she started to chatter in a way that she hadn't since she had returned home from London.

'Morgan has said he'll let me help to-morrow when they start in earnest,' she said excitedly.

'But Deborah, you know nothing about archaeology.'

'Morgan says that doesn't matter: it's a willing pair of hands he needs. He'll show me what to do.' She smiled at me as though that answered my question.

I didn't want to dampen her enthusiasm: working outdoors this early in the year might do that for me. Deborah wasn't exactly the outdoor type.

Then I stopped myself. It was good to see she was interested in something I thought, looking at her flushed cheeks. And it would be better if she had some young people of her own age to talk to during the weeks ahead.

I felt much better as we went to bed : hopefully tomorrow Simon would join us, Deborah was happier than she'd been for some time and even the weather forecast on the radio sounded promising.

I began to feel almost cheerful. Too soon, as it turned out.

ELEVEN

In spite of feeling exhausted earlier, I slept very little that night. I knew we were safe and sound in the bedrooms we had cleared in Ettrick House, but my imagination worked overtime, hearing threatening sounds and little noises from the main house downstairs.

Several times I got up in the night to check the doors were securely fastened, but it was of no help. As soon as I was back in bed, my ears attuned themselves for any noise, straining in the dark to catch the slightest change. If someone had managed to get through that stout outer door once, they could do it again. Though when I thought about it, what would be the point?

As far as I could see there was nothing of real interest to anyone in this place. You did hear from time to time of thieves targeting empty houses of this size and making off with the marble fireplaces, but this was Bute, for goodness sake. It would be impossible to move something so large off the island without being caught.

Deborah slept through it all. I peeped round the door of her room each time I was up on one of my night prowls, but she lay deep in slumber, curled up in that way she finds most comfortable. I was glad that Simon was due to arrive to-morrow.

Eventually I gave up all attempts at sleep and wrapped myself in my dressing gown and decided I'd go down to the tiny kitchen and make a hot drink.

I pulled back the curtains in my room. At home there would have been the friendly glare of the sodium streetlight. Here there was total darkness.

I opened the door to the upstairs hall and put on the lamp that sat outside on a little table, hoping that it wouldn't waken Deborah. I stood and listened for a moment but I needn't have worried: there was no sound from her room.

I crept downstairs and fumbled around in the strange kitchen. I switched on the light, but just as quickly I switched it off again as the harsh fluorescent tube sprang into life with a nausea inducing glare.

I tried to remember where I had put the teabags and struggled with the antiquated gas cooker and what appeared to be an early version of a kettle. Was it worth while buying an electric kettle I wondered, thinking about the state of the wiring in the house?

Eventually I settled for making myself a cup of warm milk and went through to the library. I sat down in the chair by the window and nursed the cup of steaming liquid. What I really felt like was a chocolate biscuit or two, but there were none in the house.

As I sat there in the dark, I caught a glimpse of a light outside coming from the direction of the archaeologists' trench. Surely there was no one out there digging in the middle of the night.

I stood up, went over to the window for a better look and tried to see through the complete darkness of a night without a moon. No, there it was again, some kind of light or torch. And it was most definitely coming from the direction of the trench.

Suddenly the light disappeared round the side of the house. Consumed as I was with curiosity, I had no intention of venturing out into the inky blackness. It would have to wait till morning.

I went back over to the kitchen, emptied out the remainder of my milk and left my rinsed cup on the draining board. I stumbled back upstairs to bed where I must have fallen asleep at long last. The next thing I remember was waking up with the sun streaming in and Deborah standing over me with a cup of tea in her hand.

'Thought you could do with this, mum.'

I looked at the bedside clock as I struggled up into a sitting position.

'10 o'clock! Why did you let me sleep so long?'

'I peeped in a couple of times, but you were sound asleep,' she replied a little testily.

'Yes, I must have dozed off again,' I said in a conciliatory way. I didn't want to start the morning by quarrelling with Deborah.

I saw she was fully dressed in her outdoor clothes.

'Anyway, I'm off. See you later.'

'Off? Where are you going?'

'You must remember. I told you I'd be helping Morgan and the other archaeologists to-day.'

I remembered nothing of the sort but I contented myself by drinking my tea while I thought of a suitable reply. For some reason I had a sense of unease, though I couldn't decide exactly what was wrong. Possibly it was all to do with this general feeling I had about the house, about the ghosts that seemed to haunt it. I didn't want Deborah to see how I felt. She seemed to have no such fears about the place.

She sat down with a bump on the edge of the bed, almost causing me to spill the hot liquid all over the covers. 'Oops, sorry. Will you be all right? I know dad will be here later, but I'll stay till he comes if you prefer.'

'Not at all.' By now I was fully awake. 'I'll go and pick dad up from the ferry. He should be in Rothesay about lunchtime.'

She laughed and leaned over to give me a quick peck on the cheek. 'Thanks, mum, I'm really glad that I came. I'll see you later this afternoon.'

With that she sprang up and made for the door. I heard her footsteps clatter down the stairs.

'Don't forget to collect the key,' I called after her.

'I won't,' her voice echoed downstairs in the hall.

I finished my tea deep in thought. At least she had found something, or someone to interest her, so the holiday would do her some good. And us, I thought a bit selfishly.

By the time I'd had a bath of sorts in the ancient bathtub, still hopelessly stained in spite of all my scrubbing, and breakfasted on two slices of toast and more tea, it was almost time to head off to collect Simon.

I decided to go into Rothesay and do some shopping before I met him from the ferry. As I drove down towards the gates I could see the feverish activity in the area of the trench, but it was impossible to spot Deborah among the huddled group.

I thought of going over to let her know I was on my way then I decided against it. She was quite capable of looking after herself without her mother fussing round.

I parked the car at the Albert Pier and went into the Co-op store. This time I made a determined effort to remember all the bits and pieces we might need over the next few days.

I carried everything over and crammed it all into the boot of the car, before walking round to the ferry terminal to meet Simon.

As I crossed the road I saw a familiar face. It was Greta. I waved to her and she came over to me.

She was immaculately turned out in pale fawn trousers and a matching jacket which made me conscious I was in an old pair of trousers and a jumper that had seen better days. But she looked much more strained than when we had met her at the Ettrick Bay tearoom, as though she had a lot on her mind. As I came close up to her I noticed her hair was tied back loosely as though she had combed it in a hurry.

She must still be finding it stressful to cope with having to sort out her mother's papers and dispose of her belongings. If this was the effect it was having on her, Harry must be concerned about her.

'How is everything at Ettrick House?' she said with no preliminary word of greeting.

I was taken aback by this direct approach. 'Well, fine, I think.' I didn't want to start a discussion with Greta about what was happening at the dig at Ettrick House.

'Have you recovered from your fright with that car business? It didn't put you off?'

I opened my mouth to say, 'Not at all, thanks, but it was rather odd,' when something stopped me. 'How did you know what had happened?'

She stared at me for a moment and then said, 'On this small island news travels fast.'

'Indeed.' My response was frostier than I had intended but as the only people we had told of the incident had been the police, I didn't think it likely they had been letting all and sundry know what had happened.

As though she read my thoughts, Greta added, 'You hear from all sorts of places if anything out of the ordinary is going on.'

I smiled. 'I'm sure that's true,' I said. In a small community there is always someone who knows what is happening and news spreads fast.

I expect she thought her reply was suitable vague. She had no intention of revealing her sources.

'I'm sorry, I really have to go. I'm meeting Simon,' I said.

She frowned. 'So you're staying on at Ettrick House?'

'Well, at the moment.' More than that I wasn't prepared to commit to.

Out of the corner of my eye I could see the ferry swinging into the bay. It provided me with a good excuse to end this conversation.

'See you later, Greta. Simon's on this ferry.' And I hurried away before she could say any more

It was a lesson learned. I should be very careful what I said about Ettrick House and Susie's inheritance.

I waited patiently until the crowds thinned out and Simon came strolling down the walkway. We hugged and then went over to the car. He drew a deep breath.

'You've no idea how good the air feels after the stuffiness of Glasgow,' he sighed.

'I think I do,' I replied, but I didn't add how pleased I was to see him. I crossed my fingers the weather would stay fine.

When we reached the car he said, 'Why don't we go for lunch somewhere? It's warm enough to go round and sit outside in the garden at the Kingarth Hotel round at Kilchattan Bay.'

'I did say to Deborah that we'd be straight back,' I replied doubtfully.

Simon laughed. 'From what you've said I think she has plenty to occupy her. I don't think she'll be too worried about us.'

'I'll try calling her on the mobile.' When I rang the number there was no reply. 'I guess she's switched it off.'

'For goodness sake, Alison, stop fussing. She's grown up now and well able to take care of herself. You didn't worry about her when she was working in London, why start now. Besides you know how bad the reception can be in parts of the island.'

So off we went to Kilchattan Bay for a pleasant couple of hours relaxing over some home cooked food in the local hotel.

Simon drove us the long way round back to Ettrick House. The island, wakening from its long winter sleep, was green and fresh with the promise of new life. The roadside verges were alive with daffodils and as we drove up to Ettrick House, the lambs in the surrounding farms appeared decidedly plumper than a few weeks ago.

'How is the mansion then, Alison?'

'Fine,' I lied. I certainly wasn't going to admit to him my previous night's terrors. He'd only laugh at my fears and I had to admit in the cold light of day they did seem somewhat silly. And there was no point in voicing my suspicions that someone had been in the house. Not yet.

I had no time to tell him even if I had wanted to. As we went up the drive of Ettrick House it was evident something unusual was going on in the new trench at the bottom of the gardens.

We parked outside the main door. There were several other cars there, none of which I recognised.

'What's happened now,' muttered Simon, no doubt seeing his few days of calm rapidly disappearing.

We got out of the car and started to walk down towards the excavation site. What was going on? What were Morgan and his team doing?

I felt angry on Susie's behalf. The archaeologists might have permission to dig but not to bring all and sundry along. This was private property after all.

As we approached the site we could see a little knot of people gathered round the latest trench. It had grown vastly in size since I had last seen it.

There was a palpable air of excitement. Everyone was peering intently downwards but there didn't appear to be much work going on.

I was determined to give them a piece of my mind. If Morgan wanted to set up some kind of viewing party he should have had the courtesy to ask us first. I rehearsed exactly what I would say to him as we walked over.

I noticed Deborah was standing at the extreme edge of the group. When she saw us she came running over, her long dark hair streaming out behind her in the wind. She looked exhilarated.

'Oh, I'm so glad you're back,' she cried, clutching at my arm.

My heart gave a lurch, though I tried to sound calm.

'Why, what has happened?'

'Oh, mum,' she said, breathless with excitement, 'they've found something in the trench.'

'Isn't that good?' Simon said. 'Aren't they looking for that kind of thing - old pottery and stuff? After all, from what Morgan has told us, he's sure must have been people living on this site thousands of years ago, given its high position.'

I was equally surprised by her reaction.

'That's just it, dad,' she said, shivering as she spoke. 'It's not pottery or anything they've found. They've found a skeleton.'

TWELVE

The only skeletons I had ever seen had been in museums, the strong glass cases distancing me from their incarnation as real people. And although the flesh had long since disappeared, leaving these bare bones, there was something so human, so much more connected about this skeleton lying on its side in the trench. From the way it was positioned it was as though the person had drifted off to sleep one night and forgotten to waken.

Deborah was intrigued by it all and apparently a little frightened, but she rallied as she came closer again to see what was going on. Her curiosity outweighed any fear.

That was just the start of it. Morgan looked more intent than I'd ever seen him and the other diggers were as excited as he was. They moved backwards and forwards, keeping up a steady stream of chatter. Brian had started on his drawing of the find in the trench but he kept stopping every now and again to talk to the others.

As site director it fell to Morgan to take control of the sequence of events and I guessed he didn't want a lot of amateurs around at this point.

'How do you know it's a female?' I asked.

'You can tell by the shape of the pelvis,' he said, bending down to my height as he pointed it out to me. 'And the shape of the skull also helps, though that's less useful.'

'Are you absolutely certain that it's not some skeleton from a previous burial ground?' Simon said.

I willed him to be quiet. This is what happens when the great British public watches *Time Team* and picks up random bits of information.

I could see Morgan was trying very hard to be patient. 'We're not absolutely sure, Mr Cameron. But there are no records of any burials on this site and the skeleton needs much more excavation - as does the site surrounding it - before we can be certain about what it is.'

'Stand back,' Morgan ordered as it looked as if Deborah might go too near the edge of the trench.

She looked at him in surprise but she moved back as she had been ordered.

He seemed to realise he had been abrupt. 'It's essential the site isn't contaminated,' he said by way of explanation.

I made sure I kept well back from the edge of the trench. From where I was standing I had seen enough. Now I would have to contact Susie and tell her that as well as archaeologists digging at the bottom of the garden of her house, the police might be swarming all over the place.

Among those gathered at the site, I recognised P.C. Killop. No doubt the police had been summoned by Morgan as soon as he had made the discovery.

Deborah interrupted anxiously.

'It's not that recent, Morgan, surely. I mean not the past year or anything?'

Morgan shook his head. 'No, not that recent. We'll have to wait till I have the chance to do a proper dating and then we can decide what to do.'

My heart sank. This complication was all we needed. I could see these people being here for a long time to come, digging up here, there and everywhere.

I heard the sound of a car coming up the hill. More police were arriving. There hadn't been this much excitement on the island for a while. I expected the reporter from *The Buteman* to be along any minute. There would be no problem about the front page of next week's edition.

'Something of interest then?' said Sergeant Trueson, as he came walking towards us.

Strange the thoughts that go through your head at a moment such as this. It seemed odd to me that Sergeant Trueson, the more senior of the two, should be shorter and slighter. But pinch faced and slight as he was, he was obviously the man in charge.

'We've found a skeleton,' said Morgan sounding very matter-of-fact though I could hear the underlying excitement in his voice, 'and we have to be clear what age it is in case we need to involve you.'

The two policemen peered into the trench, but beyond a brief 'harrumph' said nothing although I noticed P.C. Killop had his note book at the ready.

Perhaps this was not first time he had encountered a real skeleton.

After a hurried consultation we were motioned to leave.

'I have to seal his place off as a potential crime scene,' said Sergeant Trueson, 'so I'd be grateful if you would all move away.'

He went over to the car and spoke into his phone, keeping his voice as low as possible.

In spite of his command I edged my way over to the trench to have a look as the policemen unwound the blue and white tape to seal it round as much of the area as possible.

The trench wasn't as deep as I had first thought. The first trench they had dug lay abandoned and it was obvious they had found the skeleton very soon after starting to dig this one.

As I looked at it again I realised that the skeleton wasn't the least bit terrifying. From what Morgan had said it was unlikely to be a common burial ground, but was it the first skeleton of many?

I felt a great sadness. I wondered why this skeleton was here, so near to Ettrick House. Surely if it was really old it would have been discovered before now? Then I realised this trench was at the very bottom of the gardens of Ettrick House, and although part of the estate, the area so far down here bore no signs of ever having been cultivated.

P.C. Killop motioned me to step away from the trench. 'You have to keep well back,' he said firmly, gesturing me away with his arm as he positioned the last of the tape.

I stepped back obediently. I had seen all I wanted.

'How would he know if it was recent?' I said to Simon, trying to avoid being seen by the police who were back to earnest discussions at the corner of the trench. 'There must be some way of determining the age.'

'How should I know, Alison,' he muttered. 'I've never dealt with this kind of situation either.' He hadn't watched that episode of *Time Team* then.

There didn't seem to be anything we could do. The police stood together, their voices occasionally raised, but I couldn't catch any of what they were saying.

Morgan stood over at the far end of the tape, smoking a roll up. He was regarding them with some interest, but took no part in the discussions.

'What happens now?' asked Deborah who seemed to have recovered her composure.

Morgan nipped his cigarette out between his fingers. 'I'll liaise with the police and then the report goes to the Procurator Fiscal in Dunoon. Once I can do the post excavation analysis though, they'll only be interested if the skeleton is less than seventy five to one hundred years old.'

Deborah looked puzzled and Simon and I waited for his next words with interest.

Morgan smiled. 'Think about it, Deborah. I'm sure you'll come up with the answer.'

We all stood mulling over what he had said. I could see light dawning in Deborah's eyes. 'Of course,' she cried. 'There would be no point in pursuing it because the murderer would be dead.'

'Correct.' Morgan clapped quietly. 'Well done.'

She looked pleased with herself at finding the answer. Then she grimaced. 'That seems very unfair - that the murderer could be let off like that.'

'I certainly wouldn't worry about it. If my first thoughts are correct, this is a skeleton much, much older than that.'

Could Morgan have found what he was looking for? Great for Morgan, but not so good for Susie. We'd have to wait and see.

'Let's go back into the house,' I suggested to Simon and Deborah. 'We can at least make a cup of tea for everyone.' At times of crisis I find it's still a useful remedy.

Deborah and Simon and I walked back to the house and round to the main door. Deborah was very pale. She hadn't uttered a single word on the way to the house but once we were indoors she sat down heavily on the nearest chair. I saw a tear or two trickle down her face.

'Deborah, whatever's wrong?'

'It's so awful, mum, that poor person, left like that.'

'Hush, Deborah,' I tried to soothe her. ''It may be nothing at all. Morgan is probably being extra cautious. I expect this happens to archaeologists all the time. They have to call in the police even if they think the skeleton is very, very old.'

She lifted her face and looked at me doubtfully. 'Do you really think so?'

'Of course I do,' I replied, trying to convince myself as much as Deborah.

It was strange to think that this skeleton had once been a real, breathing person who had lived and died here. My feelings about the ghosts haunting this place were not so far wrong.

'Come on, now, help me to make some tea and we'll take it out to everyone outside. I'm sure they could all do with a cup.'

Simon had already filled the kettle. We put everything together on a couple of trays and I rustled up some biscuits. I considered for a moment suggesting making some sandwiches, but quickly abandoned the thought. I was sure they would be happy with tea.

Once everything was ready we set off in procession. As we reached the hall there was a loud knocking on the door.

'We're coming,' I shouted, though I was sure that we couldn't be heard through the thick walls.

'They must be desperate for a cup of tea,' grinned Simon.

The knocking came again, more furious than ever. I set my tray on the floor.

'I'll go and tell them we're bringing it,' I said to Simon and Deborah.

I ran down the hallway and pulled open the front door, prepared to say, 'We're coming.'

On the steps stood Susie. 'Hi, Alison, I bet you're surprised to see me,' she laughed.

THIRTEEN

Susie sat nodding sagely at our attempts to describe what had been happening. She looked more exotic than ever. Long silver orbs dangled at her ears, her neck was festooned by several necklaces of different colours, bracelets jangled as she spoke.

As I gazed at I her I noticed to my amazement she seemed to have turned a curious shade of orange. Susie is very dark and she does tan easily, but this colour was more than a tan acquired on the beaches of Los Angeles.

I had to ask her. 'Have you been out in the sun too long?'

She laughed loudly. 'It's not real Alison; it's all out of a bottle. Or rather, a very expensive tanning salon near Venice Beach.'

'Good grief,' I said. 'Why would you want to do that with the weather they have in California?'

She looked at me and wagged her finger in mock admonishment. 'It's much too dangerous to sit out in the sun for any length of time. Yet you must have a tan to be anybody.'

As far as she was concerned that was the end of this particular discussion but all the while we talked I couldn't help staring at her in fascination.

'You've been too long in L.A.,' I said.

'Never mind that, Alison; I want you to tell me what else has been happening here.'

I returned to the problems of Ettrick House. Susie was fretful that the discovery of the skeleton had affected us all badly.

'It's not been like that at all Susie. It's just…,' I gestured wildly, 'all this seems to have developed a momentum of its own.'

'But whose is the skeleton?' she insisted.

'Look, Susie, it's probably nothing to worry about. You have to understand that these archaeologists must be really careful. There are procedures to be followed. I'm sure Morgan will be proved right and they'll find that the skeleton has been in the ground for hundreds of years. It happens to be well preserved. Something to do with the kind of soil.'

'I feel guilty now,' she said, without the least appearance of guilt.

Simon stood up. 'I'll go out and check what progress has been made. The sooner they take the skeleton away, the sooner we'll have an answer.'

I looked hard at Susie. 'So what really made you return? I thought you didn't intend to come home till the end of June?'

Susie let out a long sigh. 'Yes, I know. I thought so too. But it didn't work out as I planned.'

I smiled. 'It or him, Susie?'

'Both,' she confessed, watching for my reaction, her head cocked to the side in that birdlike way she has. 'It all seemed to be going so well: the job, the living, the romance.'

'And then?' I prompted.

'I discovered he was married.'

'I wouldn't have thought that a little thing like that would put you off, Susie.'

She frowned at me, trying to weigh up what to say. I could almost hear her brain ticking over. 'No, I mean married in the sense he was still living with his wife and was terrified of being found out. And too frightened of the alimony payments to divorce. Especially as he was also paying alimony to his first wife,' she added darkly.

'Good heavens, how many wives had he had?' I said in astonishment.

'Only two.' Susie seemed surprised at the question.

She grinned again. 'He was such a wimp and so worried about his standing in the community. Apart from the alimony he was worried his wife might spill the beans about him if they divorced.' At this memory she laughed, throwing her head back so that her silver earrings jangled loudly.

'Ah,' I said, nodding my head, 'now it makes sense.'

Before we could have any further discussion, Simon came back into the room. I'd have to wait till later for all the juicy details of Susie's failed romance.

'They've taken the skeleton away,' he said.

'How did they do that?' I was curious. 'Surely they didn't take it in an ambulance?'

Simon shook his head. 'No. They have a special kind of box for skeletons. Morgan says the analysis will be quick as he's convinced it's more than a hundred years old. He seems to have persuaded the police.'

'What does that mean?' Susie looked at him, full of curiosity at this turn of events.

'It means the police won't be interested. Anything over seventy five years isn't investigated. Any suspects would be dead - even if it were murder.' Now that he knew the routine Simon sounded very authoritative.

'That's something of a relief,' Susie said with a shiver. 'I don't like the idea of dead bodies on my land.'

I noted with interest the use of 'my land'. Did this mean Susie was planning to stay?

'The post mortem - no, I mean the 'post excavation analysis' - will have to be done off the island but apparently Morgan will deal with that.'

'What will happen in the meantime?' Susie obviously thought Simon was the source of all information.

'Not a lot,' he responded. 'Morgan and his team can't do anything else for the moment. But he did say it shouldn't take long. He's a tried and trusted professional apparently.'

'They take his word for it?' I was astonished.

Simon smiled. 'Not quite. A report goes to the procurator fiscal but Morgan makes the recommendation.'

I couldn't face the prospect of an evening with the four of us sitting round in this uncomfortable house, with the discussion of the skeleton coming up every time there was a lull in the conversation.

Added to which Deborah had lapsed again into a profound silence. Whether it was because she was still upset about the skeleton or the thought of not seeing Morgan over the next few days was hard to tell.

'Let's go out for dinner,' I suggested brightly, 'to celebrate Susie's arrival.' In the present circumstances any excuse would do.

We drove round to St Blane's Hotel. The evening turned out to be perfect: the wind had died down and it was warm, so we were able to sit out in the gardens with a drink and watch the rose red sunset over Kilchattan Bay.

It was all so calm and peaceful. The events at Ettrick House seemed a million miles away. I sat in silence as Susie entertained Deborah and Simon with stories of her life in America, most of which seemed to involve pool parties, fast cars and lots of shopping trips. Occasionally I stirred myself to make a brief contribution, but my thoughts were far away and I had to make a determined effort.

I looked out over the bay. The sound of the oyster catchers drifted over the water as darkness fell. I wanted this moment to stay forever, without any decisions having to be made about Ettrick House or the skeleton or anything else.

By the time we'd had an excellent dinner and several bottles of wine, we were all convinced a lot of fuss was being made about nothing and our skeleton, as we now thought of it, was indeed ancient and of no interest to anyone except the archaeologists.

We left the car at St Blane's and took a taxi back to Ettrick House. Even the usual creaks and groans of the old house didn't disturb me at all. I fell into a dream free sleep, but it would be a completely different story in the morning.

As it happened, I was first to waken. There was no sound from the rest of the house.

I raised myself carefully on the pillow, wishing I hadn't drunk that second glass of red wine the night before. It might not have done my head any good, but it was some consolation medical evidence said it was good for my heart.

I swung my legs slowly out of bed, felt about for my slippers and stood for a few moments before going downstairs and into the kitchen. I put on all the rings of the cooker to warm the place up. No matter how warm it was outside, I suspected that this old house was always chilly. How could people live like this without any decent heating system? I shivered as I made an extra strong cup of coffee.

I debated if I should waken the others or not. In the end I decided to get dressed and go for a walk down along the shore. It was only just after 7 o'clock.

I went up into the bedroom and pulled on some jeans and a thick sweater and back crept downstairs. I didn't want to disturb the sleepers so I made my exit through the French windows in the dining room. I quelled any thoughts there might be a burglar lying in wait at this time of the morning.

The air was clean and crisp and I breathed deeply as I made my way down the hill to the shore. In the morning light the water shimmered and I felt happier with every deep breath I took. Beyond Ettrick Bay, past the little island of Inchmarnock, the top of the sleeping warrior on Arran was still wreathed in mist, but it was the kind of mist that promised a fine day. There had been no sign of any of the archaeologists at the trench when I left. Either it was too early or they were waiting for confirmation about the skeleton before continuing with the dig.

When I reached the bottom of the hill I crossed the road beside the Ettrick Bay tearoom and set out along the sands. I was enjoying being the only person out and about at this time of the morning. I kept to the shoreline, watching out for any jellyfish that might be lurking; though I couldn't remember if it was the right time of year for them to make their appearance. Such it is to be a city dweller.

As I walked round the sweep of the bay along the shoreline by the Kirkmichael Road, I saw a figure coming towards me. It looked strangely familiar and as it came closer, I saw it was Cassie Milne. She was dressed in jeans and a warm fleece and wasn't easy to recognise out of the outfit she'd been wearing the day we met in the lawyers, especially as her blonde hair now swung loose.

I smiled at her. 'Hi there, enjoying the weather?' Up close she was even younger and prettier than I had thought.

I wasn't sure about the reception I would get, given the way she had reacted last time we had met, but she laughed. 'I always try to come out early before I start work. Rufus likes his morning walk. One of the benefits of living on the island.'

I noticed a small black dog of indeterminate pedigree snuffling about down by the water's edge. She called and he came bounding over, tail wagging furiously.

'Be careful,' she warned as I bent down to pat him. 'He's been in the water and he's soaking wet.'

Although I'm really a cat person, I had to admit Rufus was most taking. There's always something about an animal that seems pleased to see you.

'How are you enjoying Ettrick House?' she asked. 'Apart from this business with the skeleton, I mean.'

'Well, it's not ours, of course. It belongs to my friend Susie. We were helping her out while she's on an exchange programme to America.' I shook my head. 'You must know that of course.'

She made no response.

'Are you familiar with the house?' I said to fill in the silence.

To my surprise she laughed. Not a conversational chuckle, but a really hearty laugh. 'I know the place very well. One of my relatives worked for the family right up until the time the last Ainslee died. I probably know the nooks and crannies of the place better than most. In fact my aunt …'

She stopped suddenly as though aware she had said too much and bent down to put a lead on her dog. I couldn't see her expression for a few moments.

That answered one question. Cassie also knew about Ettrick House. I frowned. It seemed many of the people on the island had worked there. I supposed the big houses provided plenty of work for the women of the island at one time. What did Cassie have to do with this? I wasn't sure at all. I tried to get her to talk about it.

'So your family have a long association with Ettrick House?' Not that I expected an answer, but it was worth a try.

She didn't seem to want to say any more. It was as though a shutter had come down on her face. 'I'd better be off. I have to go to work.'

I had the feeling she regretted what little she had told me. Well, it was too late now.

She turned her back on me with a hasty 'Goodbye' and strode off across the sands.

I was left looking after her in some bewilderment. I had only been making polite conversation. Her sudden departure was disconcerting. How strange that was, but it wasn't the first strange thing I had encountered in my time at Ettrick House. I was becoming used to these surprises.

I went over our brief conversation in my mind. All she had said was that at one time her relatives had worked at Ettrick House. Why should she feel that had been a mistake? She had mentioned something about an aunt. Perhaps the aunt wasn't keen on people knowing she had been a servant at the 'big house.' I shrugged. Even if the aunt was still alive, what difference did it make?

We should have paid more heed when we were in Mr Laidlaw's office. He had hinted he had information we should be interested in, but we were so anxious to check out Ettrick House and go back home as quickly as possible, we hadn't listened to him.

I walked along the beach and up to the Kirkmichael Road until I felt refreshed, then turned and headed up towards the main road. I sauntered back up to the house, deep in thought, pausing every now and again to look at the view over the bay. It was going to be another hot day for so early in the year. Already there was a heat shimmer over the bay but it would be cool inside Etttrick House. Was this so-called global warming? Perhaps we were to have Mediterranean weather on Bute.

As I reached the drive towards the main house, slightly out of breath from the climb up the hill, I caught sight of Morgan over at the main trench. He was deep in conversation with Cassie. She must have come up here while I was still out on my walk. While there was no reason Morgan shouldn't chat to Cassie, it was a surprise to see her up here at the house.

I wasn't going to ignore them. 'Hello,' I called out.

They sprang apart guiltily at the sound of my approach and as I came nearer I saw Cassie was very flustered. She bent down to pat Rufus to disguise her confusion.

I pretended to ignore this and proceeded as if there was nothing unusual, 'Any word yet on that skeleton, Morgan?'

He shook his head, all the while gazing with some anxiety at Cassie.

'Nothing as yet. I expect it will be another day or two. We're trying to decide if we should stay on or head back over to the mainland until we get the all clear.'

'So you think there won't be any problem, then?' Perhaps there would be some answers if I persisted.

A guarded look came over his face. 'I didn't exactly say that, Mrs Cameron.'

I turned back to Cassie who was gazing fixedly at the ground as if her life depended on it. Why had she come up to see Morgan?

I was about to say that I was going into have breakfast when Morgan's mobile rang. He whipped it out of his back pocket hurriedly. Cassie and I stood there in an awkward silence, carefully avoiding looking at each other.

He listened for a few minutes with no more than the odd 'I see,' or 'I understand', but when he rang off his face was wreathed in smiles.

'I'm afraid we'll be staying on for some time to come. The procurator fiscal's office is happy with my analysis. There's no doubt the skeleton is very old indeed. In fact it looks as if I'll be able to confirm my theory that it's Roman.'

'What happens now?' I had a sinking feeling about what his reply might be.

'Once we have confirmation in writing we start digging again. We need to see what artefacts we can find in this trench to confirm the dates.'

Cassie stared hard at him but said nothing.

He went on, seemingly unaware of her discomfort, 'We'll probably have to dig several other trenches as well. Who knows what may be there.'

Great, I thought, so much for any prospects of a peaceful Easter holiday.

FOURTEEN

The phone call had settled it: the archaeologists were to be here for some time to come. And goodness knows how many trenches they would have to dig now to find the proof Morgan was convinced lay beneath the gardens of Ettrick House.

Simon adopted that tight closed look I knew so well. Inwardly he was furious about our involvement in what was happening.

'To make it all worse,' he said yet again, 'Susie's here so there is absolutely no need for us to be here as well.'

'In a way she needs our support more than ever,' I protested, feeling as usual like piggy-in-the middle.

'Well, I'm going out for a walk,' was his reply. He made it perfectly clear he didn't want any company.

'Dad's in a bit of a mood,' commented Deborah as she came into the kitchen where our conversation had taken place. 'It's nobody's fault the skeleton has turned out to be so interesting.'

'Yes, I understand that, but we had anticipated having a relaxing holiday, not having to deal with a corpse.'

'That's a bit of an exaggeration, Mum. It's hardly a corpse. Morgan says that they always have to do this. Now they are certain the skeleton is so old, they have to find out if there are any more. They have to carry on digging in the hope finding artefacts to date it more accurately.'

'You seem to have found out a great deal about it.'

I looked at her curiously and she blushed.

'Morgan has been telling me all about it. I think it's a most interesting subject. It must be a fascinating way to earn your living.'

'Oh, Deborah.' I made a face. 'You're not trying to tell me you've developed an interest in archaeology in such a short time. What about your plans for teacher training?'

She had the grace to look sheepish. 'I don't know, but I've really enjoyed these past few days. If everything turns out as Morgan hopes, he'll be a really big name in archaeology. His reputation will be made.'

I was saved from further comment by Susie bursting in through the door. 'Did you see that dishy policeman? He can interview me any time.'

'Not you as well, Susie,' I said wearily.

'What do you mean?' She sounded indignant.

'Yes, what do you mean 'as well', mum.'

Now I had both of them ganging up against me, I decided to beat a hasty retreat.

'I think we're running a bit short on bread and milk,' I said. 'I'm going off into Rothesay to buy some more.'

We seemed to be getting through gallons of tea and plates of biscuits. Morgan's original promise of 'bringing their own tea' seemed to have fallen by the wayside.

'I'll come along for the ride,' said Susie, making to collect her jacket.

'No, no,' I replied perhaps a little too hastily because she looked disappointed.

'You'd be better to stay here in case you are needed. There may be some developments.'

'What sort of developments?' she said, astonished.

'Well, they might find another skeleton, for instance.'

Even to my ears it sounded feeble, but without waiting for any further comment, I made off.

When I arrived in Rothesay, I parked in Guildford Square and made my way slowly up Montague Street. In spite of its size you can find almost anything you want in this small town. And it's much less stressful than shopping in a city.

It wouldn't take me long to make my few purchases and I lingered as long as possible by venturing into the Bute Tool Company and pottering around all the counters. As I was coming out, lost in thought, I collided with someone coming in. It was Morgan.

'How are you doing, Mrs Cameron?' he greeted me affably, as though he hadn't seen me for ages.

'Fine, though I'm a bit surprised to see you here. I thought you'd all be too busy to take time off.'

He shrugged. 'I had some bits and pieces to collect in town. I've left the others plenty of instructions. A couple of extra diggers are coming over from the mainland and I can pick them up from the ferry at the same time.'

How many of them were there to be? I had a sudden vision of all of the gardens being turned over in Morgan's quest for proof.

'Hi, Morgan.'

We both turned to see Cassie coming towards us. She must have come out of the offices of Laidlaw and Cummings, because she was back to the severe hairstyle and clothes suitable for the heat.

'Oh, hi there, Cassie,' Morgan greeted her, touching her lightly on the arm.

There was an awkward silence as we looked at one another. There was certainly some spark between these two, of that I was sure. Oh dear, poor Deborah, I thought.

'Cassie and I have known each other for years,' said Morgan, by way of explanation, though I certainly hadn't asked for one.

There was a further silence. It was obvious they were waiting for me to leave them alone.

'See you later then,' I said but as I hurried down the street I couldn't resist having a quick look back.

Their voices drifted towards me. I heard Cassie say, 'I told you the other morning....' but the rest was lost to me.

I was now curious. Why had Morgan and Cassie not indicated they knew each other well? If he knew Cassie he must have some connections to the island. Why had he not said? He had given us to understand that he was from the mainland and that this trip to the island was prompted by the need to excavate the site at Ettrick House.

I walked a little way along the street and pretended to be hugely interested in the window display of the Electric Bakery. I tried to keep an eye on them as best I could.

Morgan and Cassie stood exactly where I had left them, outside the Bute Tool Company. As far as I could tell they were having a very animated conversation. It wouldn't do any harm if I lingered for a while longer to see what they did next.

I slipped round to the cafe side of the Electric Bakery, making sure I wasn't immediately visible. I peered round the corner.

Cassie was shaking her head furiously as Morgan leaned close to her face. Then I saw him grab her by the arm, but she went on shaking her head. Finally she jerked herself free and turned away.

She walked quickly back across the street and disappeared into the offices of Laidlaw and Cummings. Morgan stood looking after her and flung up his arms as though in despair, before heading off towards the seafront.

I moved slowly back to the bakery window. One of the shop assistants was staring at me with an expression of curiosity on her face. I realised I must have been standing there for at least five minutes watching Morgan and Cassie. There was nothing else for it. I'd have to go in and buy some of their pastries. And I'd have to make it a decent order given the time I'd appeared to take choosing them.

Before I had a chance to speak the shop assistant grinned at me, her eyes twinkling behind her thick glasses. She was a woman of about my age, so I daresay she had seen it all before.

'Watching the lovebirds, were we?'

I was about to bluster some non-committal reply but her comment intrigued me and instead I said, 'What do you mean?'

She raised her eyebrows. 'They're both from the island, you know and there's not much goes on here that's secret. Especially now that Eric is back digging at Ettrick House.'

'Eric? Don't you mean Morgan?'

She smiled. 'Is that what he's calling himself now? Did he give you that story, did he? He's a real charmer, but you have to be careful what you believe.'

This astonished me. Why on earth would he give a false name?

She answered my unspoken question. 'He thinks it makes him more interesting. Plain daft if you ask me - at least here on the island where everyone knows him.'

I was becoming more and more intrigued by every new piece of information. On this island everyone seemed to know everyone else, know all about them. I was about to ask her to explain but she said briskly, 'How can I help you,' in a way that ended this part of the conversation.

I gave my order but as she said, 'Was there anything else?' I knew I couldn't leave now before I had the opportunity to learn more.

'I think I'd better have a plain loaf - and could you slice it please.' It would take a few minutes to set up the machine.

'What do you mean, back at Ettrick House? Has he dug there before?'

She turned round from placing the loaf in the machine, obviously considering carefully what she should say.

'No, no. Not at Ettrick House. But he has dug at sites all over the island. He's some notion that the Romans were here on Bute and he seems to be intent on digging up half the island to prove it.'

As she turned back to her task, I thought hard. How could this be? What exactly was Morgan looking for? And what was the relationship between Morgan and Cassie?

Susie wasn't the only person with an interest in the house at Ettrick Bay.

FIFTEEN

I treated myself to a coffee and a scone in the café on the seafront as I considered what I had seen.

I thought about telling Simon, but it was going to be very difficult with Susie about all the time, not to mention Deborah. I didn't want to involve them until I had some answers. At the moment, answers were pretty thin on the ground.

Deborah! My heart gave a lurch. How involved had she become with Morgan in the short time we'd been here? The last thing I needed was a lovesick daughter. Certainly Cassie and Morgan seemed to know each other very well indeed. Was there some conspiracy of silence about the house at Ettrick Bay? And someone had been in the house, someone who had a key.

As I drove back to Ettrick House, I took the bend at Kames Bay too fast. I was so busy concentrating on finding answers that for a few moments my attention wandered.

I pulled up just in time as I saw a car coming straight at me from the other direction. I managed to bump over onto the grass verge, narrowly avoiding ending up in the ditch.

'Idiot,' I muttered under my breath, as much to myself as to the other driver. I briefly registered a pale blue car of some foreign make as it sped past without stopping.

'Probably didn't even notice I was here,' I said. The traffic on the island is so infrequent compared to the mainland, visitors find it difficult to resist the temptation to speed.

I waited for a few moments to recover my composure before easing the car off the verge. This time I made sure that I gave my full attention to the road ahead.

When I arrived back at Ettrick House I was still a bit shaky, but I managed to unload the shopping and take it in by the back entrance that led into the kitchen.

For a moment I was blinded as I came into the gloom from the outside light, so I failed to see Deborah, sitting in the chair by the old table.

'Hello, mum.' She sounded despondent.

'Hi, Deborah,' I replied trying my best to sound bright and cheerful and ignore the drama queen act. 'Fancy making your mum a cup of tea? I'm ready for one.'

'All right, then,' she replied without much enthusiasm and got up to fill the kettle with water at the creaky tap.

I had to say something. 'What's wrong, Deborah, you sound less than happy.'

Now that I was accustomed to the dim light I could see that she looked miserable.

'Nothing that's really important,' she said in a small voice.

I was not to be sidetracked. I'd pussyfooted around long enough with her. Now was the time to be made of sterner stuff. I could guess the cause of her problems.

'It's Morgan, isn't it?'

She gazed at me wide eyed. 'How did you know?'

'Because I'm your mother,' was my short reply. What else could it have been?

She sat back down in the chair with a thump and looked directly at me with the hint of a smile.

'Oh, it's nothing serious, nothing to get worried about. We seemed to be getting along really well. I went to see him this morning as soon as you went out and there he was with Cassie: you know, the woman from the lawyer's office. It was pretty obvious that they knew each other well.'

She looked up. 'A bit too well, if you get my meaning: at least from the way he was holding her.'

'It may have been nothing. Probably he was being friendly,' I said lamely. 'Morgan knows a lot of people on the island. It's that kind of a place.'

Deborah smiled. 'I don't think that's what he was doing. Then they seemed to have this enormous quarrel and she stormed off. I didn't have the chance to talk to him because he made off in his van in hot pursuit.'

From what she said, Morgan must have followed Cassie down into the town. So much for the story about meeting more diggers at the ferry.

'Surely you weren't smitten?' I decided to make light of it. 'You've only known him a short while.'

She gave a long drawn out sigh. 'Not really, but it did look as if it would prove a useful distraction while we're here.'

'Let's organise some sandwiches,' I said more brightly than I felt. 'Maybe there's nothing to the relationship between Morgan and Cassie. They seem no more than friends to me. You might have an enjoyable holiday yet.'

She looked at me. 'How did you know about Morgan and Cassie?'

I had to admit that I had met Morgan in Rothesay and yes, I also had seen him with Cassie. What else could I say in the circumstances?

I was saved from further discussion as with a 'Hi, everyone,' Susie came bouncing into the room. That was the only way to describe her entrance. Her dark curls were tied up in some kind of floral patterned bandana and her combination of yellow leggings and a red top was more than a little eye-catching.

'Guess what?' She looked at us expectantly.

'I can't even begin to guess,' I replied. With Susie anything was possible.

She waved a piece of paper at us that she had been keeping well hidden behind her back.

'I've had word from the State department. My funding has been approved and I can apply to stay on for another year.'

'Are you sure that's wise, Susie,' I said doubtfully. Apart from genuine concern I certainly didn't fancy being left as caretaker of this ancestral pile for any longer.

'Oh, there's no problem, Alison. You worry too much.'

And you don't worry enough, I thought.

Before I had the chance to add anything to this conversation, Susie went on, 'You never know. I may meet someone and decide to stay.'

So her earlier disaster in the romance department had been completely forgotten, then?

'What about this place?' I said in astonishment.

'Oh, I've decided I'd be better to sell it,' was her airy reply. 'Now what is there to eat? I'm starving.'

Honestly, sometimes I feel more like Susie's mother than her friend. But I set about making us all something to eat. It was nothing more elaborate than pasta with a mushroom sauce, but by then we were all hungry.

As we were sitting over coffee, chatting and relaxing, there was a pounding at the door.

'I'll go,' said Deborah, getting up from her seat rather too quickly.

I could hear mutterings and lowered voices.

'Who is it?' I called.

'Morgan,' Deborah shouted and went back to her muted conversation with him.

A few moments later she came back into the room.

'Well, that's for definite,' she said. 'The skeleton is old,' she rolled her eyes, 'extremely old in fact.'

I couldn't help laughing at her expression. Her disappointment at her romance with Morgan had been short lived.

'So what happens now?'

'Well, as he said, there will be a lot more excavation. Apparently they have to determine if there are any more skeletons. The place might be full of them.' She gave a mock shiver.

'Oh, for goodness' sake, it's nothing to joke about,' said Susie crossly. 'How am I ever going to sell this place if the gardens are full of skeletons?'

I rather doubted this would be the case, but I'd have to try Morgan for an answer.

'How does Morgan feel about it all?' Their conversation had been long enough for her to have found out more than the brief account she had given us.

Deborah laughed. 'There's only one way to describe it,' she said. 'He's like the cat that got the cream.'

SIXTEEN

I'm not sure what wakened me. By now I was becoming almost used to the quirks of Ettrick House, the creaks and groans as it settled down, the complete silence and utter darkness of the night. I no longer missed the comforting glow of street lamps.

I couldn't say I would be able live there permanently, even if the place was renovated, but at least I felt more comfortable. And with the skeleton now safely on the mainland, the ghosts seemed to have disappeared also. I had been sleeping much more soundly.

Suddenly I was alert. I lifted the bedside clock and peered at it: 2 o'clock. I lay back down on the pillow, my ears straining for any sound. Yes, there it was again. This was something more than the sounds of the old house I had become so used to.

I sat bolt upright and tried to decide what it might be. There it was again, a scraping sound. It wasn't inside the house at all: it was coming from outside. I pulled my pillow up to support me.

The curtain lifted a little in the breeze from the slightly open window. Probably an animal of some sort I thought, willing myself back to sleep. Somewhere high up in the woods behind the house an owl hooted. Yes, that's what it would be: animals on the prowl. Most likely a fox scratching around at the back of the house. Then I remembered there are no foxes on Bute.

Beside me Simon slept on, oblivious. I considered wakening him, then thought better of it. He would only tell me to go back to sleep.

I had almost convinced myself it was my imagination at work, when I heard the sound of a car door closing quietly and the mutter of voices. I sat very still. Yes, there it was again. One voice soft and low, the other high pitched, angry. There were most certainly people outside.

Who could be out there in the middle of the night?

I slipped out of bed carefully so as not to disturb Simon. Against my better judgement I had to know what was going on. It might be nothing at all, though I doubted that.

I felt in the semi darkness for my slippers and lifted my dressing gown, wrapping it tightly around me. It was distinctly chilly and I shivered as I went across to the window and cautiously lifted aside the curtain, as the sounds of voices grew fainter. I could make out the shapes of two people and they were heading down towards the trenches in the lower terraces.

They disappeared into the absolute darkness. Then I saw a small flash of light down at the bottom of the garden beside the original trench. It took me a few moments to realise what it was. At first I thought it was a torch, but then I realised it was the glow of a cigarette being lit. I squinted to try to make out the shapes over by the trench but all I could see were two figures huddled together. At this distance it was impossible to tell who they were or what they were doing.

The full moon suddenly appeared from behind a cloud and by its brief light I saw one of them turn towards the house. It was Morgan. For a moment I thought the other person with him might be Cassie, but why would she be here at this time of the night?

I shrank back behind the curtain, though there was really no way I could be seen in the gloom. Yes, indeed, with that the long blonde hair it could only be Cassie.

She turned back to Morgan and they both bent over the trench. What on earth could they be looking for? The skeleton had been taken back to the mainland to await Morgan's attention and the trench had not so far yielded any other items of interest.

Surely they weren't digging in the middle of the night? Their heads were bent close together in that intimate way I'd seen before when I'd met them in Montague Street.

Although their voices were low, they carried on the still night air. I couldn't make out what they were saying but Morgan sounded angry. He caught Cassie's hand as she tried to step back. She shook him off and turned away.

There was a brief pause as they both moved over to the edge of the trench where the skeleton had been found. I saw Morgan lift something and swing it up from the trench. The moonlight glinted off the edge of a spade. They started to move away together towards the original trench, Cassie a few steps behind Morgan.

I shrank further back into the room. My heart was beating fast. What were they up to?

By now I was wide awake. There must be something of interest in the new trench they had dug. I was hard pressed to think what it might be, but whatever it was they didn't want anyone else to know about it. Else why come up here in the middle of the night? There was no possibility of sleep until I had some answers.

I thought about wakening Susie. It was her property after all. Then I decided against it. I convinced myself there must be some perfectly reasonable explanation for what they were doing and I would look foolish if I involved anyone else.

Even so, I had to find out what was happening and went downstairs. I would be better able to see what was going on from there.

Before I ventured out into the chilly outdoors I went into the drawing room which has the best view of that part of the garden. I might have a better idea of what was happening before I ventured outside.

By now my eyes were becoming accustomed to the dark on this side of the house. There is a security light, very dim and not really much use, but it provided just enough illumination for me to see them.

They had stopped and were both squatting down by the old trench. There was the sound of scraping and then some discussion in low voices.

When they stood up, Morgan was holding something in his hand which gleamed in the soft light. So I was right. They were digging here in the middle of the night. The only reason I could think of was that Morgan had found something he didn't want the others to know about. But why involve Cassie?

I shivered, but I wasn't sure if it was from cold or from fear.

Morgan stood up and looked round. Though it was impossible that they had noticed that I was there, I drew back again. I didn't want them to know I was spying on them.

A few moments later, I screwed up my courage and peeped round again. There was no one there. Where were they? There was no sign of either of them. It was as though they had vanished into thin air. There had been no sound of a car starting up: they must still be somewhere on the site.

This is ridiculous, I told myself. What did I know about archaeology? Perhaps it was easier to search the trench at night when there were unlikely to be onlookers interfering. But I knew this was a stupid idea. If Morgan did want to dig in the middle of the night, surely he would have involved either Penny or Brian?

I waited for what seemed like an eternity but there was no further sign of either of them. I thought I heard a crunching sound from the gravel on the driveway. Had they found what they were looking for and left?

There was nothing more to see. I was chilled through standing there in the gloom and whatever had been happening, it was all over. I made to go back to bed, but realised that I was far from sleepy. So far from sleepy that even the usual tried and tested method of having a hot drink and a biscuit would fail miserably. I had to know what this was all about.

I went upstairs as quietly as the creaking floorboards would allow. At the turn of the half landing, I bumped into the small table and only just caught the lamp on it before it fell. The sound seemed to echo forever along the corridor.

I waited with bated breath, but there was no sound from anyone, except for a faint snoring from Susie's room. I went into the bedroom and felt around for some warm clothes. Anything would do: I wasn't exactly worried about colour co-ordination at this point in time.

I flung on a sweater and a pair of jeans over my pyjama bottoms and tucked them into Simon's wellington boots which were lying carelessly abandoned beside the door. They were far too big but I didn't want to waken him by rooting about for my shoes. I grabbed a jacket from the peg on the back of the door as I crept out of the room and back downstairs.

Snugly wrapped up, I tiptoed across the hall where the moonlight was filtering in through the windows, making patterns of silver on the marble tiles. I took a torch from the hook beside the back door to the kitchen.

Once out of doors, I stood for a few moments, listening intently for any sound of activity. All I could hear was the soft ebb and flow of the water in the distance at Ettrick Bay and the owl hooting again in the trees. The air smelled cold with a faint whiff of brine and somewhere in the trees behind the house, I could hear the wind gathering strength.

I took a deep breath of the cold night air. It struck me forcibly and I felt I thought I was about to cough. I held my breath, hoping I'd be able to stifle any sound. I switched on the torch tentatively, casting its beam downwards as I set off. If I'd had the courage I would have forgone the torch, but I preferred not to twist an ankle in the unkempt road around the house.

I needn't have worried, as the light from the torch did little to penetrate the inky blackness. I slowly moved the beam upwards to see where I was treading. I stopped several times, looking over my shoulder in case they had returned, but there was no sign of anyone. Had I been dreaming it all? If not, where could they be?

I went carefully along the drive and crossed as near as I could to that part of the grounds leading to the trenches. I went down the terrace steps and across the top garden. I squelched through the ground, boggy underfoot in patches, a combination of Spring rains and the overnight dew. I almost lost my footing a couple of times, but fortunately managed to recover before I fell.

When I reached the trenches I went over to the original one first and swung the torch downwards. I peered into it, moving the torch all around, as if I could gather some clue by doing so. But it looked exactly as I had seen it on all the last occasion, except that it was now completely empty. Or was it? Through the darkness I could make out something jagged peeping out of the soil.

Morgan and Cassie must have had some reason to be rooting round the trenches in the middle of the night. There must be something of value that they were looking for. But why not do it in the day light with the rest of the team? If they had found something of interest here, why had they left it?

If Morgan was a professional archaeologist, I didn't see him robbing a trench. It didn't make any sense.

I didn't want to climb into the trench. I wasn't quite brave enough for that. I did lean over to try to get a better view, screwing up my eyes as I moved the torch backwards and forwards and into the far corners.

And that's the last thing I remember.

SEVENTEEN

'Why on earth didn't you waken me?' Simon asked several times as I sat on one of the sofas in the library, wrapped in a blanket. The local hospital had been most kind but it was clear they felt as Simon did: anyone who went trailing about in the middle of the night with inadequate footwear and the poorest of torches didn't really deserve much sympathy.

'You must have slipped and knocked your head. There was a lot of rain earlier in the night and I'm sure the edges of the trench were treacherous. You must have leaned too far over.'

He didn't say that he hoped it had knocked some sense into me, but I knew that was his unspoken thought.

Simon was cross: cross because he was worried. It wasn't the first time in my life I had gone off on a chase that resulted in danger. But I hadn't imagined it: Morgan and Cassie had been out there at the trench last night. I had seen them.

When I tried to suggest it had been no accident, but that I'd been pushed, Simon pooh-poohed the idea until I began to doubt it myself.

'You must have been dreaming, Alison. You know how active your imagination is. Why on earth would Morgan be excavating in the middle of the night? And what help would Cassie be? She's a secretary to a lawyer, not an archaeologist.'

On the other hand, I'd been there and he hadn't. And what he was suggesting was too easy an option.

I wasn't knocked out cold, but I was stunned. Everyone was of the same opinion: I must have slipped. I decided it was easier to go along with this suggestion. Simon's response made me realise it would be better to keep any suspicions to myself. Further discussion would only complicate matters. Whatever was going on, there was no way I could involve the others until I had more evidence.

So I was as vague as possible about my motive for being out in the middle of the night. I pretended I couldn't sleep and had decided to go outside for a breath of fresh air.

Deborah obviously thought I'd taken leave of my senses.

'Why would you want to go outside in the cold in the middle of the night?' she kept asking, eyeing me cautiously.

There was no sensible reply to that question, so I closed my eyes and leaned back to avoid having to reply.

Even Susie, whose own behaviour can often be less than predictable, was appalled. 'I know you've done some silly things in your life, Alison, but this really is mad.'

Simon added for good measure, 'You might have broken your leg or seriously injured yourself.

And you could have come to some serious damage if you had.'

'I didn't,' I replied firmly. 'I'm perfectly fine, thank you, apart from being a bit shaken.'

I had to admit it was a stroke of luck Simon had wakened and noticed I wasn't around. Even luckier he had come looking for me.

It was evident no one believed my story. For the rest of the day I could see them looking at me warily as if they thought I might make a habit of these nocturnal forays.

After a few hours I again began to wonder if they were right. I might have imagined it all. Then I thought of the meeting between Morgan and Cassie and I knew without a doubt that something had been going on: something they didn't want anyone to see.

Later in the afternoon we were all sitting round trying to make the most of the warmth from one of the meagre two bar electric fires. The morning, which had started fine and dry, had clouded over again and now torrential rain was pouring down, beating against the windows and making desolate the view to the bay. Being Atlantic weather, chances were that by evening the sun would come out and there would be a glorious sunset over Ettrick Bay, but for the moment we were all huddled indoors trying to amuse ourselves as best we could.

I had a good book, which gave me the necessary cover to think through what I had seen last night. Deborah was engaged in painting her nails a peculiar shade of purple which was taking an inordinate amount of time. Susie was flicking through a pile of magazines, obviously not really paying much attention to what she was reading.

Simon appeared to have nothing to amuse him and he paced restlessly up and down, backwards and forwards to the window.

'Anyone like some tea?' he said at last.

'No thanks, dad, not more tea,' said Deborah.

He looked so hurt that I said bravely, 'I wouldn't mind a cup, if you're making some,' although I wasn't sure how I'd manage to force down another one. It would give Simon something to do and encourage him out of the room into the kitchen. I wanted to find out if Susie had heard anything last night. I had to find a way to make sure Deborah was out of the room also.

'Don't you think you should offer to help dad,' I said.

She looked up at me in astonishment, waving her hands in the air in an attempt to dry her nails more quickly.

'Surely dad can cope with making a pot of tea without any help?'

'Deborah,' I said as firmly as I could, 'I think you should at least ask him.'

There must have been something in the way I looked at her, because she smiled and rose slowly from her chair.

'Oh, I see. You want to discuss something without me here. Well, why didn't you say so?'

Holding her hands out in front of her in an exaggerated fashion to avoid smudging the newly applied polish, she sauntered out of the room, reminding me of Motley our cat when he wants to let you know he's not pleased with you.

Susie raised her eyebrows. 'What was it you wanted to discuss with me so privately, Alison?' she said putting her magazine down on the floor.

I took a deep breath. 'Susie, I know you all think I'm just imagining it all, but I'm certain that last night someone tried to frighten me by pushing me into that trench.'

As I expected, she looked completely amazed.

'Come on, Alison, who would want to do that? If you will go walkabout in the middle of the night, in the pitch dark, then it's no wonder you slipped. Even you agree that the ground was boggy underfoot.'

'I hear what you're saying, Susie,' I robustly defended myself, 'but I had taken a torch with me and I was careful.'

'Obviously not careful enough,' she retorted. 'If you do think someone pushed you, who do you think it was? Simon for the insurance perhaps? Or perhaps Morgan was stealing valuables from the trench?'

She laughed, but the expression on my face made her realise it wasn't a matter for laughter. We were both aware that so far the new trenches had yielded nothing of interest and Morgan was looking more and more unhappy. Finding the skeleton was an exciting first step, but without artefacts the dating process would be difficult.

'Did you hear anything last night? Any disturbance, any sound?'

She sighed, 'No, Alison, I heard nothing at all. Now stop worrying and be grateful that you came to no serious harm. And stay indoors in future during the night.' She wagged her finger in mock admonition.

That was the end of the conversation as far as she was concerned and she turned back to flicking through her magazines. There was to be no help from Susie and there was no time for further discussion as Simon and Deborah came back into the room.

Deborah put her head round the door first. 'All clear? Is the girly talk all through? Is it safe to come back in?'

'Oh, don't be so childish, Deborah,' said Simon as he came in behind her carrying a tray laden with cups, saucers, the teapot with milk and sugar and an array of small sandwiches and biscuits.

Susie perked up immediately. 'Oh, those look very tempting, Simon. I think I may have a cup of tea after all.'

Simon put the tray down on the nearest table and Deborah and he set to, pouring tea and offering round the goodies.

I was glad they were all distracted by this, because my mind was racing and I didn't feel like joining in the conversation.

I went over my conversation with Susie. What was it she had said? Something about Morgan taking valuables from the trench?

They might think I was making it up or that I had been careless enough to fall into that trench, but now I knew for sure it had been no accident.

What's more, I suddenly had a very good idea about who had pushed me. I also suspected I knew why.

EIGHTEEN

In spite of my protests that I was 'absolutely fine, thanks' I was still suffering the after effects the next morning. But no matter how I felt, I resolved to track down Cassie. She might have some of the answers I was looking for. I couldn't rest until I knew what she and Morgan had been doing that night.

I didn't want to approach Morgan. I was now sure that in spite of his charm, there was more to him than first appeared. I had to content myself for a few days pottering around Ettrick House, until I convinced everyone I had recovered.

Although the skeleton and what Morgan called 'all the necessary soil samples' had been carefully removed, Penny and Brian and a couple of the new diggers had returned and were working on the trench. They seemed to be having some success because every so often one of them would leap out and take something over to the finds table. Even from a distance I could see the pile was growing larger.

While I was desperate to see exactly what was going on, I didn't want to venture anywhere near that trench at the moment. Memories of my tumble were still too fresh.

Of Morgan there had been no sign for some time, unless you counted the other night when I had seen him with Cassie at the trench. As the days passed I was beginning to doubt even that. Perhaps I had dreamed the whole thing, made a mistake.

I didn't know whether he was still on the island or had returned to the mainland. At this stage I wasn't particularly anxious to meet up with him again until I had talked to Cassie.

By the middle of the week I was feeling fine and Simon was prepared to concede I was back to my old self and could get out and about.

I guessed Cassie was unlikely to turn up at the dig again so there was no option but to go down to Rothesay and try to speak with her at the office.

I drove slowly into the town, trying frantically to come up with a reason for my call. What on earth could I ask Mr Laidlaw that would give me an excuse to speak with Cassie?

I thought about something to do with selling the house, but then it wasn't mine to sell and he might think that very suspicious indeed.

I hoped inspiration would strike me when I arrived. Perhaps I should try to be honest with her and explain what I had found out? But could I trust her? She had certainly seemed upset by whatever it was that she and Morgan had been discussing. Would friendly overtures and offers of help work?

I parked outside Laidlaw and Cummings and sat still for a few moments, trying to think everything through. We were nearly at the end of our holiday on the island and if all went according to Susie's plan the house would be sold and our contact with it severed forever. The agent could show any prospective buyers around. But that bit of me that can't let go without having an answer made me determined to carry through my plan and confront Cassie.

As I rang the bell at the door I realised I should have checked Cassie would be here. It would be a wasted trip if it was her day off. I was in luck: Cassie was in the office and Mr Laidlaw was out.

She was at the reception desk dealing with another customer, someone who seemed to have lost the keys to a house he had been viewing. All the contents of his pockets were spread over her desk as he fumbled about and grumbled under his breath.

She looked up and smiled as I came in. 'Hello, how are you?'

I hadn't expected this cheerful greeting after our last encounter. Perhaps Cassie was one of those people given to rapid mood swings.

I prepared for a long wait but I needn't have worried. As the client turned out his pockets to look for a pen to fill in the form she pushed towards him, the lost keys fell out. He couldn't make his exit from the office quickly enough.

'That was lucky,' I said warily, not sure if there would be a sudden change of mood again.

Cassie laughed. 'It happens more often than you would think. How can I help you, Mrs Cameron?'

I went straight to the point. 'I wondered if there had been any more word on the skeleton found at

Ettrick House.' I shrugged, 'We're anxious to get on with helping Susie to sell the house. I thought that as Mr Laidlaw was involved with the house he might know something about it all.'

There was a silence. 'We wondered if there had been any more finds? Anything of significance that would cause problems for Susie selling the place?'

I wasn't exactly lying but I was most certainly giving the impression Laidlaw and Cummings would be asked to handle any sale. Fortunately she was too pre-occupied to ask why I was there instead of Susie.

She stared at me and fiddled with a lock of hair that had come astray. The welcoming smile left her face. 'I don't think I can help you,' was the reply. 'I'm afraid we're as much in the dark as you are. No doubt we'll all know soon enough.'

She stood there saying no more, no niceties, no attempts at conversation. The awkward silence extended while I thought furiously. I had said the wrong thing again and lost any chance of finding out what she and Morgan were planning.

What could I do but retire defeated? 'You'll let us know if you hear anything?'

She nodded in reply to this but said nothing, so I backed out, smiling encouragingly as I did so.

Out in Montague Street I paused and took a deep breath. That had been a complete waste of time. There was no doubt she knew more than she was revealing.

Did she guess that I had seen them the other night? But how could she? Unless, unless. My suspicion was that Morgan had returned and pushed me in, more as a warning than anything else. After all, there were plenty of tools available if he had wanted to finish me off. I had to face facts. I was no further forward in discovering what it was they were trying to find or to hide. My only worry was that by telling Cassie I had given too much away.

As I stood at my car, wondering what to do next, someone at my side said, 'Good afternoon, if it's not Alison Cameron again.'

I turned round, startled by a familiar voice.

It was Harry Sneddon, perched on a bike of ancient vintage.

'What are you doing here?' We both asked the question at the same time and then burst out laughing.

I marvelled again how Harry looked ten years younger than when I had last seen him. He even seemed to be standing more erect, rather than that hunched up way he had been when he was such a reluctant teacher at the school. Island living and retirement obviously agreed with him.

He shook my hand warmly. 'Good to see you, Alison, good to see you. Can't keep away from the place, eh?'

'Here for a short holiday and to keep Susie company,' I said though even as I spoke I realised that 'holiday' wasn't the right word for what was happening.

He shook his head and smiled. 'I think there's something about Bute you can't resist. We moved to the island a few years ago, almost as soon as I retired. My wife comes from here originally and we eventually decided city life was all too much for us.'

I said, 'I was surprised to meet Greta. I didn't realise you were married? All the time I taught with you, you never mentioned a wife.'

'An autumn marriage.' He smiled again. 'Greta and I met in Glasgow the very week I retired. I had decided I wasn't going to fade away once I left school so I joined the University of the Third Age, as they call it. I signed up for a class on calligraphy and there was Greta. We hit it off straightaway and at our time of life there seemed no point in delaying.'

A smile lit up his face. 'Her family has been on this island for years and when I first came over with her I saw immediately what the attraction was. So we both sold up in Glasgow and bought a property here on the island.'

All this astonished me. If there was one person I had thought set in his ways and unlikely to make any kind of change in his life it was that confirmed bachelor Harry. How little you knew about the people you worked with.

This was an exceptionally long speech for him. Marriage had obviously changed him for the better. Yet when we had met him and Greta that morning in the Ettrick Bay tearoom my first thought had been how unsuited they were.

'You like living here?'

He grinned. 'Absolutely: I don't miss Strathelder High and the little dears one bit, if that's what you mean.'

I well remembered how anxious Harry had been for early retirement: how he had persevered in spite of the workings of the local education department to thwart his plans.

'How is everyone else, Alison? How is Susie? Enjoying her unexpected inheritance at Ettrick bay?'

He wagged a finger at me. 'You must both come along and see us. You did promise. Greta loves company.'

This was not my impression of Greta, but perhaps I was wrong and she was shy.

For a moment he was silent and then his face clouded over. 'Truth to tell, it would do Greta good to have some more company. She's been so down lately.'

'It does take time to recover from a death,' I replied sympathetically. 'And from what you said there does seem to be a lot of paperwork to sort out.'

He nodded vigorously. 'Her mother left a box of family treasures as well. I think that's what Greta is finding most difficult. All those memories...' He tailed off, lost in thought.

There was a pause and I tried to change the subject. I blurted out a much abbreviated story about Ettrick House and why we were on the island. '...and I'm sure Susie would be delighted to see you too,' I finished, though I wasn't too sure that was the case, given some of her caustic comments about Harry over the years.

'Well, if you are here for some time, why don't you come along and see us? My wife and I live along at Ardbeg outside Rothesay.' He gave me his address. 'In fact, why don't you come along and see us later this afternoon? No time like the present. And,' he added with a frown, 'it would cheer Greta up. It would take her mind off her problems.'

I nodded in agreement. It would be some distraction for me as well and would take me away from the sight of that gaping trench with all its associations.

'I'll give you a call once I've spoken to Susie,' I said.

'Hope to see you later, then.' With a wave of his hand he jumped back onto his bike and meandered somewhat shakily down Montague Street.

I stood for a moment looking after him. Life has a habit of turning out unexpectedly. I would never have guessed that Harry would decide to marry, let alone come to live on the island.

I started up the car and headed back to Ettrick Bay to break the news to Susie. I was sure Simon wouldn't want to come so I had to persuade Susie. Pleased as I was to see Harry, I remembered he wasn't the happiest of company, though of course it appeared all that might have changed.

Anyway, better to get the visit over with. Given how long we had both known Harry it would seem churlish not to accept their kind invitation.

It would probably be a boring afternoon, but it would pass an hour or two. Apart from school talk I don't remember having much in common with

Harry. I knew I could rely on Susie though: Susie is never lost for something to say.

There was only one problem: I would have to warn her not to say too much. And certainly not to say anything about my adventure last night. If she did it would be round the island in no time. But I would make sure she understood how upset Greta was about her mother's death. So with no expectation of anything very exciting, we would go along to Harry's for some tea and chat.

I arrived back at the house, still musing over my lack of success with Cassie. Should I have played it differently? Taken a different approach? Worst of all, she must now know I had some suspicions about what was going on.

Now I had to convince Susie an afternoon spent with Harry would be a good idea. As I approached the driveway at Ettrick House, carefully averting my eyes from the series of trenches, I heard a shout.

'Over here, Alison.' It was Simon, waving enthusiastically from a spot near the latest trench.

'What's happened now?' Not more skeletons, I hoped. One was enough for me.

The diggers were gathered round the trench and you could almost feel the great excitement in the air.

Deborah came running up the terrace steps to join me. 'Isn't it great news? It's Morgan. He's been proved right. He's found some Roman artefacts in this trench. Isn't it brilliant?'

We walked down together to the site. She gazed adoringly at Morgan who was working at the finds table set with trays of various sizes.

He looked up briefly and flashed a smile but he was obviously intent on cleaning up whatever it was he had found.

Penny was still in the trench on her hands and knees, carefully scraping away in the far corner with a tiny trowel. Another of the diggers was sifting earth, stopping every now and again to lift some small object and examine it carefully before passing it to the finds table.

As I approached, she stood up and wiped her brow. 'Well, looks as if it was all worth it,' she said. 'And Morgan was right. There must have been Romans on this site.' She was flushed with enthusiasm.

I looked over at the table where Brian and Morgan were cleaning what seemed to be pieces of pottery.

'So you were right after all,' I said.

'Yes, indeed.' Morgan couldn't disguise the triumph in his voice. 'This means that the skeleton is most definitely Roman. We've found plenty of pottery in the new trenches but best of all we've found this in the trench where the skeleton was.' He opened his hand and showed me the tiny object nestling there.

Even though it had only been surface cleaned I could see the object was a brooch, finely crafted in what appeared to be silver.

'The pin is missing, but it's still a fine example of Roman work,' he said. 'Now at last I've the proof I wanted.'

'You'll be the toast of the academic world then, Morgan.'

He nodded eagerly, not the least bit aware I might be less than thrilled. I could foresee months, if not years, of digging here and all Susie's plans for a new life on the proceeds of Ettrick House would disappear.

I moved away and left them chattering excitedly. Morgan had found what he was looking for. The skeleton remains were Roman. He was right and all the other so called experts had been wrong.

Interesting as this news was, I had other matters on my mind. I still had to find a way to tell Susie we were committed to a visit to Harry and Greta.

NINETEEN

Susie needed a lot of persuading. 'Alison, I don't see why you want us to spend the afternoon in the company of someone who is the gloomiest person on earth. Surely you remember how depressing even a few minutes with Harry could be?'

I had to agree that was also how I remembered Harry, but from our brief encounters on the island he did seem to be a changed man.

'I've promised now, Susie,' I pleaded, 'and I don't want to go along on my own.'

'Only if the visit is short,' Susie said firmly. 'Think of an excuse, any excuse, Alison that will mean we have to come back quickly. I couldn't take a whole afternoon of gloom and doom.'

Although she came along with me, she kept up this tirade about how depressing it would be all the way down the Etrrickdale Road, along through Port Bannatyne and on to Ardbeg. I was beginning to wish I hadn't asked her but instead had come along to suffer on my own.

Harry's directions had been very precise and we found his house without difficulty. It was the lower half of a large Victorian villa on the Shore Road. Impossible to miss it: the bright yellow door and paintwork round the windows made it stand out from its more sedate neighbours.

There were so many of these wonderful villas on the island, a legacy from the time when the rich Glasgow merchants used to send their families to Bute for the summer. It was far enough away from the fetid air of the city to keep the family healthy but near enough for Papa to come down at the weekends or whenever business allowed.

Most of the grand houses proved too costly to maintain once those glory days were gone and many of the villas were divided up into flats. Harry's place was one of these: the lower flat in one of the Victorian mansions. It wasn't on the scale of Ettrick House, but it was substantial none the less.

We parked outside the house and as I locked the car I paused to look at the view. On a steel grey afternoon such as this the land and the water seemed as one, brooded over by hills half hidden in the mist.

I took a deep breath as we went up the path. The place looked well cared for, the windows screened by modern pale cream blinds. Susie had not yet met Harry's wife so I had to hope Greta wasn't going to be as frosty as my first impressions of her.

The door opened almost before I had finished knocking, as if he had been watching out for us.

'Come in, you are most welcome,' we were greeted by a beaming Harry.

The door to the room at the front, overlooking the water, was open and I noticed with interest that a large telescope stood ready on a tripod. Was this how Harry spent his days? We went down the long hall past the downstairs cloakroom. Harry leaned over to close the door. 'That's our glory hole; you wouldn't want to see all the rubbish that's in there.'

'Every house has one,' I said, thinking of my own cupboards at home.

And even at a brief glimpse I could see it was crammed full. Coats hung perilously one on top of another, boots and shoes lay in haphazard pairs and several stout walking sticks leaned against the wall. He pushed the coats in, dislodging one or two long black waterproofs obviously designed for really inclement weather. 'Something for every occasion,' he grinned.

'Come through to the garden,' he said, 'and make the most of what light there is. '

Given how early it was in the year I didn't think that sitting in the garden was a particularly good idea. Perhaps living on the island had made Harry impervious to the changes in the weather. I hoped the cardigan I'd brought with me would be enough to ward off the chill of the afternoon.

Fortunately he took us through to a large conservatory overlooking the well tended garden. Compared to the neglected grounds at Ettrick House, these were in a prize winning category. Carefully arranged flower beds, thick with early crocus and swathes of daffodils of more varieties than I thought possible surrounded a weed free lawn. Was this another way in which Harry was spending his retirement? I had never seen him as a gardener somehow.

Greta rose from the wicker armchair, put down her book and held out her hand to greet us. She was beautifully dressed as always, this time in a suit of some draped material, with a muted pattern of pink and yellow roses. I looked at my own outfit of jeans and jumper, topped off by what could best be described as a comfortable cardigan and again wondered if I should have made a better attempt to dress for the occasion.

In spite of her elegance she looked even more strained than when I had last seen her. Her face looked drawn, pinched and the dark circles under her eyes were a sign she had been sleeping badly. Her mother's death must have affected her very much indeed. I had the fleeting impression she had made a determined effort to look smart in acknowledgement of our visit.

At least Susie in her usual bright attire - today yellow trousers and a bright blue top patterned with daisies - looked as though she had tried to dress to impress.

'I've heard so much about you both,' Greta said as she shook hands with Susie and then with me. I glanced at Susie to see if she was as worried as I was about exactly Harry might have said, but her face for once gave nothing away. 'It's good for him to catch up with old colleagues. I often say he should do more to keep in touch.'

As far as I remembered Harry couldn't wait to leave Strathelder High. I doubted if 'keeping in touch with colleagues' ever crossed his mind. If we hadn't met on this island I'm certain I would never have seen him after he left school.

We sat down on the surprisingly comfortable wicker chairs. The conservatory was large and airy and from the piles of magazines and books scattered over the various tables, this was where Harry and Greta spent a lot of their time.

A large pair of binoculars sat on top of the newspapers. Binoculars as well as a telescope? Harry was interested in all around him, then.

'Taken up bird watching, Harry?' said Susie in her usual blunt way.

Harry chuckled. 'Birds and other wildlife - there's always plenty to see on this island. And of course there is the view of the boats from the front room.'

Greta smiled at him indulgently. 'It's one way of keeping up with all kinds of activities,' and they exchanged a look.

'Let me put the kettle on. Everything's ready,' said Greta disappearing into the kitchen adjoining the conservatory.

We made polite conversation with Harry and fortunately she was back within a few minutes bearing an old fashioned tea pot, china cups and an enticing array of home made cakes.

'I'm a member of a Bute baking club,' she said apologetically, 'and I take every chance I can to try out new recipes. You don't mind, do you?'

'Not the least bit,' said Susie quickly, eyeing the variety of cakes. So much for any diet. It would be very impolite to refuse, even if either of us had considered that option.

There was a moment of silence as Greta poured the tea. I noticed her hands were trembling and Harry was watching her intently.

'Can I do that?' he asked, getting up from his chair.

'I'm fine, I'm fine,' she snapped, waving him away.

He looked crestfallen at her words and I hastened to cover the awkward silence that followed.

'Are you from Bute originally?' I enquired as we started to make our way through the excellent afternoon tea Greta had provided.

Harry butted in before she had a chance to reply. 'More than that,' he said, 'Greta belongs to one of the oldest families on the island – the MacThreaves.'

I saw Greta hesitate for a moment and then glare at him but he failed to notice. What had he said to upset her?

I paused with my slice of cake half way to my mouth. 'Do you know Ettrick House?'

Greta sniffed. 'I spent a lot of my childhood there.'

'Was your family connected to the Ainslees?'

'My family worked on the estate for many years.'

I waited, but she didn't expand on her brief statement. Was everyone on this island in some way involved with the Ainslees? It was all very strange. Perhaps I should try to do some research, find out more about the families.

I watched Susie out of the corner of my eye but she was happily making her way through a second slice of cake, seemingly unaware of how important this information might be.

Then Greta said, 'Yes, I knew the place well, but that was long ago. I left the island, I thought for good.' A shrug of the shoulders. 'But how strange life is, isn't it? Harry and I came back for a holiday and, well, the rest is, as they say, history. Compared to life in the city, life here is so easy going.' She gazed indulgently again at Harry whose response reminded me of nothing as much as a simpering teenager.

Concerned she was about to digress into a long story about Bute and its many attractions, I came in hastily. I couldn't let this reference to the Ainslees pass without finding out more.

I swallowed a mouthful of cake. 'So who were the Ainslees exactly?' I was more than a bit curious. I ignored the warning glances from Susie, though we both knew from experience that once you started people on the history of their family you were lucky if they paused for breath.

Greta frowned as Harry launched into the story. He stopped from time to time as though trying to recall the details, but Greta sat stony faced, offering him no help. The return to this topic evidently didn't please her.

'They were very well known in the island at one time. The original Ainslee had a business in Glasgow in the 1850s.' He paused. 'Linen, I think. It was something to do with trading with the island. He made a fortune and had the place at

Ettrick Bay built. It's called Ettrick House now but I think it was originally called something else.' He stopped for a moment. 'I'm sure it was called after the owner. Ainslee House: yes, that's what it was.'

He looked over at Greta for confirmation but she did no more than give a slight nod of her head. Why was she so reluctant to tell the story of the Ainslees? She must know it much better than Harry did.

'Did they live there for long?'

This time Greta did take up the story. 'Well, you will realise that old as I am, I wasn't around then,' she said with a rare flash of humour, 'but I think they did as so many Glaswegians did then. The family came down for the summer and Ainslee escaped the city when he could. He was one of the original commuters, I guess. You would scarcely believe it now, but at one time this whole Firth of Clyde was busy with boats of every description, especially in the summer months. You can still see the remnants of the various piers around the island where the steamers landed as close as possible to the grand houses.'

Greta poured more tea for us all. 'The original owner William and his wife retired down here and then his son Robert inherited.'

'And he is the one who died and the house passed to Susie?'

'Mmm, yes, he lived to a ripe old age but he never married. The house has been empty for a good number of years.'

'Surely he didn't live all on his own in that great big house?' No wonder the place had fallen into decay.

'They were an unlucky family. Old William Ainslee had a sister called Beatrice but she left for the mainland. Had enough of the place I expect. The story was that there was a man involved. Someone the family thought not at all suitable.'

I wasn't surprised the sister had left. I had many misgivings about that house at Ettrick Bay myself. But I was curious to find out more about the family. 'Where did she go?'

Greta paused for a moment as though trying to recall that part of the story. 'That was the strange thing. I only remember what I heard from my mother, of course. I was far too young to take much interest in it all. But it was the talk of the island at the time, from what I heard later. One day she was there and the next she had gone. The story was she had run off to her lover in Glasgow, but Ainslee refused to talk about it.'

I cast a glance at Susie but she was studying her empty plate intently as if she expected another cake to materialise there.

'Did this sister have any family?' I stopped abruptly. I didn't want her to think I was too eager for information, although I most certainly was. I felt a chill run down my spine. This might be news Susie would be better not to know. If the sister had had family, Susie might not be the heir to Ettrick House after all.

Greta shrugged her shoulders. 'Who knows? I recall there was a story of some big family row but what it was about I can't exactly say.' She stopped for a moment. 'All I know is that after he died the house lay empty for ages while they tried to track down anyone who might be related.'

'That's amazing. How did you know all this?'

Harry chipped in before she had a chance to reply. 'Greta's mother worked at Ettrick House as her mother did before her.'

Greta looked at him and this time the look was one of anger. 'That was all a long time ago,' she said. Maybe she didn't like recalling that her mother and her grandmother had been in service.

'In spite of the fact they were servants, they were very well treated by all accounts,' Harry said. Another look from Greta finally silenced him.

I started to speak again but thought better of it. The story of Ettrick House was a lot more complicated than I had imagined. Greta wasn't at all happy about the direction this conversation was taking.

Susie had said almost nothing during this exchange. She yawned a few times as though bored. She had no idea the story about Ettrick House might well have serious implications for her inheritance, if this sister Beatrice had any descendents still living. I hoped Inheritors Limited had explored all these possibilities and Susie was indeed the rightful the owner.

And what was it that Morgan was so interested in? Was there more to this archaeological dig than first appeared? Did he have some claim on the place as well? It wouldn't have surprised me if he was also related to the Ainslees.

The conversation meandered through other topics: the best place to eat on the island, the local industry, proposals for bringing back tourists to the island. No more was said about Ettrick House. Susie made no move to re-introduce the topic and neither did I, though a thousand questions were buzzing in my head. While the conversation ebbed and flowed around me, my mind was working furiously.

As usual I was torn between ignoring it all and trying to find out exactly what had happened. I knew which would win. A visit to the local library was certainly called for. Perhaps there would be some information in the back copies of *The Buteman*, the longest produced local newspaper and a source of all information about the island. Once I had access to the internet I could try the *Scotland's People* website.

With some effort I dragged myself back to the conversation going on around me. Susie was looking at me strangely but neither Greta nor Harry seemed to have noticed my silence.

Time started to drag as we ran out of things to say. There are only so many times you can discuss the CalMac sailing schedule and Harry made it clear reminiscences about his time at Strathelder High were out of the question. I noticed that Greta was looking increasingly agitated.

'I think we should head back,' I said, standing up. Susie immediately stood up to join me.

We made our farewells with promises to keep in touch, but somehow I didn't think the afternoon had been as successful as Harry had hoped.

Once we were safely in the car, I turned to Susie and said, 'What's going on? Surely this is very strange about Ettrick House? What do you make of what Greta was saying?'

Susie shrugged. 'Search me. I've absolutely no idea what's happening.' I had this feeling she also had her suspicions, but wasn't going to acknowledge them. She was no fool and knew finding other heirs would spell trouble for her.

On the other hand I was now consumed with curiosity. Had Inheritors Limited had no luck in tracking down other heirs? From what I knew these people were very thorough. Wasn't there some rule about a time limit? If no heir was found the estate would go to the Treasury. I seemed to recall thirty years was the cut off point. Lucky Susie had been found in time, then.

'Let's leave it, Alison,' said Susie as we drove back. 'I can't be bothered. I have to go back to the States. I'm the rightful heir. I'm not going to keep the place on anyway. I'm going to sell it. It would be better as a hotel or something. There's no way I could afford to run a place like that as a holiday home, even if I wanted to.'

I had to agree with her assessment of the situation. You could end up pouring endless money into Ettrick House and still not be comfortable.

Now she had made up her mind to sell it, I could understand why she didn't want to open a can of worms about the ownership of the place. Even in its present state, Ettrick House would fetch a good deal of money. Enough to buy Susie her freedom, if that was what she wanted. Better to be rid of it, to sell it, to move on.

For me it was easy to say and difficult to do. I can't stand a mystery. I worry at it like a dog at a bone. And there was certainly some mystery about Ettrick House.

Once Susie had left the island, I was determined I would find out all I could about the Ainslees and especially about the sister who had disappeared back to Glasgow. Though if the probate firm had had no luck in tracing her, why should I be able to? I convinced myself I was doing it from the best of motives: I didn't want Susie to plan on the basis of the money from this inheritance and then find that she wasn't entitled to it after all.

I owed it to Susie to find out the truth. I didn't want her to discover there was someone was more entitled to the property than she was. She had asked me to get involved, I kept telling myself.

Feeling much happier that I had made a decision, I started to chatter about this and that as we drove back. As usual I was getting in much deeper than I should have.

TWENTY

Ettrick House had more than enough space for us but we closed off most of it. I didn't like going through those rooms, empty and desolate, echoing to our footsteps. Far better to pretend they weren't there. Susie's idea of selling up seemed to be to be the best option, but who would want to buy a place this size and with so much work to do?

There had been no sign of the archaeologists for several days. How long ago it seemed since the skeleton had been fully excavated, enclosed in a finds bag and stowed safely in its special box for the trip to the mainland.

Morgan was elated. Each time we saw him he reminded us of the importance of his find. 'Marvellous, isn't it? Now all those who thought I was wrong will have to eat their words. Talia will make my reputation, for sure.' Already there had been a camera crew over from the mainland and from the window of the house I could see him laughing and gesticulating to the trench. Yes, Morgan was on the way to a great career.

It was all so much worse because he had given the skeleton a name. It was no longer a skeleton in my mind, but a person. Morgan had been in high spirits when he left us 'to see what was happening with Talia.' It was as if he didn't want to let her out of his sight.

Susie had returned to Glasgow. She was due back in the States in a few days' time. She pleaded, 'I really have to see this exchange programme out, Alison.'

Much as I wanted to help, I didn't think Simon and I could devote much more time to this house either. I had sadly neglected my work for my pupils at Strathelder High: Simon was as usual fretting about the possible funding cuts at the college.

Susie went off with promises of, 'I'll keep in touch and let you know what I intend to do about selling the place.'

I wasn't very hopeful. Fond as I am of Susie I know that she forgets very easily. Once back in the States, in her other life, Ettrick House would soon become a distant memory, a problem to be dealt with at some indeterminate time in the future.

Deborah had gone back to Glasgow with Susie. With no Morgan around, she had lost interest in the whole adventure. I wasn't too sorry. I didn't want her changing direction again. Fortunately her ideas about a career in archaeology had died with Morgan's absence.

Instead she was sounding very positive about going to teacher training college and had made an appointment to see her tutor. With that I had to be content.

Simon decided to go to the internet café to check out his e-mails from work. Too late I wished I had taken the opportunity to go with him.

On my own, I was bored. I'd finished the novel I was reading, had devoured even the smallest article in the magazines lying around as a leftover of Susie's visit. I was seriously thinking about making the journey on foot down to Ettrick Bay to catch the bus into Rothesay. I'd be able to stock up on magazines or find something of interest in the Print Point bookshop. I could meet up with Simon for a lift back.

I looked out of the drawing room window. The darkening clouds rolling in across the bay heralded bad weather. If the rain started soon I would be well and truly soaked before I reached the bottom of the Ettrickdale Road. Surely there must be a few books worth reading among those in the library.

As I crossed the hall I saw Simon's wallet and his mobile lying on the table. I put them in my cardigan pocket. He must at least have taken his bank card with him or he would have returned.

I went into the library where the remaining books languished in the dusty glass bookcases. I should be able to find something here to pass an hour or two.

The bookcases lined every wall: evidence the Ainslees had owned a substantial library at one time. But most of the books had gone. Probably the most valuable had been sold and those remaining sat lopsidedly in the cabinets, carelessly abandoned.

My choice was strictly limited because I could only reach the bottom two shelves, even if I stood on tiptoe. I was in no mood to go searching for a ladder or trying to balance on one of the decidedly rickety chairs.

I pulled at the door of the first cabinet. For a moment or two I thought it might be locked but it was merely stiff with age and a determined tug or two set it free. I coughed as the dust rose from the books, undisturbed and unread for so long. If they were all like this, I thought, I might change my mind and make that trip into Rothesay, rain or no rain.

I picked a book out at random but it was so covered in mildew I hastily replaced it. Don't be so fussy, I rebuked myself. The alternative was that long trek into town.

I went across the hall to the kitchen to find a cloth, hopeful I could remove the worst of the dust and the damp from some of the volumes.

I made a start, none too successfully. On some of these copies the covers were loose and, even cleaned up, they weren't the least bit inspiring, written by authors I had never heard of. No doubt a selection of improving reads for a Victorian Sunday afternoon, but nothing to tempt me.

I scrubbed at one or two more. This only made matters worse as the colour of the binding started to come away on the cleaning cloth. Without thinking, I wiped my hands on my cardigan, leaving a long streak of red dye on the pale blue wool. If this was what was available, I'd have to go into Rothesay after all.

I stopped, cloth in hand, as I heard the sound of footsteps outside in the hall. Someone had come in at the front door. Was Simon back early? I was certain he had said he would be at least a couple of hours and scarcely half an hour had gone past. Of course, I thought, he's come back for his wallet and his mobile.

I was about to put my head round the door and say, 'That you, Simon?' when something made me hesitate.

If it was Simon, he would have called out. But no one else had a key. Suddenly I remembered my suspicions that time I had returned with Deborah, sure that someone unknown had been into the house. I started to open the library door as quietly as I could.

Then I stopped again, coward that I am. If it was a burglar he would be alerted by any noise I made. Why would a burglar come all the way out here to Ettrick House?

The disappearance of our car and my night time adventure in the trench flashed through my mind. As Simon had taken the car, whoever it was out there had assumed the house was empty.

I took a deep breath and stood stock-still. The footsteps came nearer, echoing loudly as the intruder went through the half empty rooms. He crossed the hallway and stopped outside the library. He was making no attempt to disguise his presence, judging by the noise he was making.

This is stupid, I told myself crossly. Go and see what's happening. I wanted to discover exactly what the intruder was doing.

There was a creak as, ever so slowly, the door handle started to turn. I held my breath, transfixed by the sight of the movement. I'd have to find somewhere to hide. I looked around the room but there was little choice. The bureau was far too small to hide behind and I was certain to be visible underneath the legs of the ancient sofas.

I made a quick decision. There was only one place where it was possible I wouldn't be seen. I crept over to the window and reluctantly pulled one of the large dark red chenille curtains over. I wasn't sure how safe this would be and, even worse, as I pulled it over, small clouds of dust rose in the air. For a moment I though I was going to sneeze and summoned all my energy to stifle it.

The musty smell was so overpowering I had to make a conscious effort not to faint. I stood rigid, hardly daring to breathe. If the intruder was a burglar, intent on malice, there was nothing I could do to stop him. The mildewed book I still held in my hand would be no defence.

For a few moments there was no sound at all. I tried to convince myself the burglar had sensed he wasn't alone and had thought better of it. Or else he realised there was nothing worth stealing in this crumbling old pile.

As I listened I heard footsteps head towards the drawing room next door. I knew beyond a doubt there was nothing of any value there. Thank goodness whoever it was had decided to leave the library alone. I strained my ears to catch any further sound.

Silence. I relaxed a little, moving stealthily out from my hiding place, trying to brush off the worst of the dust. But too soon: suddenly the door to the library was pushed open. I flattened myself back against the window and pulled the curtain in front of me again just in time.

The intruder came slowly into the room and then stopped. I heard a cough. I was desperate to know what was going on. Dare I risk a quick look? Then I decided to be sensible. The curtain gave out little clouds of dust if I made the slightest movement and I would be spotted immediately.

Silence again, then the sound of one of the bookcases being tugged open. I peered round the side of the curtain, moving it as slowly as possible. This was madness, but I couldn't help myself.

The intruder had his back to me and was going through the books one by one. Were these remaining books much more valuable than I had imagined?

The figure moved and turned round. I retreated quickly behind the curtain again. This was someone who knew his way around the house. I heard the sound of furniture being moved, the bureau being opened and closed. Then another long silence.

Was it safe to move out again? I don't know how long I remained in that position, willing whoever it was to go away, conscious I was developing a cramp in my leg from being so long in this awkward position.

Footsteps moved towards the door and it shut with a loud bang. I waited a few minutes to make sure, before I slowly pulled back the curtain. The room was empty. I tiptoed out of my hiding place and took several deep breaths to calm my rapidly beating heart.

I heard the front door close, much more quietly than I would have thought possible. So the intruder did have a key. It must surely be the same person who had been in the house last time.

I sneezed violently as the clouds of dust rose again. Thank goodness I was released from my uncomfortable hiding place.

I gazed round. There seemed to be no damage done though it was impossible to tell if anything was missing.

A sudden thought struck me. I had better move away from the window in case he looked back and spied me, but before I did so I glanced out quickly in time to see a figure retreating down the driveway alongside the house. He must have come up to the house by car, but it was well hidden out of sight.

It was impossible to tell who it was. The person was tall but the long hooded coat the intruder was wearing was a good disguise. If only he would turn round, I might get a glimpse of his face. And I certainly didn't want him to know I was in the house.

It could only be Morgan. Whatever was he up to? And what was he looking for?

I stood for a moment, thinking furiously. How on earth had Morgan acquired a key to the place? As far as we knew from the lawyer we had the only means of entry to the house. It wasn't the kind of key you could get copied in the Bute Tool Company without arousing suspicions.

Had it been Morgan in the house the last time? The mud beside the basement door made it more than likely it was him. What was he after? And why the secrecy? He could surely have asked if there was anything he wanted, anything relevant to his work at the trenches. As far as I knew there was nothing of value left in the house.

I wished Simon would come back. It wasn't even possible to phone him as his mobile nestled in the pocket of my cardigan. What if the intruder returned? At the very thought the knot in my stomach grew tighter.

I went out into the hallway and quickly looked into all the rooms, hoping somehow I could determine what he had been looking for. There was nothing else out of place as far as I could see. Even in the library the disturbance had been minimal. This was the work of someone who was looking for something very specific.

I went back into the hallway and stood wondering what to do next. To my horror I saw the door to the basement kitchen was very slightly open, as though someone had closed it in a hurry. I thought back to the time Deborah and I had come in to find that mud on the floor. So this was where the intruder's interest lay. There was something down there he wanted - and wanted badly.

I went over and pushed the door gently. It swung closed with a loud click. For a moment I considered leaving it as it was or at least waiting till Simon returned. But this might be where I would find some answers. Had Morgan discovered whatever it was he was looking for down here? Besides what harm could there be now in having a look, now he was safely off the premises.

I promised myself I would take no more than a few minutes, go no further than the bottom step. If there was nothing obvious I'd come straight back up again. I could make a proper inspection later when Simon was here to give me courage.

I took a deep breath and opened the door. I felt about on the wall and eventually managed to locate the switch. I pressed it a couple of times before it sprang into light, if you could call the dim glow a light. No doubt this had been installed to counteract the gloom of the basement: a place of darkness even in summer, but it was most certainly the economy model.

I went down the steps slowly, holding on to the wall as I descended. This part of the house was in even worse condition than the rooms above. Plaster flaked off in my hand as I fumbled my way down. The steps were of stone, worn in the middle from years of servants' footsteps.

I stood on the bottom step and looked round. From here I could make out in the gloom the entrance to what appeared to be the old kitchen, a pantry and a couple of other rooms of indeterminate use.

A large spider scuttled out of the darkness over my foot. I let out a little scream as it disappeared into the pantry. The spider and her friends had been busy: there were cobwebs everywhere.

I shuddered. I couldn't possibly go any further. I looked down, but there was no sign of footprints in the dust. If Morgan had come down here he hadn't come this far.

I rubbed my hands together. There was a chill in the air here, a dampness of a place long shut up. I was doing no more exploring on my own.

I turned to go up the stairs, back up into the comparative safety of the library. Suddenly, as I reached the step halfway from the top, there was a loud bang and the door slammed shut. A gust of wind, no doubt. Thank goodness I had thought to leave it on the latch.

I climbed the next few stairs quickly, anxious to be out of this dank place. I would go into Rothesay and find Simon and never again remain in this house on my own.

Suddenly, with no warning, there was a soft popping noise as the light fizzled and went out.

TWENTYONE

I stood there, frozen with fear. The blackness was complete: I could see nothing.

Keep calm, keep calm, I said aloud as I tried to remember which step I was on. Somewhere about the middle was the best I could judge. I sat down, heedless of the dirt and dust. I breathed deeply in a vain attempt to stop my heart from pounding.

I realised with a sickening feeling in the pit of my stomach that this was no accidental gust of wind. Morgan had seen me at the window of the library and had returned. He might even have left the door to the basement open deliberately to lure me down here.

My best hope was to climb the rest of the steps and make it back up into the main house. I began my ascent cautiously, feeling my way along the wall as I did so.

There could have been no more than ten steps to the top but they seemed to take forever. When at last I reached the landing, I reached out and felt the solidness of the door. I breathed a sigh of relief. A few more moments and I'd be safe.

I pushed the door. It remained resolutely closed. I pushed again. I turned and twisted the handle, but it refused to give. It was locked. This was no accident. Even worse, someone must still be in the house, someone who wanted to scare me.

I stood there for a few minutes, thinking furiously. Simon wasn't due back for some time yet. Could I wait all that time, here in the dark, worried that at any moment Morgan might appear, intent on doing more than merely frightening me?

There must be a way out. Of course - the kitchen: there must be a servants' door out of the house from the basement kitchen. If I could face making that journey down the stairs again I would surely find a way to escape. The thought of Morgan waiting in the house above gave me courage.

I turned and started down the steps again, slowly and carefully. If I tripped and hurt myself goodness knows when I would be found.

The walk down was slow, very slow. Once or twice I almost missed my footing but my hold on the wall saved me. With each stumble I paused till I had gathered the will to continue. When I pushed my foot out but couldn't feel another step I realised I had finally reached the bottom.

I tried to remember where exactly the entrance to the kitchen was. I made a couple of wrong guesses, bumping once into the door to the pantry. The bang on my forehead would result in a lovely bruise - a small price to pay if I managed to find a way out of here to safety.

Finding the kitchen was only a start. As I inched my way round, everything I touched was covered in dust or cobwebs. I had to concentrate hard to stop myself from being physically sick but

I was determined Morgan wouldn't have the satisfaction of terrifying me.

Bit by bit I edged along the walls until I encountered the wood of a door frame. That was strange. If this was an outside door, why was there this inky blackness?

I soon discovered the reason as I pushed this door open. It gave way with a groan as though resenting being disturbed after so many years.

I blinked. What I had thought of as the kitchen had been some kind of lobby or storage place leading to the dank room that was the original kitchen. Light filtered in through the window set high in the wall. This must be one of the windows half hidden from sight by the top terrace. To my relief my guess had been correct: there was a door to the outside and no matter how much effort it took I would prise it open.

The door was locked but the ancient key was still there. I tried and tried to turn it till my hands were aching and stained with rust. No movement: it refused to give. I couldn't bear to think I had I gone through all this only to be defeated at the last hurdle.

I went back into the lobby, now a little illuminated by the light from the window in the kitchen. There must be something here that would help.

Shelves were ranged all round the walls, stacked with long out of date tins and containers. Many were so foul with black and decay it was impossible to read the labels, but after a few false starts I found what I was looking for: containers of what appeared to be cooking oil. It took three attempts before I found one I could open and the cork popped out with a loud whoosh.

I stumbled into the kitchen and prised the key from the door lock. There was no finesse about the amount of oil I poured into the keyhole and onto the key. A puddle of oil accumulated at my feet, soaking my shoes, but I was past caring.

From time to time as I worked, I thought I heard noises overhead and resumed my task more fiercely. I would not be defeated now. It took several attempts and the entire contents of the container of oil but finally, to my relief, the key turned with a groan and the door eased open.

I staggered out into the yard at the back of the house, panting for breath. I stood for a few moments, bent double, before I lifted my head to look round. Was Morgan still about? Even worse, had he seen me? But there was no sign of anyone.

I went slowly round to the front of the house, keeping close to the wall and on alert in case Morgan might still be in the vicinity. When I reached the front door I went up the step and sat down beside the lion with the broken nose. I stroked it absentmindedly for comfort. I was shivering, but not with cold.

From here I could see down into the bottom of the garden, beyond the terraces, but there was no sign of activity in the trenches. Morgan must have moved quickly once he had trapped me in the basement. I pondered what I should do next.

I could start out for Rothesay, but if Morgan was lurking around he might spy me. I tried to come up with all kinds of reasons or even excuses to explain his presence in Ettrick House, but none made any sense. What was the name of that company he worked for? I closed my eyes and tried to picture the old battered white van with some of the letters missing. Strathmore, that was it, wasn't it?

I must be able to check it out. The strange thing was that they seemed to know what they were doing. There was no doubt the trenches they had dug were the work of professionals. I thought back to that first day Morgan had showed us the letter of permission. Neither Simon nor I had paid much attention. So overwhelmed were we by the unexpected vastness of Ettrick House we hadn't given the piece of paper he produced more than a cursory glance.

On the other hand, the procurator fiscal seemed to know him well. He had been happy to accept Morgan's estimate of the age of the skeleton. Others on the island knew all about him. A change of name didn't make him a criminal - or did it?

How stupid we had been not to pay more attention, ask more questions that day in Mr Laidlaw's office. Not for the first time I wished we hadn't become involved in Susie's problems. If we hadn't agreed to help, she would have had no choice but to come straight back from America and sort all this out for herself.

I had to go down into Rothesay and find Simon. We'd be able to look up the details of Morgan's company and Morgan in the internet café.

This time I would have no trouble convincing Simon. I know I have a very active imagination but I hadn't imagined Morgan in the house. He had most definitely been there. And someone had locked me in the basement. It wasn't very likely there would be two people prowling round the house.

Even if I had been able to get back into the house there was no way I was going to risk it. I'd have to go off as I was. I stood up and shook myself: I rubbed at my clothes to remove the worst of the dust. I could go back into that basement kitchen: there would be water there to help me clean myself up. At the moment, that was not an appealing prospect. I shivered again, this time in the wind which had sprung up. I only hoped I would be able to cope with the walk down the hill.

I set off, determined not to be frightened by the thought of anyone lurking about. For all I knew Morgan might still be around and I didn't want to risk meeting him because I had no idea what I might say or do.

I walked down the driveway, past the lodge house, to the wooden gates, stopping suddenly as I reached them. The only other person with access to the keys was Cassie. I thought back to my last visit to her office. Her job at the lawyers gave her access to all the keys. Had she been the person in the house? Or had she passed a set of keys to Morgan? The more I thought about it, the more it made sense Cassie had somehow been involved, though it didn't answer the question about what Morgan had been looking for.

I set off again, quickening my pace. The road down was easier than I had anticipated. Fear gave speed to my steps and as long as I was careful not to stray on to the muddy verges, I managed to keep my footing.

As I went down I thought about it all. Why had none of us questioned Morgan more closely about what he was doing at Ettrick House? Were the archaeologists here because there was a proposal for the new road? Was there really any possibility of siting a wind farm here? Somehow I didn't see Penny and Brian and the others diggers being part of any plot.

We had asked so few questions. We had been so engrossed in the problems of Ettrick House we had taken everything Morgan had said at face value. Once Morgan and the others had started on the work, the trenches became another part of the landscape.

I was almost at the bottom of the hill and came out from the high hedges lining this part of the road. I was so busy pondering all of this I didn't notice the van at first. It was Morgan's van and unfortunately it was in the car park beside the Ettrick Bay Tearoom. He must have left the house as soon as he shut me in the basement.

The stop for the bus that would take me into Rothesay was close beside the tearoom. If Morgan was inside he would be sure to see me, realise I had managed to escape.

I had a choice. I could either brazen it out and go over and wait for the bus, though I might be there for some time as I had no idea of the bus timetable. Or I could skirt round the back of the tearoom and walk into Port Bannatyne. I wasn't sure I could manage another couple of miles in these shoes: neither option was attractive right at this moment.

The decision was made for me. As I stood there, weighing up my next move, the doors to the tearoom swung open and out came Morgan with his fellow diggers, laughing loudly. I shrank back behind the hedge, trying to see as much as I could through the tangle of leaves.

Morgan and the others were so busy talking they didn't even look in my direction. They climbed into the van, slammed the doors shut and started up, the van coughing and spluttering in a cloud of blue smoke as it swept past my hiding place on the road leading to Rothesay.

I stood up, rubbing my aching back. What a relief. There was no way they would see me now. Then I thought: how did Morgan manage down here so quickly? His van must have been parked out of sight of the house. But it appeared he had been with Penny and Brian and the other diggers in the tearoom. Surely they weren't all involved.

I went over to the bus stop and scanned the weather beaten timetable. In the salt air the writing had faded badly in spite of its protective Perspex covering. From the little I could make out I had missed a bus and the next one wouldn't be along for some time.

A cup of hot coffee in the Ettrick Bay tearoom was the answer, while I considered my options. I would have to persuade them to let me pay later.

Then I remembered and felt in my cardigan pocket. Yes, Simon's wallet was still there. I silently thanked him for his absent mindedness in leaving it behind.

It was quiet at this time of day so I ordered a mug of coffee and a fresh scone. If anyone thought my appearance odd, they were too polite to say so. As I sipped the steaming liquid I realised I had no alternative but to walk the extra couple of miles into Port Bannatyne to pick up the more regular bus service to the town and hopefully catch up with Simon.

I paid for my snack and started out on the road to Port Bannatyne. I walked at a steady pace, deep in thought, wondering what might be the best approach to take. I would have to speak to Simon about what had happened - but how much should I tell him?

Pre-occupied as I was in making these decisions, I didn't hear the noise of the vehicle till it was too late. It shuddered to a halt beside me, startling me. I turned round and could scarcely believe my eyes. It was the archaeologists' white van and Morgan was driving.

He wound down the window. 'Out for a walk, Mrs Cameron?'

'Not exactly,' I replied and then could have bitten my tongue. Far better he thought I was out for a stroll, even if it made him think I was a bit mad to be doing so.

I craned my neck to see if there was anyone else in the van with him. But as far as I could make out he was alone.

'Well, if you're heading for the Port or Rothesay, I can give you a lift. I'm headed for the ferry myself.'

'Thank, Morgan,' I replied hastily. 'I'll be absolutely fine. It will do me good to get some exercise, even in this weather,' I went on, laughing hysterically.

He didn't move. 'I think that would be very foolish.'

I looked at him. Surely he wouldn't attempt anything out here in the open.

He glanced up at the sky, 'The weather is set to get worse and you don't exactly look as if you're dressed for it.' He leaned over and gazed pointedly at my shoes.

I hesitated and that was my undoing. 'I'm heading for Rothesay,' I said.

Morgan opened the door to the van. 'Come on, hop in. It won't take long to get you into Rothesay, even in this old wreck.'

What choice did I have? Surely nothing would happen here on the short drive to Rothesay? But as I looked at him, the gleam in his eyes told me otherwise.

He must have seen me at the house, must have come back to find me after he had dropped the others off somewhere. It was too late now.

TWENTYTWO

I could see no way out. If I climbed into the van with Morgan, would I be safe? If I didn't, what would he do? Surely after all that had happened up at the house, I wasn't to be trapped now.

'Come on,' he said more impatiently, 'I don't want to miss the ferry.' This was a side to the easy going Morgan I hadn't seen before. I looked around, but there were no other walkers in sight and I was now too far from the Ettrick Bay tearoom to run back for help.

I looked again at Morgan. He reminded me of nothing so much as the wolf in the story of *Little Red Riding Hood*. There was nothing else for it. I had to act normally, give him no reason to suspect I realised what he was up to.

I moved forward to climb up into the van and as I did so a car I recognised came whizzing round the corner and drew up alongside me. I couldn't believe my luck: it was Simon. He wound down the window and leaned out.

'Alison, where on earth are you going?' he asked.

I could have wept with relief at seeing him.

'Thanks, Morgan.' I smiled brightly. 'I'll have to have a word with Simon and go into Rothesay later.'

'Suit yourself.' He shrugged, slammed the passenger door and drove off at speed in a cloud of smoke.

'What was all that about?' asked Simon as I joined him in the car. 'And what have you been doing to yourself?'

I wasn't in the mood for long explanations. I sat still and waited for the beating of my heart to subside. 'I'll talk about it later. Any chance of a lift into Rothesay?'

'What have you forgotten now, Alison?' he said.

'If it's a problem I can come back up with you to the house and then take the car in myself.' I wasn't up to a long interrogation. 'And talking about forgetful,' I said as I pulled his wallet and his mobile from my pocket.

He took them from me with no comment. 'Well, it's not as if I have much else to do here, Alison. Of course I'll come in to Rothesay with you. Where are you headed?'

'I want to check out a couple of ideas in the internet café or the library,' I said.

'Not enough to occupy you at Ettrick House, then?'

'I don't mind going on my own.'

'I'm happy to go with you, but I think you should tidy yourself up a bit first. You look as if you've been cleaning the whole of Ettrick House.'

He was right. After a wash and a change of clothes I felt much better, though not yet up to telling Simon the full story.

The distance to Rothesay by car is very short, especially as there was little traffic on the road. At Simon's suggestion we headed for the library. 'The internet café was very busy,' he advised me.

Thankfully the library was quiet. We went in to the computer room and through the window I could see a solitary librarian at the desk. She looked up when she spied me.

'What's really going on?' Simon hissed.

In spite of my protestations about 'doing a bit of research' I couldn't actually lie to him but the version I gave him was very much shortened.

'Why are you so interested in the Ainslees?' He frowned. 'It's all years ago. Didn't he live in the late 1800s? Besides, it's Susie's problem, not ours.'

'I have this feeling it has something to do with what's going on at Ettrick House.' I couldn't be more specific than that. If I could find out more about this family and their history, I might begin to understand what had been happening.

'It might take some time,' I added. In the corner of the computer room beside the book section there was a waiting area complete with armchair, sofa and small table. 'You could have a seat and wait for me.'

He frowned. 'If you intend to spend the whole afternoon in the library, I think I'll go over to Scalpsie Bay and have a walk. And I want to call in at the Discovery Centre for one of their brochures on walking the West Island way. While we're here we may as well have some exercise. I'll see you back here in a couple of hours.'

The afternoon had cleared up. The rain had stopped and the sun was out, glinting on the gently steaming pavements. I was almost tempted to abandon my search and go with Simon over to Scalpsie Bay, but my curiosity about the Ainslees won.

Simon left and I pushed open the door to the library, lighter of heart now I was on my own. Surely I would find some answers to the puzzle of Ettrick House?

It didn't take me long to sign up for the library services and I returned to the computer section where several people were already staring fixedly at their screens. Good - there was still one computer free.

I logged on and started by looking for Strathmore Archaeological Services. I found it very quickly. It had all the appearance of a proper company, but then it was so easy these days to set up a company as a front for anything. That didn't seem to answer any of my questions.

I turned my attention to the problem of the family who had owned Ettrick House. The more I thought about it, the more difficult I found it to understand why Inheritors Limited hadn't made a greater effort to find Beatrice's descendents. The only explanation I could come up with was that she had died without having any children, but no mention had been made of her in any of the papers Susie had received.

I didn't want to upset Susie, but it would be worse if she sold the place, only to discover she wasn't entitled after all.

The librarian was most helpful. 'If you want to know about the Ainslee family you'd be best to look at back copies of *The Buteman*,' she said. 'Not much of interest has escaped their notice over the years. Some of the earlier editions are on microfiche but we do have some paper copies still.'

She brought me the microfiches and the bound copies for the period of time I requested. I erred on the side of safety so she had to make two trips. She lingered beside me as I began to slot in the first microfiche.

'Anything I can do to help?' she enquired.

'Not at the moment, thanks.' Then, not wanting to seem rude, 'Perhaps later, when I've had a chance to have a first look through?'

She brightened at the prospect and bustled off to the desk. Another customer had appeared, obviously someone she knew well. I could hear them chatting and laughing quietly as I started on my quest.

I wasn't sure where to begin. No one seemed to know when exactly William Ainslee's sister left the island for Glasgow. It would be a laborious task to trawl through all the back copies of *The Buteman* of roughly the time I thought might help me and I was already beginning to regret my decision to dispense with the services of the librarian.

I looked over, but she was engaged in a conversation which entailed a lot of head shaking. I guessed it must be an interesting tale of island life.

I turned back to the next edition. One of the difficulties was the numerous possibilities for distraction. There were too many of them, interesting stories of bygone Bute, when it was the favourite destination of so many people from Glasgow who came 'doon the water' for that much longed for summer break.

I scrolled further and further into the past: still no mention of this elusive sister.

The Buteman went as far back as 1855 and I was beginning to think it was a fruitless quest. I sat back and rubbed my eyes. I looked down at my watch. I had been there for almost two hours and made no progress, though I now knew so much about the history of the island I felt I could write a book about it.

Without some help I was going to sit here all day and do no more than entertain myself. I needed someone who had local knowledge so I stood up and waved to the librarian. She waved back to indicate she had seen my call for help and came through from the main part of the library, smiling broadly.

I leaned back in my chair and said to her, 'I have to admit I'm rather at a loss. Any chance you could spare a few moments to help me?'

'Give me a minute to put this book back,' she replied.

She returned promptly and drew up a chair beside me as she adjusted her spectacles. 'What is it you're looking for exactly?'

I explained as briefly as I could, concocting a story about how I had recently read a book about life on the island in Victorian times and story of the Ainslee family had intrigued me. Fortunately she didn't ask me the name of this mythical book. For good measure, in an attempt to add authenticity to my request, I told her we were spending some time on the island and it seemed a good opportunity to track down any local reporting of their activities, especially the quarrel between William and his sister.

I'm not sure that she believed me because she did stare at me rather hard before briskly saying, 'Oh, I remember all about that. Not personally, you understand. She left the island, you know. It was one of the scandals of the time though it wouldn't raise an eyebrow nowadays.'

She scrolled through the earliest editions of the copies of *The Buteman* and frowned. 'I wonder if I can remember the date. I'm sure it was towards the end of the 1890s or the early 1900s.'

With a rapidity that astonished me she went quickly through edition after edition, refusing to be distracted as I had been, before saying, 'Ah, this is it, I think. Yes, here it is.'

She stood up to leave me more room to look at the screen, satisfied she had passed the test I had set her.

'Thank you so much,' I smiled. She smiled back but showed no signs of moving.

'I think I'll manage now,' I said, as politely as I could.

She realised I wasn't going to give way and respond to her unspoken questions so she sighed and said, 'Well, if you need any more help, give me a call. I'll be over in the children's section, sorting out the books.'

As she left she looked so wistful that for a moment I felt a pang of guilt. I steeled myself not to give way. After all there might be nothing at all to this story. I might be on the wrong track entirely.

On screen, the newspaper was faded but still easy to read. As I scrolled down I came to a small story at the very foot of page two. "Well Known Resident leaves the Island" was the headline.

This in itself was a bit odd. Surely it was a bigger event than this according to what I had heard. I read on. "Beatrice Ainslee, sister of William Ainslee of Ettrick House, leaves for new residence on the mainland." 'I shall miss her,' said Mr Ainslee, 'but she has gone to stay with relatives in Glasgow. She always wanted to live in the city and now she has her wish.'

I sat back, puzzled. This was so brief; no wonder it merited no more than a small paragraph in the local newspaper. Why put it in at all? People in those days went backwards and forwards all the time. Why should it be of any consequence that she had gone to live in Glasgow. Then I remembered the story about Beatrice's lover - no doubt that was the cause of the scandal and William would want to keep it as quiet as possible. Far better everyone assumed she had tired of living on the island.

There was nothing else for it. I would have to call the librarian over again. She might know something about this. Thank goodness she was so willing to help but before I enlisted her I would have to make up yet another story about why I wanted the information.

I stood up and waved to her through the window. She had obviously been watching me because she responded immediately.

'Can I give you some more help?' she said.

I explained the problem, telling her in brief about our current residence at Ettrick House. I suggested (I didn't actually lie) that Susie was also keen to find out a bit about the history of the place and especially the last Ainslees. She seemed satisfied with that.

'He lived to be almost one hundred, you know,' she said, 'William Ainslee.'

This did astonish me.

'And what happened to Beatrice? She would be Robert's aunt?' I waved towards the story in the paper. 'Did she return to the island?'

The librarian looked thoughtful for a moment. 'It's all lost in the mists of time a bit, but no, I don't recollect hearing or reading anything that suggested she ever returned to the house.'

'Someone must know what happened to her?'

The librarian frowned. 'I assume she stayed on in Glasgow. Island life didn't suit everyone, even then.'

I re-read the short article but it gave me no clues. I would have to find out where in Glasgow she had gone. Relatives? That was the most likely explanation. Had she and her brother William ever made up their quarrel? Such things did happen in families as I knew only too well.

The trouble was, now I was on the trail, I couldn't let go. I had to find out if the history of the Ainslees was anything to do with what was happening at Ettrick House.

The librarian suddenly spoke. 'You could always check through the census returns, you know. They are all on line now and it would give you some information about where she went.' She understandably implied she thought I must have plenty of time to waste to pursue this story about someone I wasn't even remotely connected to.

'Mmm, that might be a very good idea,' I said, more than a bit uncertain about the work involved.

I ordered a photocopy of the story from *The Buteman* and browsed the morning newspapers as I waited.

My exit was well timed as Simon had returned from Scalpsie Bay. He was outside, leaning over the railings to watch the antics of the ducks in the moat at Rothesay Castle.

'Any luck?'

'Some,' I replied,' but there's still very little information of use. Nothing to take us forward in making sure Susie is the rightful owner of Ettrick House.'

'You, Alison, not us. You're the one who seems to imagine there's a problem. I think you should leave it to Susie.' Then as he saw my crestfallen face he added, 'Let's go along to the Pier at Craigmore for a bite to eat. All this fresh air and exercise is making me hungry.'

I was only too happy to agree, especially as I remembered the supplies up at Ettrick House were at the moment very sparse indeed. I had intended to make a foray to the local supermarket but somehow with everything that was going on I hadn't had the time nor the energy.

As we drove along in silence I thought about what little I had discovered. I knew I would be unable to let it rest. I had to find out what had happened to that sister. If she had married and had offspring it was more than likely Susie wasn't the rightful heir to Ettrick House after all.

Was Simon right and I was being disloyal to my friend by pursuing this investigation? If an heir with a better claim turned up, Susie would lose Ettrick House. I had the distinct feeling that now she had decided to sell up, she was depending on the money to set her up in some comfort, possibly even on the other side of the world, if our recent conversations were anything to go by. Much as I would miss her, I could understand why she would want to take the opportunity.

I resolved to put it out of my mind for a while. Perhaps after we had eaten I would be more focused. I was now eager to return to Glasgow and begin the internet search for the sister, Beatrice. Until I found out what was going on, best to keep any information to myself. If Susie wasn't the rightful heir, far better she knew soon. At least so I convinced myself.

Before I could return to the mainland something happened to change all our plans.

TWENTYTHREE

It was Simon who heard the news first. I was glad I hadn't been anywhere near when it happened. An accident, they said.

Cassie Milne had been found dead on the far stretch of the beach at Ettrick Bay. Her dog had raised the alarm. It was found wet and whining outside the Ettrick Bay tearoom when it opened that morning. Jenny, who worked there, was always first to open up and had found Rufus shivering on the doorstep.

She knew at once there was something seriously wrong. She followed the distressed dog at a rapid pace to the beach and there in a crumpled heap on the sand, in the receding tide, was Cassie's body.

Simon had decided to go into Rothesay early to collect the newspapers as they came in on the first ferry. As he drove down he saw there was something strange going on over by the Ettrick Bay tearoom: the police car, the buzz of activity, a couple of policemen unrolling the blue and white tape. He stopped at the side of the road and spoke to Jenny who was being comforted by some of the others from the tearoom.

'It's so awful,' she sobbed. 'How could something like this happen?'

At first Simon assumed it was a holiday maker who had come to grief. That was bad enough, but the news that it was Cassie, someone he knew, even slightly, was enough to make him forget his errand and come straight back up the hill to Ettrick House.

I couldn't believe Cassie was dead. 'What happened?'

Simon shook his head. 'It's all rumour at the moment, but the suggestion is that she was out with her dog and tripped or had a fall of some kind and banged her head. With the tide coming in she would have stood little chance.'

While this sounded possible, my first thought was the quarrel between Cassie and Morgan I had witnessed in Montague Street and then again at the trench a few nights' ago. When I put it all together with the terrifying experience I had had in the house, I found it hard to believe Cassie's death had been an accident.

I thought back to Morgan's offer of a lift into Rothesay only yesterday. Had I had a lucky escape? I shuddered at the thought.

It didn't make any sense. Morgan might want to scare us from the house for some reason known only to himself but why on earth would he want to kill Cassie? Even Deborah had been convinced they were more than friends.

Not for the first time I thought it might be better if Susie were found not to be the rightful owner. It would be a terrible disappointment to her at first, but she would recover and we could leave this house with all its ghosts and its problems to someone else.

Neither of us said much for the rest of the morning. We sat around, re-reading yesterday's papers, but finding it hard to concentrate.

By mid afternoon we were weary and fretful.

'Let's go out for a while,' said Simon, throwing down one of the colour supplements.

I was in no mood to disagree with him. I hurried to get ready before he could change his mind.

As we drove down into Rothesay I could see in the distance the area taped off where poor Cassie had been found. The blue and white tape fluttered forlornly in the breeze behind the solitary policeman left on guard. I had been talking to her such a short time ago and now she was dead. Whatever she knew had died with her and I berated myself for not being more persistent when I'd had the chance. If only I had been more determined, followed up what she had said, I might have been able to save her.

We reached the Ettrick Bay tearoom and I saw Morgan's van in the car park. If he was here I wanted to talk to him. With Simon around, I found I had courage again.

'I think I fancy a cup of tea before we go back into Rothesay,' I said to Simon. 'Can you pull over?'

Simon started to say something. I could guess it was on the lines of, 'But we've only just finished a cup of tea back at the house,' but instead he said nothing at all.

To confirm my request I said, 'And a piece of that chocolate cake they do so well.'

He shook his head, deciding to humour me, though I'm sure he thought I was heartless to be worrying about chocolate cake in the circumstances.

The tearoom was unusually deserted except for one elderly couple over in the corner, greedily scoffing scones liberally spread with cream and jam. They were too engrossed in each other and in the scones to notice anyone else.

At the table nearest the door Morgan sat on his own. His back was to us and he was gazing out over the water as though he might find some answer there.

I strode over. 'Hello, Morgan.'

To my surprise, when he turned round to face me, his eyes were red as though he had been crying.

I was taken aback. This wasn't at all what I had expected.

He nodded but didn't speak.

'Can I sit here?'

Again he nodded but said nothing.

Simon, seeing what was happening, had decided to retreat to the car and leave me to deal with Morgan.

'I'm sorry to hear about Cassie. I didn't know her well, but she seemed a lovely young woman,' I said.

He stared hard at me but still didn't speak. If he was acting it was a fine performance.

I had no idea what to what to do next. I could hardly interrogate him when he was in this state and all my carefully rehearsed questions faded away.

I patted his arm as I got up to leave. Perhaps he was genuinely upset about Cassie.

Suddenly he grabbed my wrist. 'It was all a terrible mistake you know. Nothing like this should have happened.'

I hesitated, appalled by his tone. Was he confessing to Cassie's murder? Or had something else gone horribly wrong?

'She shouldn't have been out on the beach at that time of day. She's lived here all her life. She would have known how treacherous the currents can be round here and how quickly the tide can come in.'

This was the answer then: he was trying to convince me it had all been some kind of an accident. Whatever had happened to Cassie had nothing to do with him.

'Well, I daresay the police will find out the true story,' I said briskly with more conviction than I felt. 'I'm sure they'll question everyone very thoroughly. We'll all be willing to tell them everything we know, won't we?' I dared him to contradict me but he didn't answer. I had liked Cassie, even though her behaviour puzzled me. I hated to think of a young life cut short in this way.

If Morgan noticed anything in my manner that seemed threatening, he gave no indication.

I tried to remember what I knew about drowning. She must surely have hit her head or she would have been able to swim away and save herself. Why had her dog not drowned with her if the tide had come in as quickly as they said? The only explanation for an accident I could think of was that she had been trying to save Rufus. You heard about it so often - people giving their lives in an attempt to save a pet.

Morgan had lapsed into silence again. I longed to confront him directly, to ask him what he and Cassie had been doing up at Ettrick House that last time I saw them together, but now was not the time. I left him sitting staring into his cup of coffee, long since gone cold and congealing.

Outside I rejoined Simon who was sitting on one of the benches overlooking the bay. The waters were calm, lapping quietly on the shore. Far in the distance a solitary yacht bobbed about, its white sail waving like a handkerchief against the blue sky. It all looked so ordered, so peaceful, it was impossible to believe what had happened here only a few hours before.

We sat together in companionable silence for a few moments, each of us busy with our own thoughts. Simon stood up. 'Let's go Alison, there's no point in sitting here any longer.' He didn't even remind me I hadn't bought my chocolate cake.

When we arrived in town we parked outside the Co-op and went for a walk round the marina. It was full of yachts from all corners of the world. Usually we would have spent a good half hour there, trying to identify home ports. Today we didn't have the inclination.

Before we headed back up to the house, I went in to the shop to stock up, but my heart wasn't in it. What did it matter what brand of peas I bought when this dreadful thing had happened to Cassie?

As I came out I saw a figure I recognised peering into Grandma's Attic, the antique shop on the corner. It was Harry. For a moment I thought about ducking into the car and telling Simon to drive off as quickly as he could, but then I realised that was just being cowardly. I didn't want to have the problem of refusing another invitation to spend an afternoon with Harry and Greta.

Guilt got the better of me and I went up to him. 'Spot anything interesting.'

He looked up, startled. He had obviously been deep in thought. 'Oh, hello, Alison. How are you doing?' Then without pausing for my reply he shook his head and went on, 'Terrible news about Cassie Milne, isn't it?'

How quickly news travels. 'Yes,' I agreed. 'She was so young. You would have thought that she would have known her way round the island, not been trapped by the tide as she was.'

He nodded. 'It can happen to anyone you know. A moment's lack of attention, a slip and you can be dead in no time.' This was much more like the gloomy Harry I had known at Strathelder High. Sympathetic as I was to the fate that had befallen Cassie, I didn't want to have a conversation about it with everyone I met.

I made to move away. 'I have to go, Harry. Simon is waiting for me in the car.'

His next words stopped me in my tracks.

'Greta is really upset about it all. She was quite distraught this morning before she left for the mainland.'

I was surprised. 'Did Greta know her well?'

'Oh yes, indeed. Cassie was her niece.'

'Her niece? She didn't say.'

'Almost everyone on the island is related, Alison. That's one of the things about living in a small community.'

Was that what Cassie had started to tell me that day before she thought better of it? It was another piece of the puzzle and one with unforeseen consequences.

TWENTYFOUR

Simon decided it would be a good idea to go back to Glasgow. He was fretting about work and there was nothing more for us to do on the island at the moment. Everywhere you went on the island there was only one topic of conversation: Cassie's death.

Besides, I think he was worried about what I was doing. He said several times, 'Susie's inheritance is no concern of yours, Alison. Leave any further investigations to her.'

Even worse, the C.I.D had come over from the mainland, fuelling the strong rumour going round that her death had been no accident. This put a completely different perspective on what had happened. Someone on the island knew the truth - and knew why she had been murdered.

It was all becoming too complicated, all these threads. I couldn't believe Cassie and Greta were related for a start. The more I thought about it the more I became convinced this was what Cassie had started to tell me when I last saw her at the lawyer's office. For some reason she had suddenly decided it wasn't wise to continue. Yet I couldn't understand what might be the problem. As Harry had said, so many people on the island were related.

Now Greta had gone back to the mainland for a while, no doubt to distance herself from all the gossip about Cassie. Poor Greta. No wonder she was distraught: first her mother and then Cassie. Even the most robust of people would have found it difficult to deal with.

There were other compensations for returning to Glasgow. I could log onto the internet and continue my search for information about Ettrick House and the Ainslee family although I didn't say to Simon that was why I so readily agreed to his suggestion.

We had a rapturous welcome from Motley who came purring round as we opened the front door. My kind neighbour had looked after him above and beyond the call of duty, evident from the weight he had put on in the short time we had been away.

'Next time I think we should take him down with us,' I said to Simon.

Simon frowned. 'How many more times are there likely to be, Alison?'

He dumped our suitcases on the floor of the hallway. 'I'm fond of Susie too, but I think you have to be a bit firmer with her. It is her house, her responsibility, not ours.'

'But she has this contract in America. It won't be forever. And she is going to sell the place as soon as she can.'

Even as I spoke I realised how lame it sounded.

'Well, we also have jobs,' was his reply. 'And it's not as though I can get any work done while we are down there.'

'I'm sure the rest did us good,' I said stoutly.

Simon raised an eyebrow. 'I'm not sure I would describe it as a rest, Alison,' he said.

I had to agree it was good to be back in Glasgow. What bliss to be back to our own cosy house, warm and draught free.

There was no time to waste. Without wanting to seem too eager, I said, 'I think I'll leave the unpacking till tomorrow, Simon.'

As Simon made for his study with a pile of mail, muttering all the while as he did so, I made for the room I call my study, though it's a study cum guest room and usually in a state of chaos.

I logged on to my computer and clicked through to the *Scotland's People* website within a few minutes. So far so good.

But where to begin? I knew that William Ainslee had been almost a hundred when he died so I was able to calculate his birth date roughly. Thank goodness it had been after 1855, when the registration of Births, Marriages and Deaths became compulsory. I typed in the details as far as I knew them and pressed enter.

No sign of his being born in Bute. Hadn't someone said he was a successful merchant? Perhaps Glasgow? I tried 'all districts.' Yes! There he was: born on the fourth of October 1875.

I sat back. A good start. Now for the census to find out the names of any brothers and sisters.

After an hour or so, punctuated only by Simon bringing me a cup of tea and saying nothing, but silently shaking his head as though in sorrow, I had located plenty of details about the Ainslee family.

There had been four children, a small family by the standards of that time, but one of them had died and a brother had disappeared from the records. I had to assume Inheritors Limited had checked that out. At a guess this brother had emigrated to America and probably died without producing any children. I could confirm that later by combing through the shipping lists if necessary.

I sipped my tea. It looked as if there had only been two children left, William Ainslee and his sister Beatrice. By 1891 they were living on Bute, in Ettrick House, with a whole host of people who could only have been servants.

I wasn't any further forward about Beatrice. In 1901 she seemed to have disappeared from the Bute census. I tried Glasgow, going round all the various districts but no trace of her could be found in the city of Glasgow either.

Then I had a bright idea. Perhaps she had married in Glasgow? I logged on to the marriages but there was no one of her name recorded. No marriage either: but even in those days it wasn't uncommon for people to live together rather than marry. And the story I had heard was that her lover, whoever he was, was deemed unsuitable. The other possibility was that she had also emigrated, gone to join her relatives.

I heard the phone ring downstairs and eventually Simon picked it up. There was a murmur of voices but I was too far away to hear anything.

Simon came bounding up the stairs. 'Alison, there's word from the island. Morgan is holding a press conference about the skeleton he found. He is now able to prove that it is indeed Roman. He sounds as pleased as punch and reluctant as I am, I think we should go down. After all we've been through we don't want to miss the big event.'

This time I was the one who was reluctant to return. Then I thought, why should there be a problem? I only had to make sure I wasn't left on my own again.

But when the weekend arrived there were unforeseen problems.

'It's a bank holiday weekend,' Simon grumbled. His initial enthusiasm seemed to have evaporated rapidly. 'I have to pull out of the college golf match.' It had obviously slipped his mind.

'The island will be busy,' I replied. 'If you remember it's the Jazz Festival weekend.'

Simon frowned. 'What's that about?'

'Well, I don't know any more than I read in *The Buteman*. It looks as if people come from all over to enjoy a weekend of jazz.'

This appeased him somewhat: there would be plenty to do.

It was settled then. We would go back to Bute this first weekend in May in time for the press conference. Obviously Morgan wanted as much publicity as possible. The island would be busy, but in typical bank holiday fashion there wouldn't be much in the way of other news. Making his announcement this weekend would guarantee good coverage.

I was becoming more and more worried about Susie back in America. Goodness knows we could have done with her at Strathelder High at the moment. Two staff on long term sick leave, one on maternity leave and one 'unable to cope with difficult classes' didn't make life easy for any of us.

She showed no enthusiasm for returning. 'I can't possible live there now,' she said in our last phone call. 'I want the place sold as soon as possible. I'll sort it out as soon as I can.'

That was looking increasingly tricky. Even had we not been in the middle of a credit crunch I didn't see that there would be many people who would want the house, with all its ghosts and the possibility of more skeletons in the grounds. If the wind farm went ahead that would make it all the more difficult. Any hope of a sale would have to wait until all this was settled.

As though she had read my thoughts, Susie went on, 'Any more word yet on the skeleton?'

'No word yet, Susie, except that Morgan has confirmed it is Roman. No doubt he is keeping all the details quiet so that he can extract maximum coverage from the press conference.'

The news of Cassie's death had made the Glasgow papers, but the police were remaining tight-lipped about any progress.

While Susie was upset about Cassie's death her own problems were of greater concern to her. 'I'm going to instruct an estate agent to put the house on the market.'

'Do you think that's wise? Wouldn't you be better to wait until this whole business is cleared up?'

'Why? It might take ages for that to happen. And meanwhile I'm responsible for the upkeep.'

I had to agree with her. 'It's your choice,' I said. I was glad she couldn't see the expression on my face.

Her voice took on a more wheedling tone. 'Can you possibly help, Alison? I'm so far away that it makes it difficult to make any arrangements.'

I should have expected this. She was going to ask if Simon and I could possibly go to the solicitor or estate agent and start proceedings.

'You'll have to come home at some stage,' I said doubtfully. 'We don't own the property and I don't think they would take our word for it that you want to sell it.'

She agreed reluctantly that she would come over for a few days to 'start proceedings' as she put it and organise the estate agent to show any prospective buyers round the place. I was mightily relieved, though she refused to commit herself to an exact date.

'I might manage a few days,' she conceded. 'That should give me enough time. If you could keep an eye on the place meantime, I'd be very grateful.'

I sighed. It would be churlish to refuse and by the looks of things we would soon be free of this house forever. A few days would most certainly be sufficient to organise a sale. I didn't think it would be a difficult task. I didn't envisage queues of people wanting to spend the money that would be needed, not just to buy the place, but to modernise it to meet the standard of comfort required. With all that was happening in the grounds any sensible person would want a firm assurance about the viability of any purchase.

May can be a tricky month: hot with cloudless blue skies or bitterly cold with driving rain. This year we were lucky and the weather was hot and predicted to stay that way for the weekend.

Ettrick House welcomed us back like long lost family.

'I might even miss this place when Susie sells it,' mused Simon.

I wasn't so sure. It would take a lot to persuade me to come here if I weren't helping a good friend. I still thought the place was creepy. Too many ghosts lingering around in the dusty corners for my liking. I was glad Simon was there, though I still hadn't told him the full story about what had happened last time I had been there on my own.

We had no sooner arrived and unpacked the few items we had brought with us when there was a thunderous knocking at the door.

'I'm coming, I'm coming,' I said as I went down the hall knowing full well it was unlikely that whoever was making all the noise would be able to hear me.

Morgan stood on the doorstep. My heart gave a leap, remembering the last time I had seen him.

He smiled at me as if he had completely forgotten our last meeting. 'I was wondering how things were going with you,' he said. I had to admit he looked much better than when I had seen him in the Ettrick Bay tearoom.

'Come in.' I stood back to let him pass and he bounded in almost eagerly to the hallway. I was very brave, knowing Simon was around. And I didn't want Morgan to realise I had my suspicions about him.

I ushered him through to the drawing room. He turned to face us. 'Are you going to be staying here for a while this time?'

'Very unlikely. Susie has decided that she wants to sell the place. Though that may take much longer than she anticipates.' I waved my hand around. 'Who would want to buy this place with all that's happened?'

'When did she tell you?' Morgan was frowning, an anxious look now on his face.

'Why, a couple of days ago when I spoke to her on the phone. She's making a flying visit to set up the details with an estate agent and then coming down here for your press conference. She says she wouldn't miss it for anything,' I added wickedly.

He hesitated for a moment as though about to quiz me further but all he said was, 'Well, I'll be off then. I came in to tell you we'll be opening a new trench further up in the kitchen garden. The finds we've had to date are really exciting. I knew you would be wondering what the next stage would be.'

He winked. 'And wait till you here what I've got to say at the press conference.'

That was a short visit, I thought, as he went out the front door. He didn't look back. Somehow I felt uneasy. What had been the real purpose of his call?

He hadn't mentioned Cassie and the news of the post mortem must be due very soon. Or else he was waiting to see if I would mention the subject, tell him what I knew.

He had known Cassie so well and yet he hadn't said a word about her. Or was there another reason? Had my first thoughts been correct and Morgan was somehow involved with Cassie's death?

TWENTYFIVE

I was dreaming, in a deep sleep, only vaguely aware of Simon slipping out of bed and going downstairs. Blearily I fought my way out of a desire to fall asleep again as I realised the noise I heard wasn't in my dream, but was Simon talking to someone.

I sat bolt upright, now fully alert. What had happened now?

Simon came back into the bedroom. 'Good, you're awake.' He looked grim.

'That was the local police. They've been contacted by the police on the mainland. It's o.k., it's o.k.,' he added, seeing the look on my face. 'Keep calm.'

'My heart was pounding. 'Is it about Deborah? Something has happened to Deborah? I knew we should have insisted she come with us instead of going to stay with that friend of hers.'

Simon held up his hand. 'No, it's not Deborah, it's Susie, but she's going to be absolutely fine.'

This was hardly better news. Susie had been involved in some kind of accident, the details of which were somewhat vague, but my name had been the next of kin in her diary. Thankfully it was the one thing she always carried with her. There was no time to lose.

I swung myself out of bed and scrambled for my clothes.

Simon was, as usual, much calmer about the situation than I was. 'There's no point in rushing, Alison, the first ferry from the island doesn't go till 6.30.'

I sat back down on the bed, feeling defeated. There was no way I could go back to sleep. 'I'll make some coffee,' I said.

I went downstairs, shivering in the early morning cold. As soon as we could I wanted to leave this house and never return. There had been nothing but bad luck since we had arrived.

The kitchen looked even gloomier in the half light. Nothing had been touched for years. The walls were thick with the grease of long forgotten meals and I was sure more than a few mice were living in the dark corners, eager to make good use of any food that might be dropped.

I pottered about, went into the library, walked about the hallway, packed and repacked my small bag a dozen times. With no more information available, I had no idea how long I would be gone. All I knew was that Susie had had some kind of accident. Thank goodness she was still alive.

At long last it was time to go down to the ferry. Simon drove, muttering about how early we were. 'You know CalMac is scrupulous about timekeeping. It won't go any earlier than stated in the timetable,' he said.

The journey across the waters of the Firth of Clyde seemed to take forever, although it was no more than the usual smooth thirty five minutes.

Once off the ferry, there was no problem about finding the hospital. I don't think I could have coped in my present state with a long argument about directions.

The hospital had that look of so many modern buildings, square and impersonal and at this time of the morning we were able to park easily. A few staff were wandering in: there was a general air of calm of a place which had not quite woken up from the night before.

We made our way up the hill to the main entrance, hurrying impatiently through the automatic doors. The reception desk was easy to spot because it took up about half of the available floor space in the entrance lobby. The receptionist was reassuringly plump in a motherly kind of way and her dark blue suit and brisk demeanour made me feel a good deal better. After a brief phone call she directed us to the fourth floor.

Neither of us spoke as we went up in the lift. I stole a glance in the mirror. The harsh lighting made me look totally washed out. At least I blamed the lighting.

My imagination was working overtime. By now I was convinced we would find Susie on a life support machine. Perhaps we had been called as next of kin to ask if we wanted it turned off. I shuddered, but didn't dare say a word to Simon. He would only tell me to be patient.

The corridor was hushed, though in the distance we could see a nurse with her trolley making the rounds.

As though he could read my thoughts Simon whispered, 'Well, it's not intensive care, Alison, so that's something to be grateful for.'

The nurse on duty at the station in the middle of the corridor stood up as we came in and introduced herself. 'I'm Sister Mackie.' Her smile was warm and friendly. 'Are you the friends of Susie Littlejohn?'

I nodded dumbly, too choked to speak. Surely if it was really bad news about Susie she would look a good deal more solemn?

We dutifully washed our hands with the gel displayed prominently outside each ward before going in to see Susie. She was in a side ward on her own. Her eyes were closed and she looked deathly pale, as white as the bedcover which was drawn up almost to her chin. There was extensive bruising to her face and one arm was in a plaster cast while the other was attached to a drip. She was lying so still, my heart gave a terrible lurch.

As we came into the room, she heard us and she opened her eyes. 'Oh, Alison, am I glad to see you.' Her voice was so faint I had to lean forward to catch what she was saying.

I bent over and kissed her. 'What on earth happened to you?' My words came out much more briskly than I intended. It was the release from all that worry, I suppose.

I had to move even closer to catch her reply. 'A car accident, if you could call it that. Someone tried to run me off the road.'

I opened my mouth to say, 'You really should be careful about your driving,' but the look on Susie's face made me think that there was something more to this accident than her erratic driving.

Simon hovered in the background, making sympathetic noises, but it was obvious he felt he could contribute little at the moment.

'I know what you're thinking, Alison, but it wasn't my stupidity,' she whispered. 'Someone deliberately tried to make me crash. I was lucky I wasn't killed.'

She lay back on her pillows, as though exhausted by these few words.

I sat down on the chair next to the bed. Simon stood over at the door as though reluctant to intrude but I knew he was watching both of us keenly.

I held Susie's hand. She wasn't up to being questioned. That would have to wait for later.

If she was sure someone had been deliberately trying to kill her, I had no idea why. What on earth did Susie have that was worth killing for? The only possession she had was her inheritance of that house at Ettrick Bay. And the only people to benefit if she was killed would be the Treasury.

Yet there had been so many strange goings on since we had come to Ettrick House: the theft of our car, my 'tumble' into the trench, the intruder in the library, my suspicions about the incident in the basement kitchen, Cassie's drowning and now Susie's accident.

There had to be a connection between all these events, if only I could understand what that connection might be. Every time I thought I had found an answer, I only came up with another question.

As I looked again at Susie who lay there with her eyes closed, a terrible thought struck me. Morgan must have something to do with this. Was it because he had more than passing interest in the house? Was his work in the trenches no more than a decoy?

As all these thoughts went through my head I realised what an impossible scenario this was. Morgan had most definitely been on the island when Susie had her accident and as far as I could make out, he was a genuine archaeologist.

I was back to my original idea. Morgan had an accomplice, someone he could rely on to do his bidding. I didn't see it being Penny or Brian somehow. But what about those other 'diggers' who had come over from the mainland? I knew nothing about them, hadn't been introduced to any of them.

We sat with Susie for a while as she drifted in and out of sleep; the result of the heavy sedation she was under, we were assured. Simon went off in search of a newspaper and I sat on, my mind in turmoil. I had to find an answer before there were any more deaths.

Whatever was the secret of that house at Ettrick Bay, I was determined I would find out.

TWENTYSIX

Susie's recovery was much quicker than any of us expected. Apart from a broken arm, most of her injuries were superficial. Being the kind of person she is, she made sure that her stay in hospital was short.

'I'm fine to go home,' she wailed when the doctor said she should stay in for another couple of days.

'Be sensible, Susie,' I retorted when she made this complaint for the umpteenth time. She agreed, though very reluctantly, when she saw that she would get no sympathy if she discharged herself.

The next problem was where she should go to convalesce. As she lives alone in a tiny flat in Glasgow there wasn't really room for me to stay with her. She would have been welcome at our house, but the way it's designed wouldn't be a good idea in the circumstances.

It was finally agreed the best option would be for all of us to go back to her house in Ettrick Bay. I was determined to start on my quest to find out exactly what was happening there and the best place to do it was on Bute. Whatever the secret of that house, the answer lay somewhere among the families on the island. Someone knew what was going on and why. My task was to find out who that could be and the sooner I started the better.

Simon was appalled. 'I can't afford any more time away from college,' he said crossly. It wasn't that he was unsympathetic to Susie's plight, but he wasn't convinced that her injury was any more than an accident. Susie is pretty scatterbrained at times and I'm sure he was convinced it was the result of her poor driving.

'Anyway,' he said, 'what about her return to the States? What is she going to do about that?'

'There's no way she can go back at present.' I was determined I wasn't going to agree with him. I knew Susie would sort out her problem about the States in her usual way and no employer, no matter how much in need of her, could be unkind enough to force her back to work in the present circumstances.

I went on, 'If the worst comes to the worst, she can cut short her American exchange and return to Strathelder.' I wasn't too sure how Susie would feel about this but Simon said no more.

At the very last minute his plans to come over changed. A phone call from college was the cause. 'Funding problems again: we have to review the development plan for next year,' he muttered as he rang off. 'Will you and Susie manage on your own?'

I nodded. 'We'll be fine,' I said. 'We've missed Morgan's press conference, but I'm sure we'll find out soon enough what is going on.' Things would be easier if he wasn't there to curtail my activities, even with the best of intentions.

Susie and I set out for Bute and Simon headed back to Glasgow. While I was sorry about the work he was facing, at least there was a real reason to encourage him to go.

My next difficulty was exactly how much to tell Susie. I didn't want to alarm her, but if her life was in danger she had to know. I had to find a way of telling her without causing her undue alarm.

As it happened the decision was taken out of my hands. We reached the house at Ettrick Bay in the late evening and settled ourselves in as best we could. In the interests of basic comfort we had acquired some extra bedding and curtains found in our attic in the house in Glasgow now adorned the windows of the bedrooms. The ancient cooker still gave me nightmares though. We might be having lots of takeaways during our stay.

We sat together later that night in front of a fire which barely took the chill off the room, nursing our second glass of wine with the excuse that it would warm us up even if the fire didn't.

Susie suddenly turned to me and said, 'Alison, do you think there's something strange going on with this house? Too many things seem to have happened for it all to be mere co-incidence.' She paused and took a sip of her wine, eyeing me over the rim of her glass, watching carefully to see my reaction.

I thought furiously for a moment before I replied. This was the difficult bit. If I told her I agreed with her suspicions then we were both involved, even though there was very little proof of anything. And once my doubts were voiced then it would be impossible to retract them. On the other hand, it was Susie's house and Susie's problem.

I would have preferred to have more information before I told her, especially in her present state of health. If anything else did happen to her I would feel responsible.

Before I could reply Susie's mobile rang. She frowned as she took the call. I wasn't really paying much attention. I was too glad of the breathing space to consider what I should say.

I heard her say, 'Are you sure that's the latest?'

She snapped her mobile shut and looked at me. 'I don't think I need you to answer my question, Alison. That was my friend Russell who works for the *Morning News*. There is some word about poor Cassie from the procurator fiscal's office. It seems the decision it wasn't an accident was right. She was dead before she went into the water. It will be in all the papers tomorrow.'

This was the news I had been expecting, but equally dreading. I should have realised Susie hadn't been as unaware of what was going on as she had pretended.

If Cassie had been murdered both Susie and I were in danger, so the sooner I found out the answer to my questions, the better for us all. I would need all the help I could muster.

As anticipated, the news about Cassie's death spread quickly. Given it was a small community, I shouldn't have been surprised. As she was well known in that community, I should have been even less surprised.

There was someone with a more than passing interest in Ettrick House. Someone who was prepared to kill. The answer had to be somewhere in the house and it was something to do with the inheritance, of that I was sure. If all the efforts to frighten us off weren't working was Susie next on the list?

The front page of *The Buteman* was dominated by the news of the press conference. The confirmation that Cassie's death had been no accident came too late for that edition. There was a large picture of Morgan displaying various objects they had found, including the brooch. There was no doubt about it. He had found a Roman skeleton and proof that there had indeed been Romans on Bute.

'It's almost impossible to provide an exact date, but my best guess is between 99 A.D and 110 A.D.,' he was quoted as saying.

Morgan had achieved what he wanted at Ettrick House. There would be more excavations, more searches for evidence and his reputation was made. But I couldn't stop wondering about the extent of Cassie's involvement. Was this the reason for her murder?

The ghosts of Ettrick House haunted my dreams and one night after what seemed like hours of tossing and turning, I gave up any hope of sleep and went downstairs to the kitchen. Instead of having all these thoughts rambling round in my head I thought it would be a good idea to try to set them all down on paper. If I looked at everything in black and white I would be seized by inspiration, or so I hoped.

I scolded myself for my obsession with the place. It was Susie's concern and her only interest now was in selling the place and moving on.

It was hard to imagine why someone would want to cause problems for Susie. I reminded myself if something did happen to her and if no other heirs could be found, the money from the estate would go to the Treasury. So what benefit was there in harming Susie?

I smoothed out a piece of paper on the table and sat for a moment wondering where to begin. There seemed to be so many people involved. I wondered if I should include the skeleton. It was all connected somehow, everything that had happened. If only I could find the common thread, the mystery would be solved.

I listed everyone in the order we had met them. I frowned as I reached Harry and Greta. Did they count? After all we knew Harry from our days together at Strathelder High and it was pretty unlikely he would suddenly have turned killer over a property with which he had no association.

And what about Greta? It was true she had some connection with the house, but she seemed not very much bothered by the fact Susie had inherited it. She and Harry seemed perfectly contented with their spacious house and garden along the Shore Road. Then I thought about the bereavements Greta had suffered. Had they affected her mind somehow? But that idea seemed too ridiculous to merit any further consideration.

I frowned as I lifted my pen to strike both of them from the list. If I deleted Harry and Greta the list was very thin.

Then there was Morgan. What was he up to? It was obvious he knew Cassie well and I still had my suspicions about his credentials as an archaeologist.

There was a lot of checking to do. And yet and yet - somewhere in the past the answer to this problem lay hidden. There was something nagging at the back of my mind, something I had seen. I knew would be important if only I could remember what it was.

The piece of paper in front of me was covered with spider diagrams, names and lists but nothing on it that would take me any further forward. At least I had the satisfaction of knowing that I had committed it all to paper.

Now it was all out of my head and written down I could let it go for a while and go back to sleep. I folded the piece of paper carefully and put it in my dressing gown pocket.

What is it that they say about that time last thing at night when you are dropping off? When the mind is in a state of being half awake, half asleep and the thoughts and ideas that have been lurking at the back of your mind all day suddenly crystallise into coherent thoughts.

As I lay in bed, listening to the creaks of the old house as I gradually nodded off, I remembered what had been nagging at me.

I suddenly realised that I knew the identity of the intruder to the house. It wasn't Morgan in that long coat but Greta: Greta dressed in the long black coat I had seen hanging up in the cloakroom at their house in Ardbeg.

All possibility of sleep vanished with the realisation that Greta had some connection with Ettrick House. A connection that made her determined enough to get into the house. But where had she obtained the key? And what was she was looking for?

I had to find some more information about Greta. I wondered if I should tell Susie, ask her to help. But she can be so volatile I was afraid she would either tell me to stop or try to involve herself in such a way she would be a danger to us both.

If it had indeed been Greta she had taken very little time to go through the house. Either she had quickly decided it was a fruitless quest or else she had abandoned it temporarily. Or was it possible she had found what she was looking for?

I slipped out of bed and went downstairs into the library. I stood gazing round me, wondering where to begin. Although many of the books had disappeared there were still many left, most of them in very poor condition. As I tugged open the glass case and went to lift out the first one from the bookcase nearest me, a cloud of dust rose, making me sneeze violently. If they were all like this it would take me forever to go through them all. I remembered last time I had attempted this. Surely no one would appear to startle me this time.

The majority of the books were very old indeed and in no particular order. What seemed to be history was all muddled up with fiction, ancient tomes on religious subjects side by side with tales of travels in foreign lands.

I wondered again if any of these books was of particular value. Perhaps that was all that Greta had been looking for. Maybe she was no more than a common thief. But somehow that didn't square with my impressions of the cool elegant Greta. How would she know what remained in this house and in the library?

By early morning I had managed to make my way through only three of the shelves. Part of the problem was I had no idea what I was looking for. There didn't appear to be anything in the books I had looked at so far to give me a clue.

I heard stirrings above me. Susie was awake at last. I decided I had better abandon my search meantime. I hastily replaced the pile of books lying at my feet back on the shelves, but I didn't bother to put them back in any special order. After all, who would know? Most of them seemed to me as if they would even be rejected by the most desperate of charity shops.

I began fiddling around with the damp cloth, giving the impression of trying to clean up a bit. No need for Susie to know what I was up to.

'Been up long?' she said as she came into the room, stretching and yawning.

'Not long,' I lied.

Fortunately she didn't seem interested in pursuing the matter any further. She sat down heavily on one of the few chairs in the room. 'Any plans for today, Alison?'

She was bored and looking to me to come up with some idea to amuse us. I shook my head. In truth I had no plans at all.

'I suppose in days gone by, ladies like us would have spent some time writing letters at the little bureau,' she said, idly wiggling her toes.

'Who writes letters these days,' I said. 'It's a lost art.'

'What are you on about Alison?' It was obvious Susie was only half listening. 'I think I'll go back over to the mainland later. I'm going to make an appointment with an estate agent to start the process of selling this house. Then I can organise my flight back to L.A.'

'Won't you use one of the agents on the island?' It seemed to me there was no need to trail all the way over to the mainland when there were perfectly good facilities on the island.

Susie shrugged. 'I know this estate agent. He's a friend of a friend. I think he could do with the business.'

I didn't reply. This wasn't the kind of property that would sell overnight - quite the opposite. If Susie thought she would make money quickly she was very much mistaken.

'And you'll go back to America?'

'Who knows? I have to square it all with the Education department, not to mention Strathelder High.'

'Anyway,' she waved her hand around vaguely, 'if this sells for a good price, even after Inheritors Limited have their commission, I may never have to work again.'

So I was right. She thought this house would sell for a fortune. I didn't want to disabuse her, but there was so much work to be done, it might be more likely that someone would want to buy the place to knock it down and re-build. I didn't think the Council would be likely to give permission for that.

'I'm going into town,' I said. 'Do you want to come?'

Susie yawned again and stretched. 'No, I think I'll stay here. I honestly can't be bothered moving.'

'Suit yourself. Are you sure you'll be all right on your own?' I was beginning to get more than a little fed up with the whole sorry saga but I worried Susie was still fragile after her accident.

'Don't fret, Alison, I'm absolutely fine.'

I headed off, leaving Susie sitting in the armchair, looking as if she was about to doze again.

Rothesay was busy, much busier than usual. There was a gala event up at Mount Stuart at the weekend and some people had decided to take advantage and come over early. I didn't blame them. The sun was shining, glinting on the boats swaying in the wind in the marina and even the shops along the front had a brighter, chirpier air.

I stood for a moment, leaning on the railings, letting the breeze blow over me. The smell of the seaside was in the air, that distinctive mix of salt and brine mingled with the appetising scent of fish and chips from Zavaroni's on the block opposite, reminding me so much of childhood holidays. As I stood there reminiscing, lost in memories, I heard a voice I recognised at my side.

'Enjoying the sea air, Mrs Cameron?'

I turned, startled by the sound, and came face to face with Greta.

'Oh, hello, Greta,' I said. 'I'm in town to pick up a few things and I thought I might as well take advantage of the fine day.' I hesitated for a moment. 'I was so sorry to hear about Cassie. I didn't know you were related.'

She acknowledged my words by the merest nod of her head. Perhaps coming so close on the death of her mother it was too painful to talk about.

'You're still all at Ettrick House then.' A statement more than a question. She looked cross and her hair appeared hastily put up. Little tendrils were escaping at the back and even the pale blue suit she was wearing wasn't as immaculate as the last time I had seen her. The skirt was crumpled and there was a small stain or two on the collar of her jacket. She must still be very upset about her mother's death. Was she one of those people who felt guilty about their parent dying in a care home?

I was strangely reluctant to give her any information.

'Well, Simon has gone back home. He couldn't afford any more time away from work. Susie and I are there, but not for much longer.'

'The lure of the mainland too much for you? Some people shouldn't be on the island.'

I gazed at her. Was she making a threat?

I shook my head. 'No, I think this time we'll be going for good. Susie has decided to sell Ettrick House.'

She looked startled. 'Sell Ettrick House? Why would she want to do that?'

'Why would she want to keep it? It's not exactly the kind of place you could use as a holiday home, is it?'

Greta looked at me sharply. 'Don't you think she was really lucky to inherit a place like that? Many a person would give their eye teeth for such a fine house.'

'I'm sure it must have been a great place once,' I replied, taken aback by the strength of her words. 'In the days when you could afford plenty of servants to help run the place. But it's been allowed to go to rack and ruin over the years…'

She put her face up close to mine. 'That's more than a bit of an exaggeration,' she hissed. 'It's still a wonderful house, I can assure you. I think you should dissuade her from selling.'

She must have realised how startled I was because she took a step back and gave a very false laugh. 'Sorry, Alison, I got a bit carried away. We Brandanes can be very defensive about our historical places on the island.'

I wasn't convinced. And what on earth was a Brandane? Was it some kind of society to which she belonged?

She must have seen the look on my face because she said, 'I should explain that the name Brandane is given to anyone who was born on the island.'

This was taking us away from the point. I was more interested in Greta's sharp riposte to my words. And I wasn't at all convinced by the way in which she was trying to make things better by engaging in idle chit chat.

'Let me know if Susie does decide to sell up, won't you?' She was back to the old Greta as though nothing at all had happened.

'Why, do you know someone who might be willing to buy the place?'

'Well, I do have some contacts,' she replied vaguely.

I was very doubtful there would be anyone on the island with the sort of money Susie would be looking for willing to buy Ettrick House. But you never could tell.

There was an awkward silence. 'I'd better be getting along,' I said. 'Perhaps we'll meet up again soon. Regards to Harry.'

She said nothing as I walked away. I could feel her eyes following me.

I was totally perplexed. Why had the mention of selling the place caused such a violent reaction in Greta? Surely she and Harry didn't want to buy the place? It wasn't only the likely price but the amount of money that would have to be spent bringing the place up to date. Perhaps it was all part of her grieving process.

I had no more time to ponder on this dilemma. I had to go to the Post Office before it closed.

It didn't take long to do what I wanted, even with the opportunity to chat that always happens on the island. A more leisurely pace of life might suit me very well I thought, as I made my way back to my car parked in Guildford Square.

As I came along Montague Street I passed the offices of Laidlaw and Cummings where we had started out. That day when we had gone to pick up the keys to Ettrick House for Susie now seemed so long ago.

To my surprise, I saw Greta come out of the main door. Then I thought, why on earth should I be surprised? There could be a million reasons why Greta was there.

But something made me shrink back. It wasn't only because I didn't want to get into another conversation with her about Ettrick House or anything else for that matter.

I had to see which direction she was taking, then I could claim my car and leave town.

As I watched, she crossed the road, looking neither to left nor right. Even at this distance I could see there was a look of real anger on her face. And then I saw her go to the little square and sit down on one of the benches. Damn! She looked as if she was waiting for someone, Harry most probably.

I would have to turn back and go down on to the front and come round to Guildford Square by the longer way. Not that anything takes very long in Rothesay and I felt very foolish indeed, giving myself so much trouble.

As I was about to make my way down the side street and across through the putting green on to the promenade, I saw someone come down from the High Street beside the castle and sit down on the bench beside her. As curious as ever, I squinted to see who it was. Unfortunately my view was blocked by the enormous stone pots, abloom with flowers.

Whoever it was, he was well covered up by an enormous parka and a black woollen cap pulled right down over his ears. I was certain it wasn't Harry - this person had no shock of white hair.

They seemed to be having some kind of argument but I was too far away to make out what they were saying. And then the person beside Greta turned round as though in despair. He pulled off his cap and I saw the mass of red hair. It was Morgan.

What on earth was he doing sitting here having an argument with Greta?

TWENTYSEVEN

The new edition of *The Buteman* was taken up with Cassie's murder. Everyone seemed to have a theory about what had happened and not a few were in complete denial such a dreadful event could have happened here on Bute.

Several times I lifted the phone to call the police, voice my suspicions. But what proof did I have? Absolutely none.

Most people on the island were in a state of shock. Who would have expected murder in this tranquil place? Much better to assume that it had been an unfortunate accident.

Susie was becoming restless. She prowled about Ettrick House complaining all the time about the lack of facilities.

'We could shut the place up and go,' I said. 'After all, the estate agent will show it to anyone who is interested.'

She shook her head. 'I know, I know, but I want to make sure that once we leave we don't have to come back.'

I wasn't any more anxious to stay than she was. My idea of a holiday on Bute is a week being cosseted in a good hotel, not being stuck in this old creaking house with the ever present smell of decay and the wind whistling through every crack and crevice it could find. 'Let's compromise,' I said firmly. 'We can stay on for a while longer till you make up your mind what you are going to do.'

That seemed to satisfy her. I was sure it would also please Simon when I next spoke to him. He had been calling at least once a day to ask when I was coming home. On the last phone call he had resorted to the sort of emotional blackmail he thought would most certainly get to me. 'I miss you - and Motley is pining terribly.'

Somehow this didn't ring true. Motley, like most cats, is only interested in whoever provides food. While there is plenty of food, he has no other loyalties.

'You could always come down and join us,' I said, knowing he had no intention of doing so.

'You know I can't do that, Alison, not at the moment.' His voice sounded plaintive.

'Is Deborah not looking after you?'

He snorted. 'Deborah has such a social life I scarcely see her.'

There was no way of pleasing everyone. Susie was absolutely determined as this would be her last trip to the house she needed me to support her in making arrangements to sell.

'Perhaps we should attempt a clear up,' I said, though I knew there was too much to do to make more than a very little impression on this house.

Susie waved her hand. 'Oh, don't let's bother Alison. Be realistic. This place need a bomb put under it. Far better that any buyer should see it as it is and make their decision on that.'

I didn't fancy sitting around for days on end doing nothing. Something about the place made me disinclined to settle and though it was now late June, a period of torrential rain had set in, alternating with brief spells of bright sunshine. Unfortunately the spells of sunshine didn't last long enough to let us make any real plans to go outdoors. We had to hope the good weather being predicted would arrive before we left the island.

I hadn't yet had the opportunity to speak to Morgan again. I couldn't think of anything to say that might not sound accusatory or plain silly.

'Tell you what,' I said finally, 'I'll go down into Rothesay and collect some books and some magazines. Then we can have a lazy day and if the weather clears up this evening we can go for a walk.'

Susie raised a hand from where she was now ensconced on the sofa, which I took to be a sign of agreement, though I wasn't too sure.

'I'll take that as a yes,' I said firmly as I made for the door. I'd hold her to that later if the rain stopped.

A few minutes later I was in the car and heading for Rothesay. The rain had started again after a brief spell of sunshine and I had to put the windscreen wipers on full to cope with the deluge. I stopped twice by the side of the track when the rain got too much even for the wipers at full speed.

It took me longer than usual to reach Rothesay and as it was Saturday, the town was crowded with day trippers and holiday makers seeking the delights of the Clyde coast in spite of the rain.

The last seagoing paddle steamer *The Waverley* was making its majestic way into the pier and I hurried to avoid the crowds of pedestrians who would disembark for their brief stop in the town.

By the time I had made a selection at the Print Point bookshop, bought some magazines and made a trip to the Electric Bakery for some goodies to sustain us through our marathon read, it was close on 5 o'clock when I at last retrieved and loaded up the car.

As expected, the rain clouds had begun to disappear and the sun had come out. These long nights of summer allow you to linger outdoors till late and it looked as if we might have that walk after all.

I felt my spirits lift. Once Susie had sold this house, or at least placed it into the hands of an estate agent, Simon and I could enjoy a break on the island somewhere other than Ettrick House.

I opened the front door and called out, 'Susie, are you there? I could do with some help. I bought much more than I meant to.'

I was greeted by silence. That was strange. Had Susie decided to go out for a walk on her own, now that the rain had cleared? Most unlikely, as she has to be cajoled, if not downright pushed, into activity of any kind.

I stood still and listened. I called again, but still there was no response. This was very odd. It is a big house, but as a teacher I am well used to projecting my voice. I was sure she must have heard the front door open. My heart began to beat faster as I thought back to last time I had been in this house on my own. Had someone come in and threatened Susie?

Then very faintly from the library, I heard a sound.

As I pushed the door open, dreading what I might find, I could see Susie sitting on the floor, a dazed expression on her face. One of the old books was lying on the floor in front of her and in her hand she was clutching a piece of yellowed paper. She thrust the sheet of paper towards me.

'I think you'd better come and have a look at this, Alison,' she said.

I had a feeling of foreboding as I approached her. 'What is it you've found?'

She waved it at me. 'I thought I'd have a look in that little bureau while you were out and I found this.'

We sat down together on one of the sofas and she handed the paper to me.

'It was stuck inside this book.' She nudged the book on the floor with her foot.

I opened the paper out carefully. It was yellow with age and cracked along the folds so that some of the words were difficult to make out. But as far as I could tell there was little doubt that it was a letter and something to do with the house.

'What do you think it means, Alison?'

I hesitated. Even at a brief glance I realised this could cause problems for Susie. She knew this as well as I did and I suspected she saw her inheritance disappearing before her eyes.

The letter appeared to be a declaration of some kind, signed and dated 1895. 'Where did you find it?' I asked. 'Last time I looked the bureau was empty.'

She laughed. 'I pulled and pushed all the drawers and there is a little button hidden in the lid that opens a secret drawer. My grandmother had a bureau very like this one, that's how I know.'

'Is it a will?' Susie squinted at the paper.

'I don't think so.' I wasn't entirely sure what it was and the signature was difficult to make out, no matter which way I turned it.

'1895,' I said, 'that would make it at the time of William Ainslee. He was the original owner of this place if you remember. He had one son, Robert. He was the one who died with no children and that's why you inherited the place, Susie.'

'How do you know all of this, Alison?'

I looked a bit shamefaced. 'Well, you know how curious I am about these things. I have to admit that I did some investigation.'

'So what is this all about?' Susie returned to the piece of paper.

'It seems to be talking about making some financial provision for a Jane Blair on her proposed marriage to one of the coachmen, David MacThreave.'

'Who was she?'

'I'm not quite sure,' I said slowly. 'But didn't Harry say Greta was related to the MacThreaves?'

'I thought Greta told us it was her mother who worked up at the house? Did this William make provision for everyone? And why is this note hidden here?'

I shook my head. I had no answers to Susie's questions.

I turned the paper over. 'It's addressed to his son Robert and seems to be charging him with taking care of Jane Blair and her family.'

'Wait a minute.' I stood up and went over to the table where there was a folder of all the information I had collected together on Ettrick House. Sure enough, there in the 1891 census a Jane Blair was listed. But the strange thing was she was only eleven. This wasn't making any sense.

'I'll have to log on to the internet, Susie. It looks like another trip into town.'

I left Susie with the task of taking the other books out of the bookcase, more to keep her occupied than anything and headed into Rothesay.

As I drove along I tried to find some pattern in it all. No one had ever mentioned this Jane Blair, yet she must have some importance in the story.

The Rothesay library was quiet and I was able to check and re-check everything as I went. Thank goodness Scotland has good records, I thought, and then felt guilty remembering how often I had complained about bureaucracy.

Within an hour I had accumulated a pile of information detailing births, marriages and deaths as well as the full censuses for 1891 and 1901.

The complicating factor seemed to be that both William and Robert Ainslee had lived to a ripe old age. Robert had been born when William was well into his fifties and Robert had died without any children.

I found the birth certificate for Jane's daughter. As I suspected she had been born before Jane's marriage.

I did a quick calculation. Jane had been barely sixteen when her daughter, Greta's mother, was born and there was no father mentioned on the birth certificate. So that was it - Greta's mother was illegitimate.

A strong suspicion began to form in my mind. It would explain why William felt bound to provide for Jane and her family and Jane's sudden marriage only two months after the birth of her daughter.

I looked at my watch. It was almost closing time. The librarian who had been so helpful last time came over.

'Sorry, I'm just going,' I said, starting to gather all my notes together.

'I'm not rushing you. I wondered if you needed any help. You seem to have done a power of work.'

'I'm almost there,' I replied and promptly dropped all the papers on the floor.

She bent down to help me pick them up.

'I see you're still researching the Ainslee family?'

'I thought they sounded very interesting. I might write a book on them,' I improvised, hoping she would believe me this time.

She handed me the papers and smiled. 'You'll be opening a can of worms there.'

I stopped trying to assemble the papers into some kind of order. 'Yes?' I waited for her to continue.

'Well,' she shrugged. 'There were all sorts of tales about the old Ainslee, William. A bit of a rascal by all accounts. Treated his servants very badly and got more than one of the girls into trouble, if you know what I mean.'

Seeing my astonishment she said, 'Memories are long on the island.'

I didn't want to discuss this any further, but if I was right, there was a very good reason why Greta was so interested in the house at Ettrick bay.

TWENTYEIGHT

High summer and the town was bustling with day trippers every weekend. Where people once came down from Glasgow on the many steamers, crowding into any available accommodation for their precious two weeks away from the grime and toil of the city, they now came for a day. Many left their cars at the station at Wemyss Bay and made the crossing on foot. Even these shadows of the past were welcome to boost the economy of Bute, suffering, as so many Scottish seaside resorts are, from a misplaced preference for exotic locations.

As soon as you left the town you could feel why this island was such paradise. A sunny day and the sea sparkled turquoise and the seals came out to bask on the rocks at Scalpsie Bay. The hedgerows were lush with the promise of juicy brambles and yellow sedge lilies flourished in the still boggy ditches at the road edges. The whole island was alive again after its long winter sleep.

Up on the hill where Ettrick House stood it was also summer. Somehow the house didn't seem so menacing, so daunting. It was still a place of shabby grandeur, but you could open the windows wide and let the house breathe. We had cleared a space in the patch of garden nearest the house and began to assume the ritual of taking our morning coffee out there, perched on a couple of the ancient garden chairs we had found in the old outhouse. That part of the garden commanded a view across Ettrick Bay and with each passing day I felt calmer and much more optimistic about the future. It would all end soon.

'The weathermen say this is to be the hottest week of the year,' mused Susie as she sipped her second cup of coffee.

My mouth was too full of buttered toast to reply but I nodded my head. If we were to suffer a heat wave, better here on the island than stifling in the dusty and dirty city.

Time and time again I had tried to broach the subject of the inheritance of Ettrick Bay with Susie but each time I couldn't find the words. If I was right, then Susie was about to lose more than the house. She was about to lose the new lifestyle it would provide.

And if I was wrong, what was the point of upsetting her? I had no positive proof, only a strong hunch that seemed to be borne out by the information I had discovered.

'There's been no word from the agent,' Susie went on gloomily. 'That's another two weeks and no sign of anyone wanting to buy the place.'

'Perhaps you should think of trying one of the estate agents on the island,' I suggested tentatively. 'They know all the properties here well. Or even wait for a while - enjoy the summer here?'

Susie stared at me. 'Why would I want to do that?' she said. 'I couldn't possibly. No, I want this place sold. Once I know how much I can sell it for, I can decide what I'm going to do.' She shook her head in a way that brooked no argument.

I sighed. I could see us being trapped forever in this situation: I couldn't help but feel friendship owed it to Susie to continue to support her and yet I knew the plans she was making might all come to nothing.

If Susie could sell the house quickly would it matter if she turned out not to be the rightful owner? I tried to remember what the legal position might be. I'd need to ask someone. 'Perhaps the price is putting people off?'

'Nonsense. A house this size with all this ground? David says it's worth every penny.'

'But David hasn't actually seen it?'

For a moment she looked shamefaced but she recovered quickly. 'Well, no. There was no need for him to come all the way over to the island. I can give him all the information he needs. And I sent pretty good photos over with my e-mail.'

I could imagine what the photos would have been like. Not exactly enough to entice the kind of clients David was used to dealing with in the West End of Glasgow. I didn't think Susie's photos would enhance the house somehow.

'What will sell for that kind of price in the fashionable West End won't necessarily be the same here.'

There was no budging her. She had made up her mind: David would handle the sale and nothing I could say would make her change her mind.

No more had been said about the paper she had found in the bureau. I attempted to raise the subject once or twice but she dismissed me. 'It's only asking that provision be made for this family,' she said crossly, when I had raised the subject yet again. 'I'm sure that was dealt with properly: it was all so long ago.'

In spite of her protestations I was sure this had a lot to do with Susie's eagerness for a quick sale.

Somewhere inside the house I could hear a phone ringing. 'Your mobile?' I asked.

'Gosh, yes. I must have left it inside.' She sprang to her feet. 'It might even be David with some good news,' she called over her shoulder as she hurried indoors.

I sat back and let the sun drift over my face. If the weather kept up like this, spending more of the summer down here would be no hardship. The only problem was that Simon refused to have any further involvement. His pleas of 'too much work' were met by a cool reception from me. Even the head of a very busy department in a further education college is entitled to some time off.

So I was torn between going back up to the dust and heat of the city and remaining here. With the weather so warm and sunny there was really no contest.

Suddenly Susie erupted from the house, clattering down the steps. 'We've a viewer, we've a viewer,' she cried elatedly.

I could scarcely believe it. 'Who? When?'

'Tomorrow - it's a guy coming down from Glasgow on an early ferry. He'll be here about 8 o'clock. According to David he seems really keen to see the place as quickly as possible. It sounds as if he's some kind of developer.'

'Fortunately there's not much to be done about that,' I said.

'We might spend some time tidying up a bit.' Now that there was the possibility of a sale, Susie had changed her mind and was keen to have the house look its best.

I laughed out loud. 'Susie, we should have tackled the clear up when I suggested it. It will take more than a bit of 'tidying up' as you put it to get this place into order.'

She looked so crestfallen I regretted the words as soon as they were out of my mouth. 'All right,' I said hurriedly, 'we'll see what we can do to make it look presentable. The sunshine should help.' Though at the thought of the effort required to go round cleaning all those windows my heart sank.

I was certain she hadn't said much to David about the archaeological work going on still in the grounds, let alone the possibility of an access road to a wind farm running alongside the bottom gardens.

She was becoming more and more excited at the prospect of selling Ettrick House. Her talk was peppered with prices, stamp duty, capital gains tax, lawyer's fees, how much Inheritors Limited would charge and the changes she would make to her life once it was sold.

I began to feel seriously worried about her. If everything went according to plan all would be well. But if she were to be disappointed, if another heir were to be found, she was the kind of volatile person who would take it badly.

Desperate times call for desperate measures and I had made up my mind I would speak to Greta. What did I have to lose? I might be fortunate enough to have some answers this time. She must know something about the Ainslee family she hadn't told us.

I was in luck. Susie had decided in the light of her possible fortune she was going to the local hairdresser for a radical makeover. 'I need to make a start,' she said. 'I've let myself go since I came back here.'

I had telephoned Greta the night before Susie's appointment expecting some resistance, but to my surprise she agreed to come up to the house.

I was crossing the hallway to make a reluctant start on cleaning the kitchen when she arrived. 'Come in, Greta. You are very welcome.'

She said nothing, not even a word of greeting, as she followed me into the drawing room. She stood still and gazed all around, her eyes taking in every inch of the room.

'Do you remember much about this house?' I asked, eager to break the silence.

She turned to look at me as though she had suddenly realised I was there. A strange expression crossed her face. 'Oh yes, I remember lots about this place.'

'Please sit down,' I said.

She looked even more unkempt today. She was wearing a decidedly grubby jumper and her hair was a mess, tangled and lacklustre, as though she hadn't bothered to comb it. Should I speak to Harry about her? He must have noticed the change in the usually immaculate Greta.

I shifted uncomfortably on my chair. There was something about the way she was talking that made me feel very uneasy indeed. I glanced at my watch. How long would Susie be? I tried to calculate how long it would take her to have her hair done and potter about for a while. She had mentioned going to the Post Office. At my most optimistic guess she would take at least another hour. Chatterbox as she is, she would be sure to stop and talk to several people. Would that give me enough time to find out the information I wanted from Greta?

'Tea, Greta?' I asked brightly.

'I didn't come for tea,' she answered. 'I came because you asked me to and because I wanted to find out what was happening to this house.'

I hesitated. How much exactly should I tell her? But she looked so insistent I felt myself quail before her. I have never been much good at lying and I didn't want to upset Greta even more than she was. She looked nervous, fraught, like someone on the edge of a precipice. I didn't want to be responsible for tipping her over. Given how distressed she was could I come right out with it and ask if her mother had been illegitimate? I though not.

I took a deep breath. What I said next would I was certain get some reaction from Greta. I wasn't going to lie, merely stretch the truth a little.

'Well, I know she has had an offer,' I said meekly.' But I'm not sure if she is going to take it.'

'Who has made the offer?'

'A company, I think. They want to turn the place into a series of flats.'

'That's impossible,' Greta cried, rising from her seat. 'I need more time.'

I was taken aback. Why was Greta so concerned? It's one thing to be nostalgic about the places of your childhood, quite another to feel that you will always have some say in what happens to them.

I shrugged. 'But Susie can't possibly afford to keep this place as a holiday home.' I waved my hand around vaguely, encompassing the gloomy décor of the room, the worn carpets. 'It would cost a fortune to do up and it's better that someone who can care for it buys it.'

'Someone who is interested in making a lot of money out of it, you mean,' she said bitterly. By now she had sat down again in the chair opposite me.

I stared at her. What had she meant by 'needing more time?'

'You don't understand, do you, Alison? This house can't be sold at the moment, no matter what. I'll oppose it as much as I can. No one will ever turn this into holiday flats.' She spat out the words 'holiday flats'.

While Greta might not want to see the house renovated, there were plenty of people who would be only too happy for that to happen. A collection of upmarket holiday flats would bring some much needed income to the island.

'You have to decide what you will do, but Susie will sell. Anyway,' I added, hoping to progress the conversation, 'this deal may come to nothing. And there is the problem of the archaeology. But you'll know that from talking to Morgan.'

She stared at me but didn't deny she had spoken to Morgan.

Unnerved by her silence I went on, 'Susie can't afford to keep this place on. Even the cost of the council tax would be far too much for her. She might want to go back to America for a time. She likes it out there you see…' My voice trailed off as I saw that Greta was gazing at me as if I were talking a foreign language.

'You're not listening, Alison. This is nothing to do with you. What you don't understand is that my family suffered because of the family who owned this house and I have every right to be interested in what happens to it. My grandmother…'

She stopped abruptly as we heard the front door opening. What bad timing, Susie, I said under my breath. Just as it looked as if I might get some real information from Greta. Now I would also have to explain to Susie why I had asked Greta to Ettrick House.

Susie breezed in with a, 'You'll never guess where I've been…' Her voice tailed off as she saw Greta sitting there, stiff and solemn.

'Yes, we have company, Susie,' I said weakly.

Susie sat down. There was a strange expression on her face as she faced Greta. It was as though all the exuberance had suddenly gone out of her. She reminded me of nothing as much as a deflated balloon.

'I though you might come, Greta,' said Susie quietly, 'but I didn't think you would come as soon as this.'

Now it was Greta's turn to look startled. I glanced from one to another in some astonishment.

As though she guessed my thoughts, Susie said, 'There is a reason that Greta has a more than passing interest in this house. Isn't that right Greta?'

She turned to me. 'Sorry, Alison, but my hair appointment was only an excuse. I was in town to see Mr Laidlaw and what I learned was very interesting, very interesting indeed.'

Greta nodded but did not speak. It was as though she was waiting for Susie to make the first move, to identify what she had found out.

'Will one of you tell me what is going on,' I said crossly. 'After all I've done to help with this house, it's the least that I am owed.' I thought of all the hours I had put in trying to trace the Ainslee family, hoping to make sense of all that was happening.

'Will you tell her? Or will I?' Susie looked as grim as I had ever seen her. This was a Susie I didn't recognise.

As Greta sat and made no move to talk, Susie said, 'Have it your own way. I'll fill Alison in as best I can.'

She turned to me and said. 'Greta thinks that if anyone is the heir to Ettrick House, she is.'

For a moment there was silence. I tried to digest what Susie was saying and looked from her to Greta and back again. Each seemed to be waiting for the other to speak.

Finally I could stand it no longer. 'What on earth is going on? Didn't that firm of heir hunters exhaust all possibilities before they came to you, Susie?'

It was Greta who answered. 'Oh, yes, in legal terms it might well be Susie who is the heir to the place. But it is rightfully mine. Our family were the servants here at Ettrick House for several generations. My mother worked here for years for old Mr Ainslee, slaved for a pittance and he always promised her that he would leave the place to her.'

'Mmm,' I replied weakly, 'that may be so, but there was no trace of a will, was there? And why would he leave his house to a servant?' I thought about the letter Susie had found. 'Why would he want to leave the place to your family, Greta, when you weren't even related?'

Greta ignored my question. 'Not unless she,' pointing a finger at Susie, 'has found the will and destroyed it. I have in my possession the letter my mother left me among her papers. It's all perfectly clear. And no matter what happens, I have to carry out her wishes, make sure Ettrick House comes into my family at last.'

There was a disturbing gleam in Greta's eyes, making me even more certain her state of mind wasn't rational. Was this the time to tell them both what I had found?

This was a step too far for Susie. 'Don't talk rubbish, Greta. It's all been legally verified. I'm sorry about your mother but,' with a shrug of her shoulders, 'these things happen. People make promises and don't keep them.'

Susie sounded very determined. What proof was there that Greta had any letter from her mother? The whole thing might have been no more than the imaginings of an unbalanced mind.

Greta rose slowly and glared at Susie. 'We'll see about that,' she said. 'There's more to this than you could ever know. Robert Ainslee was doing no more than repaying a debt: a debt of honour.'

'Greta, won't you explain to us what is going on? Why do you think this place is yours?'

Greta shook her head. 'It should never have been allowed to happen like this. I will have what is mine.'

She rose quickly from her seat, went over and leaned in to Susie. 'You will never sell this place, never. Do you understand?'

Susie drew back but she said nothing. She had learned something of importance from Mr Laidlaw then, something she didn't want to discuss in front of Greta.

I went after Greta as she stormed out, her face suffused with rage. As she left she turned to me and said quietly, ' If I were you I would warn your friend that she's meddling in more than she knows.' It sounded even more like a threat.

'Oh, I think Susie is able to look after herself,' I said stoutly in defence of my friend. I wasn't going to let her get away with this intimidation.

She said no more but merely gave me a long hard stare as if defying me to get any more involved. She had succeeded in frightening me once, but she wouldn't be as successful with Susie.

I watched her as she made her way back down the drive to where she had parked her car. She roared off at a speed I wouldn't have expected from a woman of her age. And there was something strangely familiar about the colour of the car. It looked very like the car that had almost run me off the road.

I was still thinking about this as I went back into the house. Susie was sitting in exactly the same spot as I had left her, staring into space.

'Well, what did you make of that?' she said angrily.

'Are you all right?' I was more concerned about Susie than I was about Greta. 'After all, what can Greta do? She doesn't seem to me to be the kind of person who would have the money to spend on legal help.'

Susie roused herself and smiled. Her thoughts had obviously been miles away.

'I'm furious at Greta,' she said. 'It's ridiculous what she's saying. Apart from anything else we only have her word that her mother was promised the house.'

I had to agree. And it was obvious from Susie's attitude that even if Greta came up with a will, Susie would fight it tooth and nail. When she decides on a course of action, it takes a lot to change her mind.

I sat down on the chair in the corner opposite Susie. I told her as briefly as I could about my hunt for information on Greta's family.

'More or less what I learned from Mr Laidlaw. He knew about it all the time, if only we'd bothered to consult him in the first place.'

'So it looks as if Greta's mother was the illegitimate daughter of this servant Jane and William Ainslee. She was married off to another of the servants to save a family scandal.'

I waited for her reaction before saying, 'And that might cause some problems about your inheritance.'

Instead of being upset by this, Susie said, 'But there's no proof, no concrete proof.'

'I suppose Greta could try to get a DNA test or something but no, apart from that, there is no proof.'

Susie sat back. 'Fine, then. The house is still mine and I go ahead with the sale'.

It wasn't as simple as she thought however. I had a phone call from Simon later that evening.

'Someone left a strange message on the answering machine, Alison, and I thought I'd better let you know. I can't make head nor tail of it. Something about Romans on Bute and problems about the excavation. Is it something to do with Morgan?'

Of course. I had phoned my friend Liza whose husband is an archaeologist and asked if she could find out discreetly anything about Morgan Connolly. The phone message was to call her back.

'Thanks, Simon. And are you coming over again?'

'Yes, but I'm not sure when. I suppose I may as well come over for a few days and say goodbye to the house that has caused you so much grief.'

'It's not quite sold yet, Simon. There are a few complications.'

'Complications or not, this is going to be my last visit. And yours, Alison. Let Susie handle it. You've done enough, friend or no friend.'

I ignored this last comment. 'The weather makes the place much more cheerful somehow,' I said. 'You would enjoy a break.'

He promised to phone me within the next couple of days and make a definite arrangement. Deborah had gone off with some friends to a villa in Greece. Possibly he was getting fed up with only Motley for company.

No time like the present, I thought as I called up my friend's number. After the usual exchange of pleasantries we came round to the questions I had asked.

'You're lucky,' Liza said. 'The world of archaeology is small and most people know each other pretty well. Morgan, as he calls himself, changed his name by deed poll.'

'How strange. Why would he want to do that?'

'There's another archaeologist with a similar name so perhaps it was to avoid confusion?'

A possible explanation.

'Or maybe he thought his new name would look better on the academic papers.'

Again possible: Morgan was someone who took his status very seriously.

'By the way, Alison, your questions about the skeleton have stirred up a bit of a hornet's nest. There's to be a further analysis, undertaken by someone completely independent.'

'Ah, now that is very interesting.' So I wasn't the only one who was suspicious.

I rang off and she promised to phone me as soon as there was any more news. I stood looking at the receiver for a moment, lost in thought.

I still wondered why Morgan would have changed his name. What was that story he had told us about his father and the classic cars? How very odd.

I went through to the library and looked out of the window. There had been very little activity in the trenches for some days now although, even from a distance, I could see one of the archaeologists was still there. It appeared Morgan was spending a lot of time on the mainland, talking about his discoveries. I even heard him being interviewed one morning on Radio Scotland. He sounded happy, elated with his new found fame.

I thought again about that skeleton. No doubt there would be further details released soon. Between that and the artefacts discovered in the adjacent trenches, there was enough to keep Morgan and his colleagues in work for many years to come. Unless the independent analysis came up with something different.

There were too many loose ends for my liking. Before we left this place for good, I wanted to speak to Morgan one last time. I wanted to have some answers.

I glimpsed movement over by the original trench and wandered out to see what was going on. Penny Curtis was standing by the finds table, carefully cleaning something small and delicate.

'Another interesting find, Penny,' I said.

She shook her head. Today in deference to the continuing hot weather she was in shorts and a tee shirt, which made her look younger than ever.

'Not really. We've found very little since Morgan came up with those Roman artefacts. Probably there was a concentration of them in that one trench.' She sighed. 'No doubt Morgan will have an explanation.'

It was becoming increasingly hot, but in the far distance I could see a few dark clouds beginning to gather.

'Would you like to come indoors to cool down?' I felt sorry for her working there, now abandoned by the others to carry out the final part of the excavation.

'No, thanks, Mrs Cameron.' She gestured to the bottle of water sitting at the end of the table. 'I'll make do with this. Brian is coming to pick me up soon. We're scaling back as it is and if there are no more finds within the next couple of days we'll start closing up the trenches.'

I wandered back to the house along the little track beside the drive. I would phone Morgan and make that appointment to meet with him. This time

I would have some answers and would find out what he and Greta had been arguing about.

Our time at Ettrick House was coming to an end. A few more days and the archaeologists would be gone and the house would be sold eventually, in spite of Greta's determination.

I should have known it couldn't be as simple as that.

TWENTYNINE

I was right about Morgan: he was a fraud.

Would I have known for sure if Liza hadn't phoned me back so quickly? Her call solved part of the puzzle.

'There have been some developments in the analysis of that skeleton of Morgan's,' she said. 'I'm not sure you'll want to hear this, but it's not what it appears to be.'

'Nothing would surprise me now,' I said. 'What's the outcome of the tests?'

There was a moment of hesitation. 'It is a female skeleton, but there's evidence of more than one skeleton.'

Now I was confused. 'But it was identified as a female - there was no indication there was more than one in that trench. I know I'm no expert, but I'm sure I would have noticed more than one skull.'

'It wasn't so much another person in the trench with the original skeleton. It was the tiniest remains of a foetus. It was in the finds bag used to gather up all the bits of animal bones and any other material like that. Some of it had been deliberately removed but there was enough remaining to allow analysis.'

'And…?' I knew there must be more.

'And it's not Roman.'

I wasn't surprised. 'What happens now?'

Liza sighed. 'There will be a lot of controversy and Morgan will be called to account. But the detail of what will happen, I'm not sure about. Watch this space, as they say.'

I thought furiously. If Morgan had removed some of the bones, he must have had a reason. His motivation was now becoming very clear. How could I ever have known when we first agreed to come to Bute to help Susie there would be such problems?

I would have some answers from him. It was the least he owed us all. I thought about telling Simon what I intended to do, but he would only have tried to stop me.

I waited until Simon had gone off for a walk and Susie had set off into Rothesay before going into the yard at the back of the house. Mobile reception isn't good, even out of doors, but I managed to get through to Morgan after a couple of failed attempts.

I should have known something wasn't right when he agreed to meet me without question, but I was too involved to pay any attention to the little nagging voice of doubt in my head.

There was no one to blame but myself for the situation I found myself in. Here I was, trapped on this lonely beach, with someone who was possibly a madman and most likely a killer. Why on earth had I agreed to meet him down at Ettrick Bay?

I should have declined his suggestion, should have proposed somewhere more public, but he had been most insistent. Why was I not immediately alerted by the quick way he responded, seemingly unsurprised by my call?

'We can go to the Ettrick Bay tearoom and have a chat over a cup of tea. I'm sure you'll be tempted by a slice of their chocolate cake.'

It all sounded so normal any suspicions I might have had vanished. After all, what could go wrong in such a busy place? But Morgan had rightly counted on my forgetting the tearoom would be closed. There was no cup of tea, only a long stretch of deserted beach and a shuttered and silent tearoom.

All because I wanted some answers.

I had been so stupid. He was beyond any rational talk. The very mention of a second analysis of the skeleton and the charming young man vanished. His eyes were cold as he listened to what I was saying.

'It could happen to anyone,' I gabbled. 'If you have made a mistake, surely it's best to come clean.'

He shook his head. 'You have absolutely no idea, Alison, how hard I've laboured for so many years as an underling, to see my work stolen and built on by others who then take all the credit. Credit that should have been rightly mine.'

I stared at him in disbelief. 'But I don't understand, Morgan. Why did you do it?'

His voice was bitter. 'I don't expect someone like you would understand what it was like. To be passed over time and time again, to have your theories ignored and your hopes destroyed. The academic world isn't the cosy niche some people think. It's a cut throat place where people will do anything to get the better of you, to discredit your ideas, to move one place ahead of you in the rankings. I'm right, I know I'm right. It's proving it that's the problem.'

I know academics can be precious about their work, but even in my terrified state I couldn't but think this was ridiculous.

'What do you mean by someone like me?'

He glared at me with those hazel eyes. I felt myself quaking again in front of his great height and that mass of red hair as he towered over me menacingly.

'Exactly what I say, Alison. Someone from a comfortable background, who's never wanted for any thing, who's lived an easy life and thinks she can just come in here and take over, trample over someone's ideas, get involved in what doesn't concern her...'

'Stop there, Morgan.' I held up my hand. At this moment anger overcame my fear. I resented the notion that I had somehow barged in and taken everything over as he seemed to imply. There was a tiny seed of doubt he might be correct, but I wasn't going to admit it.

'I'm only here because I agreed to help a friend and I came down here in good faith, knowing nothing about the past. Nor, I'm sure ...no let me finish, Morgan...' as he made to speak. 'Nor, I'm sure did Susie. She may have been a bit bowled over to discover exactly what she had inherited, but it didn't occur to either of us that we were causing any problems.'

'You're completely missing the point,' he shouted. 'If you hadn't interfered when that skeleton was found, my explanation would have stood, I would have been able to write my find up as a Roman find, as evidence the Romans had been here after all.'

I had stopped listening. This was madness. He was saying that it was fine to tamper with evidence. Surely he didn't for a moment imagine that no one else would have investigated the skeleton?

Suddenly I realised what I had seen that night I had been pushed into the trench. He hadn't been taking artefacts out of the trench: he and Cassie had been putting items in, making it look as if the objects he had supposedly found had been there from the beginning.

More than ever I wanted justice for the poor woman whose skeleton had been found. I know it was illogical, but all Morgan wanted to do was to use her as a means to an end. He didn't care who she was or how she had met her end.

'Stop there, Morgan. You are saying that if I hadn't wanted the truth you would have been prepared to go on with this farce? I thought academics were seekers after truth? How old was that skeleton?'

He sneered as he said, 'I don't suppose it matters much now, Alison. The real artefacts I found dated it as Victorian.'

I felt a shiver run through me. There was only one person it could be: Beatrice Ainslee. Poor Beatrice. She had never left the island. She had been pregnant, a disgrace to the family. If the stories about her brother were true it was likely he had been responsible for her death. Had he murdered her because she was pregnant - or because she had found out about his activities? Had there ever been an 'unsuitable lover'? No one would ever know. She had been left in that makeshift grave all those years, left unmourned.

'It was Beatrice Ainslee in that trench, Morgan. How could you use her in that way - rob her of a decent burial?'

I thought Morgan might have had the grace to look contrite but if anything his face grew darker. I started to walk as though to leave, but he didn't move to let me through.

Now that I knew the truth, knew what had been going on, the question was, would he let me get away? If only I could somehow convince him it was in his best interest to let me go, not to make the situation any worse than it was.

I took a deep breath. 'Look, Morgan, this is ridiculous. All this happened so long ago. Surely there's no way that there can be any recriminations. I'm sure once everyone finds out what was really going on, they won't blame you in the slightest.'

In my nervousness, I couldn't stop talking. 'You're still a young man; you still have your whole career ahead of you. There's plenty of time for you to make that big find, the one that will show everyone how good you are.'

I knew I was probably talking nonsense, but I couldn't help this last attempt to appeal to him. Vanity had got him into this situation, would it save me now? Yet what did I know about the ways in which the world of archaeologists worked?

My ploy failed: he wasn't so easily convinced. He looked even angrier.

'I wish I could believe you, but I think it's too late for all of that. The word will be out that I've tried to falsify data. My reputation will be in shreds. No one will believe me ever again.'

He jabbed a finger at me. 'And I know I'm right. If only other people could see the truth.'

Privately I thought what he had done was a whole lot worse than trying to falsify data. He had planted artefacts to give a false date to the skeleton in the grave. No matter how desperate he was to prove his idea of Romans on Bute, nothing excused his actions.

Standing here discussing the situation wasn't helping. Now I had to try to appeal to his better nature, if there was any of that left. I pleaded with him, 'No one else knows the truth except you and me and I certainly won't be telling anyone.'

He shook his head. 'Sorry, Alison, I'd like to feel that it would all end that way, but there are bound to be questions, bound to be problems. Once the independent analysis is published and the truth is out, my academic reputation will be in ruins.'

It was on the tip of my tongue to say, 'Well, you shouldn't have become involved in all this fraud in the first place,' but the way things were at the moment I thought that discretion was by far the better part of valour.

Instead I said, 'Look, Morgan, I think you're making far too much of this. After all you haven't actually completed the work, so there's no harm done surely. Could it not all be put down to error? In fact,' I added a lot more brightly than I felt, 'you could help with the new investigation.'

All the time I was trying to read him, to decide if he was the kind of person who would kill for what he wanted. Surely no matter how much he wanted fame and fortune in the academic world he wouldn't have murdered someone to achieve it?

Then the thought struck me. He had murdered Cassie. How could I not have realised? Perhaps she had had a crisis of conscience, threatened to tell what he had done. If he was prepared to go to these lengths to make his reputation, he was unlikely to stop at murder.

I glanced over his shoulder. The tide was coming in fast, not only behind Morgan, but all around us. If we didn't move soon, we would be cut off. I grew bolder.

'Exactly what is it that you plan to do, Morgan? We can't stay here all night, talking.' I realised he hadn't thought that far ahead. Having cornered me he had achieved his first objective and had no plan ahead of that.

He seemed to make a decision. 'I think, Alison, you'll have to have an accident here - a stumble, perhaps, a broken ankle and the sea will do the rest.'

'Like poor Cassie you mean? Don't you think it will look a bit suspicious if we both of die in the same way. You committed one murder, Morgan. Don't make the mistake of being found out by committing another.'

He stopped and looked astonished. 'You surely don't think that I murdered poor Cassie. I had nothing to do with that, nothing!'

'I believe you, I believe you,' I said, anxious not to anger him further.

He appeared not to hear me. 'Why would I murder Cassie? She was the only one who understood what I was doing, why it was so important. If you want to know about that, ask Greta.'

I had to believe he was telling the truth. Why would he lie to me now? But if he wasn't responsible for Cassie's death, could Greta be?

It was increasingly looking as if we would be trapped by the incoming tide. There was no way I wanted that to happen. I've never been a good swimmer, even with all my limbs intact.

My only hope was the element of surprise, if I could manage it. How was I going to put him off his guard? I thought furiously. He knew this beach much better than I did.

For a moment he turned away to hoist his rucksack on his back and I took my chance. I started to run. I had the advantage of being untrammelled by any baggage. Desperate as he was to be rid of me, I didn't think he would want to lose the rucksack he was carrying to the sea.

I knew there was no way I could outrun him but perhaps if I could find a hiding place and throw him off my track? My hope was that somewhere not too far from here there would be people. I had somehow to get off the beach and on to the road.

He had paused for a moment, looked away to tighten up the straps on the rucksack, no doubt so that he could deal with me. That instant was enough to give me a chance. I might fail but I wasn't going to 'have an accident' here if I could help it. Not without a good fight.

I leapt into action and scrambled up the bank, holding on to the grass on the dunes for support as I did so. I clawed my way over the rocks, completely ignoring the effect the jagged rocks were having on my hands. I was scraped and bleeding, but that was of little consequence.

I heard Morgan shout out as he suddenly realised what had happened. I stupidly turned back briefly to see him only a short distance away. He was rapidly gaining ground. I could hear him panting behind me. As he was much younger than I was and much fitter it wouldn't be any time before he gained on me.

Goodness knows how, but somehow I managed to make a final effort and scramble up to reach the road. I scanned desperately in every direction but there was still no sign of life.

Against all my expectations there were no late evening walkers at Ettrick Bay, no seekers after a snack at the Ettrick Bay tearoom. I was quite alone on this beach with only the cattle in the nearby field to witness what was happening. Was it to end here? I wished I had never heard of Ettrick House.

I stood doubled over, breathing heavily, my heart pounding. No matter what was to happen to me, I couldn't run any further. And all the time Morgan was gaining on me. He was near enough so that I could see that manic look on his face. He had me cornered and he knew it.

I thought furiously. Whatever I did next, my life might depend on it. Unfortunately I was rooted to the spot. My brain wouldn't work and it appeared to have shut down all communication with other parts of my body. If there was no one here to help, how was I ever going to get away?

All Morgan had to do was to drag me back towards the shore and let the waters in the bay do the rest. It could be a very long time before I was found and there would be no one who would think it was other than an accident.

How I wished I had listened to Simon when he had told me to back off, to forget all of this. It was too late now.

They say your life flashes in front of you just before you die, but all I could think of was how I had managed to put myself into such a stupid situation. I didn't have the breath to run anymore.

On what was left of the beach, Morgan had slowed to a stroll. He was grinning from ear to ear. He knew there was nothing more I could do unless a stray motorist happened to pass along this way, most unlikely at this time of the evening.

'There's no point in moving, Alison,' he called. He was now near enough for his words not to be carried away on the wind.

Well, if it was going to be all over, there was nothing to be lost. The edge of the road was littered with rocks of all shapes and sizes, put down to combat the tidal erosion round the coastline. Some of them had not been there long enough to become embedded and were loose, as I had found out when I tried to scramble up on to the road.

I wasn't sure I could hit Morgan from this distance but I could at least throw him off guard and buy myself a bit more time.

If I was to be successful I had to disguise what I was doing and I had to choose my moment. I made as if to start walking.

He called out again, 'You may as well stay where you are, Alison. There's no one here to help you.'

I pretended to stumble and as I did so I grabbed at one of the larger rocks. For a moment I thought it wasn't going to budge. Surely out of all the rocks on the beach I hadn't chosen the wrong one?

One last furtive tug and it came free. I staggered for a brief moment, but I managed to put the rock behind my back as I pushed myself up again.

He was coming closer and closer. I tried to remember all those cowboy films I had seen as a child where the important thing was not to shoot till you could see the whites of the enemies' eyes.

I didn't think I had the nerve to wait for that, but I would hang on as long as possible.

He was almost at the edge of the beach, confident he had me cornered and there would be no escape.

I waited. I could hear my heart pounding. What if he saw the missile coming towards him and ducked out of the way in time? If he did, I was certainly done for.

I summoned all my strength, took aim and threw the rock as hard as I could, willing it on its way to find its target.

Morgan did see the rock coming, but he was too close to do anything about it. The look of surprise on his face as the missile caught him on the side of his head was something I would always remember. He went down with a thump.

I didn't wait to see what happened next. As soon as he fell, I stumbled off down the Ettrick Road. There was a little knot of cottages near the old Knockencroyf church. Surely someone would be at home at this time of the evening.

As I rounded the bend in the road, panting heavily, I couldn't help but look back. My last sight of Morgan was as he started to get unsteadily to his feet, blood pouring from the wound on his forehead. He looked about him, but he was too dazed to be able to see where I had gone or too hurt to do anything about it.

I would contact the police, but I somehow knew that whatever happened it would be a long time before I would see him again.

THIRTY

For a moment I was completely disorientated. In that drowsy state between sleeping and waking, I thought someone was having a barbeque. But why was the smell so strong here inside the house? I coughed in my sleep.

Suddenly I was wide awake. This was no barbeque: it was real smoke.

'Simon, wake up!' Even as I spoke I leapt out of bed. There was a wisp of smoke in the room, but not enough to overpower us. Not yet. We had to move quickly.

I pushed Simon hard and he wakened with a start. 'What's up? What are you doing?'

'Fire, fire,' I shouted and pushed him hard again.

He jumped out of bed.

'Susie, where's Susie?' She was sleeping in the room at the far end of the corridor. Had she realised what was happening?

Before Simon could stop me, I rushed along and banged hard on the door. I needn't have worried. Susie was already on her feet. Together we moved to the top of the stairs, only to be greeted by thick smoke billowing up from the ground floor below.

'We can't possibly go that way,' I yelled.

Simon pushed me aside. 'Too right,' he said grimly. We were well and truly trapped.

It was Susie, usually so scatterbrained, who took control.

'There's the back stair the servants used to use,' she shouted. 'Come with me.'

At the end of the corridor, next to Susie's room, there was a small door to stairs leading down the back of the house.

'Wait a moment. Stand back.' Simon pushed Susie aside as she tried to wrench the door open.

Susie and I edged back a few paces as he pushed hard. Although the smell of smoke was still strong, there was as yet no sign here of that choking blackness swirling up from the main hallway below.

We clung on to each other for comfort as we felt our way down the back stairs, expecting at every turn to be met by roaring flames. The fire appeared still to be confined to the front of the house. But for how much longer?

As we stumbled down to the bottom of the steps and almost fell into the basement kitchen.

'If we can get through the boiler room there's a back door from the outhouse to the gardens,' said Susie.

I was too distracted to ask Susie when she had explored all of this, but thank goodness she had.

The entry to the boiler room from the kitchen was much easier than expected, but my sigh of relief was premature.

'This won't budge,' yelled Simon tugging and twisting as hard as he could at the outside door.

I gazed around wildly. Had we come this far only to be trapped here as the fire spread? This door, unused for so many years, was firmly jammed shut. I remembered the pantry and the cans of cooking oil I had used last time, but somehow I didn't think it would help to go back and start scrabbling around for those.

Simon rummaged around beside the boiler and as I tried to stifle my feelings of increasing panic. 'I'm sure we saw some tools here that first day we came,' he said. A few moments later he emerged from behind the defunct boiler, triumphantly grasping a very rusty crowbar.

'Don't just stand there, come and help,' he instructed us as Susie and I stood there, too frightened to move.

His words galvanised us into action and we lent what weight we could to his efforts.

We all three pulled and pushed but the door was stuck fast. Simon stood back, exhausted by his efforts.

'This is no good,' cried Susie hysterically. 'We'll never get out of here.'

'One last try,' said Simon, ignoring her.

I stood behind him. Already the smell of smoke was stronger, its acrid smell making us choke. It wouldn't be long before it seeped its way in here too. And if it did there was no way we could go back up those stairs. We would perish here.

Spurred on by our predicament, Susie and I pushed hard as Simon levered the crowbar. Fear or determination, or perhaps a combination of both, gave us the strength needed.

First there was a grinding noise and then inch by inch the door, almost as if in slow motion, began to move.

One last desperate effort and with a sudden crack it gave way and we were in the outhouse. The door from the outhouse to the garden was broken and easy to shift: we stumbled thankfully into the night air.

For a few moments we stood there, panting, doubled over, exhausted from our efforts. Simon was the first to speak. 'Come on, we have to move away from here.' With gathering speed we stumbled over the grass to somewhere safer.

Behind us we heard the crackling and spurting as the dry wood of the old house surrendered to the flames. We moved further and further back as the flames leapt higher and higher in the air. Sparks danced like fireflies in the darkness.

'The fire must be visible for miles,' coughed Simon, 'so help should be on its way.'

Thankfully he was right. A few minutes later we heard in the distance the welcome sound of the fire engines. I sat down with my back against one of the trees for support.

'Get up, Alison,' ordered Simon, 'we're not finished yet. We have to open the gates to let them in.'

Wearily I rose to my feet and trudged after Simon as he and Susie made for the gates. I wondered if I could gather any strength to help them, but the gates gave way easily - we'd had plenty of practice over the past few months. We pulled them as wide as we could and stood back as the fire engine came thundering up the driveway.

I knew it was too late. The long hot spell the weathermen had predicted had indeed come to pass and the dry as dust timber was too far alight. There was a roaring and whooshing as the roof caved in completely. With a great shudder it fell downwards into the main body of the house.

I grabbed Simon's arm as the fire-fighters motioned us to move back. 'Keep away as far as you can,' one of them said. 'There could be an explosion at any time.'

I remembered the old canisters out in the outhouses. Were they a danger?

'Simon,' I said urgently, 'we need to warn them about those canisters,' but it was hard to be heard above the noise of the fire.

The volume of water hosed onto the fire seemed to me to be enough to empty Ettrick Bay, but it made very little impression on this hungry beast as it fought back against all attempts to quell it.

We stood and watched as slowly, very slowly the fire was brought under control. Not quite extinguished, it was too far gone for that, but reduced so that the terrifying flames were no longer leaping into the dark night.

As the fire abated the smell of the smouldering ruin was, if anything, worse. The bitter smell of black smoke filled the air.

I made to move forward but one of the fire-fighters shooed me away.

'It's not safe yet,' he warned. 'Fires like this have a habit of suddenly flaring up again. I'd rather you moved away completely. Is there somewhere you can go?'

'We can find somewhere,' said Simon, 'but will it be all right to leave the house like this?'

'I very much doubt if there's much left of the house,' the fire-fighter said, looking at us curiously. 'You certainly won't be able to go in and investigate for a long time yet.'

We trudged down the drive, past the lodge house and on to the far side of the road where Simon had moved the car.

My mind was full of questions about what had happened. For sure Ettrick House was old and no doubt there would be plenty of speculation about faulty wiring and old wood, but a little gnawing feeling in my heart was sure that the destruction of this place had been no accident.

I stopped and gazed back as the flames died and then flickered again, consuming what was left of the house. Suddenly I felt a knot in the pit of my stomach.

'Simon, there's someone inside the house.'

Simon shook his head. 'Don't be silly, Alison, there were only three of us in the house. How could you be seeing someone else?'

I looked again and whoever had been at the remaining window in this part of the house had vanished. Perhaps Simon was right and it had been no more than a figment of my overactive imagination. But what if someone had started the fire deliberately? Could that person still be in the house? There was only one person it could be - Greta.

Much as I thought she was mad, this wasn't how I would have wanted her to die. There was no way I could persuade either Simon or Susie of what I had seen and even the bravest of fire fighters couldn't go back into that inferno now.

The fire smouldered on for hours. At one point I remember Simon suggesting we should go, should leave it to the firemen, but there was something mesmerising about it. After all that had happened and all I felt about the house, it would have seemed like an act of betrayal to go and leave it in its final hours. We stood together through that long night as the house at Ettrick Bay crackled and growled in its death throes.

The first grey streaks of dawn were lighting the eastern sky as the smouldering abated. Occasionally little plumes of smoke leapt from one part or other of the building, but they faded just as quickly.

'Will you come away now, at last, Alison?' Simon tugged on my arm. 'There's nothing more to see here.'

The crumbled, blackened remains of the building that had been Ettrick House would smoulder on for some time yet. All that was left was a blackened shell, with the remains of the single turret grotesquely pointing skywards.

We left our car and were taken back to the Police station and offered help by a kindly lady from the local Salvation Army in the form of clothes, a very welcome bath and some hot food.

Strangely, Susie didn't seem to be too upset by the loss of the house. 'It's been nothing but trouble, let's face it,' she said. 'I never really felt any ownership of the place.'

'But the money?' said Simon. 'Your chance of a new life?'

Susie shrugged. 'Unfortunately the house wasn't insured, though I can still sell the land. I guess I'm one of those people who will always have to work for a living. Unless of course,' a gleam in her eyes, 'I happen to meet someone rich enough.'

I sighed. This was the old Susie back again.

'Anyway,' she went on, 'all this has helped me make a decision. I'm going back to America. I like the lifestyle, not to mention the weather. I'm going to apply for a green card. I have a friend who will help.'

'What will I do without you Susie? And what about your job at Strathelder?'

'Oh, you'll all manage somehow,' she said. 'You can come out and visit.'

I was weary, yet curiously saddened by it all. What had it all been for? Who had benefited from this house at Ettrick Bay? Had I been superstitious I would have said that it was cursed, but I didn't really believe in all that. It's people who make the curses, not places.

And when the smouldering ruins of the house were finally extinguished, they did find the charred remains of a body.

Even before the DNA results, I knew it had to be Greta. How awful to have wanted something so badly that you would go to the lengths she had. She had succeeded as she wished. She had been the last person in the house: no one else would ever own it.

We heard nothing again of Morgan. I wasn't sure how he had managed to evade the police, especially on an island, but somehow he managed to disappear. He had changed his name once, re-invented himself. There would be no problem about doing it again, starting somewhere else.

I didn't want to think about it any more. I had had enough.

EPILOGUE

Was it really all over?

In a way I felt most sorry for Morgan. He was so young and talented though he didn't recognise it. He had wasted what might have turned out to be a really promising career on a desire to get well known quickly. It all seemed very odd to me, but then what did I know about the vagaries of the academic life?

We had stayed on for a few days in the comfort of a local hotel. There were still a number of loose ends to be tied up, but we could come back over for that.

'I wish you would stop getting yourself into these scrapes, Alison,' Simon admonished me. 'I don't know why you keep becoming involved.'

I opened my mouth to say that it wasn't exactly always by choice, that these things seemed to happen to me, but then I stopped myself. He was right: many difficulties were of my own making.

'And Morgan was the person who murdered Cassie?' Susie frowned as she spoke. 'I can understand he would do a lot to get the recognition he felt he deserved, but murder?'

I must confess I was also baffled. 'It was certainly a great 'discovery' he had made and would have sealed his academic reputation for a long time. Or at least it would have if it had all been true. But no, he didn't murder Cassie.'

The truth had come out at last and it was another sad part of this story. There had been the remains of a foetus with the female skeleton and although tests were still being carried out, there was little doubt it was indeed Beatrice, the sister of William Ainslee, who had supposedly gone to Glasgow.

'How could they have missed the foetus?' Simon said. 'I know Morgan took the remains out deliberately, but the other archaeologists must surely have been aware?'

'I asked Liza,' I replied. 'Apparently it's not as unusual as you might think. In an excavation like this there are often remains of small animals and they bag up all the bits and pieces not directly related to the major skeleton.'

'Morgan knew?'

'I guess so. But when the second analysis was done, they decided to check the bag of bits and pieces and mixed in with the animal bones they found a tiny femur which was most definitely human.'

Susie shuddered. 'That William Ainslee must have been a very wicked man,' she said.

'Yes, else why would he kill his sister? It's possible she found out something he wanted to keep hidden. Jane must have been no more than fifteen when he seduced her. Or perhaps her pregnancy was the reason.'

As I spoke I wondered about Beatrice's lover, if indeed there had been one. Or had that story also been a lie, put about by her brother to cover his own misdeeds?

'Did Harry know about Greta and her family?'

'I'm sorry to say he did.'

I'd gone to see him after the fire.

'I did try, Alison,' he said, shaking his head. He had gone back to the old Harry and seemed to have shrunk again, become more dishevelled. 'She became obsessed with that house, convinced it should have been hers. And when Susie inherited it, she couldn't take it.'

'So her mother was promised the house?'

'It was worse than that. It was all lost in the mists of time. William Ainslee was reputed to have seduced Greta's grandmother who worked at the house, then married her off to one of the coachmen when she became pregnant. I don't know if the story was true but it was passed down to Greta's mother, then Greta.'

'But why did she take so long to do anything about it? Robert has been dead for a long time now.'

'It was in the papers and the other stuff her mother left her, including a key to the house. Until then she had no idea she was related to the Ainslees.'

I was astonished. 'So that's why she felt she was the rightful heir?'

Harry grimaced. 'Stupid, wasn't it. After all,' waving his hand around, 'what more could she have wanted than what we had here. Now it's all gone, all lost. If only she hadn't bothered to go through all those papers her mother left. If only she had burned them without reading them. She tried to get Morgan to help her, but he refused. Didn't want his own ploy uncovered, I'm sure.'

For a moment he was silent, lost in thought. 'It wasn't as though we would ever have lived there, in that gloomy house. It was a terrible burden Greta's mother left her. All that stuff about family honour: what does it matter now?'

'Did you know what she was doing?'

Harry sighed. He looked more crestfallen than ever. 'I loved her, Alison. It was a chance of happiness I never thought I'd have. Yes, I agreed to help her. I dropped her off at Ettrick House that first day when we met you in the Ettrick Bay tearoom and said I'd pick her up further down the road.'

'And she stole our car? How could she have known what to do?'

'I don't think she did. I think she intended to talk to you but seeing the car sitting there, thought she'd take the opportunity to frighten you instead.'

I could scarcely believe what I was hearing. 'Will you stay here?'

He shook his head. 'No, I'm going back to the mainland. How could I stay here with all these memories? And the memory of poor Cassie.'

He looked so sad, so wretched that I hesitated to ask the next question. 'So Greta was responsible for Cassie's death?'

'Oh, yes. Cassie wanted Greta to stop all the nonsense, said she would tell what was going on, how Greta was trying to frighten you all off. I think it was a genuine accident. Greta was a very strong woman, you know.'

'And Greta was on the mainland when Susie had her car crash?'

An almost imperceptible nod was the reply.

I didn't want to upset him further, but I knew Cassie's death was no accident. Yet what point was there in pursuing it with him now? They were both dead, both Beatrice and Cassie. So far apart in time, yet both dead so young.

I had said goodbye and left him sitting looking out over the calm waters of the bay. How could such awful things happen in such a lovely place? I gave him my phone number, made him promise to keep in touch, but I knew he wouldn't. He wanted no reminders of what had happened.

'Let's drop it all then, shall we?' said Simon curtly as we sat drinking our coffee. 'It's in the hands of the police now and nothing more to do with us.'

He turned to Susie. 'Are you going to take the offer on the property, Susie?'

She nodded. 'I think so. This developer now has a free rein so although the offer isn't as good, it's still good enough for me.'

Simon looked relieved. No doubt he saw that at last we would be able to move away from here and return to normal.

We packed up our few possessions after dinner. It was important to make an early start.

As we drove along to the ferry terminal next morning I thought about William Ainslee and what he had done. He must have lived out his remaining days worrying that someone would find out what had happened to Beatrice, come across her grave down at the bottom of the terraced gardens.

Susie was happily talking about her plans for her new life in California. I hoped it would all work out as she wished.

There was nothing else for us to do here: we had to leave the remains of Ettrick House to its ghosts.

ACKNOWLEDGEMENTS

Grateful thanks to the following:

Nyree Finlay and Paul Duffy for advice on matters archaeological (any errors are my own), Dr Joan Weeple for help on medical queries, Judith Duffy for editing assistance, Kenneth Bowie for answers to technical questions, the Rothesay police for advice, the staff of Rothesay library for information on access to documents and Peter for his never failing support.

Cover photographs by kind permission of P.J. Duffy

MYRA DUFFY

WHEN OLD GHOSTS MEET

An Alison Cameron Mystery

READ AN EXTRACT HERE

www.myraduffy.co.uk

PROLOGUE

EDINBURGH, NOVEMBER 199-

Two days before my forty-ninth birthday, I saw a ghost.

I'd taken the short cut from the High Street down towards the back entrance to Waverley Station in Market Street. As I clattered down the steep stairs I held onto the iron handrails for support, hampered as I was by my very smart, but very uncomfortable, new boots.

All I could think about was getting home and relaxing in front of the fire with a glass of wine. With a bit of luck, I'd catch the early train back to Glasgow and be home by five. It was the end of a long hard week and the meeting I'd just left hadn't helped. I'd been closeted all day in the Cowgate Hotel, wrestling with colleagues over so called 'innovative' teaching methods.

As soon as I could, I gathered up my papers and said a hurried goodbye. I pretended I didn't hear the 'Going to the station, Alison?' as I made a hasty exit to catch the lift.

A few minutes later I came out of the hotel by the back door into that fierce Edinburgh wind that takes your breath away. Once down in Market Street, I ran across the pedestrian crossing as the lights went to amber and battled my way to the station.

I picked my way carefully down the steps and then speeded up across the busy concourse. I ignored the angry comments of an irate taxi driver who had to brake sharply to avoid me.

I nudged my way through the crowds mesmerised by the illuminated arrivals and departures board. Even in winter, Edinburgh had plenty of tourists. But I was out of luck.

As I briefly flashed my ticket at the collector and ran onto Platform 14, the whistle blew and the train began slowly to slide off down the track towards Glasgow.

I stopped abruptly. 'Damn,' I said under my breath, or what breath I had left after all that rushing.

As I glanced up at the last carriage, I suddenly caught a glimpse of a face I was sure I recognised. Where had I seen that man before?

For a moment I thought my heart had stopped. He was older certainly than when I last saw him, but there was no mistaking that profile.

Even after all the time that had passed and all that had happened, I was sure it was Gabriel.

CHAPTER ONE

'You all right?'

The ticket collector eyed me cautiously. No doubt he was worried I was ill, or even worse, suspected that I'd had too liquid a lunch.

I tried to gasp a reply but it came out as more of a croak. 'Absolutely fine, thanks.'

I sat down heavily on the nearest bench. My legs refused to support me.

He shook his head in some disbelief. 'You shouldna be running for a train like that at your age, ye ken.'

As this evidently failed to make any impression on me, he added in a kindly voice, 'There's one every half hour back to Glasgow.'

Still unable to speak, I nodded in agreement, though I was a bit put out at this mention of my age. He didn't look so young himself.

'I'll go and get a cup of coffee,' I eventually managed to gasp by way of reply.

He watched me carefully as I lifted my briefcase and got to my feet. I made my way unsteadily over to the station buffet, trying my best to look calm and collected, but feeling neither. I hardly remember buying the coffee in the busy café-bar. I do recall I perched on a high stool facing the wall as I sipped the scalding hot liquid.

Suddenly, I caught sight of myself in one of the mock Art Deco mirrors over the table top. With my windswept fair hair standing up on end and my face pinched and drained of all colour, I looked positively ghoulish. No wonder the ticket collector had been alarmed.

I skimmed the froth off my cappuccino and ate it absentmindedly from the spoon. I began to reason with myself. Perhaps it was some trick of the light? At this time of year the artificial light casts long shadows. It all happened so long ago, that business with Gabriel.

I shivered as I thought about my car accident. The trauma had affected me badly, caused me to forget so much. Surely after all these years I had recovered? Or were there memories as yet unlocked?

There was tightness at my heart that wouldn't go away no matter how hard I tried to talk myself round. And I couldn't deceive myself, though I wanted to. It had to be Gabriel.

'You finished with that cup?'

The abrupt question from an obviously bored waitress broke in on my confused thoughts. She hovered over me, extending a nail bitten hand.

'Yes, yes,' I said without thinking and pushed the half-empty cup towards her.

I glanced at my watch and discovered to my horror that while I'd been lost in thought almost another half-hour had gone by.

I jumped off the stool, scrabbling for my handbag and my briefcase and had to hurry again. I caught the next train with a minute to spare by the station clock.

I managed to ease myself into a corner seat, hoping I wouldn't be trapped by some chatty old lady wanting to tell me about her shopping trip to Princes Street.

Fortunately the sleek young man next to me buried his head in some complex report which seemed from what I could glimpse to consist of column after column of boring figures.

The train journey to Glasgow seemed to take forever. I gazed out of the window as darkness fell over the familiar landscape, my mind racing from one jumbled thought to another. I shut my eyes for a moment, trying to recall the details of Gabriel's face.

I was so agitated I couldn't focus. I kept seeing his face dissolve into the faces of the others who had lived in that house in Hampstead all those years ago.

If only I could remember exactly what had happened. Had I chosen, deliberately or not, to let some memories stay buried?

I opened my eyes to see the woman opposite me looking at me strangely. Although I responded with what I intended as a re-assuring smile, she quickly retreated behind her copy of the "Edinburgh Evening News".

By way of cover for my thoughts I pulled my notebook
from my bag and pored over it. Soon that was abandoned in favour of gazing out of the window. In the fading light all I could see was my worried face reflected back at me in the glass.

At that time of day crowds of noisy schoolchildren crammed the carriages and it was a relief when many of them tumbled off at Falkirk, whooping and yelling as they disappeared into the frosty evening.

I had plenty to worry about. My husband Simon, who works in further education, was seriously concerned about his job. And, by extension, so was I: I didn't want to work any more than the part-time teaching job I had at the moment.

There was also the problem of our youngest daughter Deborah threatening to abandon her Art College course and, even worse, come home.

It was pitch dark when we pulled into Queen Street station in Glasgow. I shivered as I crossed the main station and jostled my way through the rush hour crowds to the suburban railway line, pausing only to buy an evening paper from the street vendor beside the station.

The hall clock was striking the hour as I turned the key in the lock. On Fridays Simon goes out to the pub after work with some of his department: 'stress relief' he calls it. I knew he wouldn't be home for a good hour. I tugged off my boots (what bliss to be rid of them at last) and dropped my coat on the nearest chair.

'You'll just have to wait,' I said to Motley the cat as he came purring round looking for his tea. Huffed that I was giving him no attention, he began to miaow loudly.

As he's a good few pounds overweight, Motley is on a diet, which doesn't put him in the best of tempers.

Much as I sympathised with his plight, I ignored him and ran upstairs. I would open his 'Weighless Cat Cuisine' later. What I had to do was far more urgent. It had to be somewhere, I thought, as I began my search.

For fifteen minutes I rummaged fruitlessly in my desk and the various boxes which serve as my excuse for a filing system. I was seriously hampered by Motley who had followed me upstairs. He insisted on sitting down on anything I pulled out and refused to budge.

I had almost given up my search in despair and was about to go downstairs to start making the meal when I suddenly thought about the glory hole that is the hall cupboard.

After ten minutes of disciplined searching (it's so easy to get sidetracked) that's where I came across it. Right at the back of a jumble of old programmes, postcards and assorted letters.

It was one of several photos stuck between the pages of a souvenir programme for "Hair" at the Round House at Camden.

I lifted it out. The photos had been taken none too successfully with the first Instamatic camera I ever possessed.

There we were, frozen in time: all of us, smiling and relaxed and youthfully optimistic. It was difficult to tell where the photo had actually been taken.

It was out of doors. Primrose Hill perhaps? A Sunday afternoon in summer? Impossible even to tell who had taken the picture. Some passing stranger probably, pressed into service for the occasion. It's the only one I remember of all of us together - Gabriel, Melanie, George, Josie, me - even Kara's there.

Apart from this one, there was only one other photo with Gabriel in it: a drunken party in a dingy basement somewhere.

In that one it's hard to identify him among the crowd. Only the merest glimpse of him is visible in a corner. He's partly blocked by someone's head, not to mention the smoke from the burning joss sticks.

But in this one, taken on that bright summer's day long ago, he was fully visible. His head was slightly inclined towards Melanie so that there was no mistaking that profile, the same profile I had seen on the train to Glasgow.

I sat back on my heels and stared at it, hardly conscious of time passing. I tried to imagine myself back there on that summer's day. I tried to look for any sign that I might have made a mistake.

I scrutinised the photograph again, scanning every inch of it. The past stared back at me.

It was no use. There was no mistake. The accident might have wiped much from my memory, but of this I was sure. The man I had seen on the train from Waverley was, without a doubt, Gabriel Santos.

Gabriel, who had been dead for over thirty years.